SIDESHOW

SIDESHOW

The North Shore Trilogy - Book 3

Poe Iannie

iUniverse, Inc.
New York Lincoln Shanghai

Sideshow
The North Shore Trilogy - Book 3

iUniverse, Inc.

For information address:
iUniverse, Inc.
2021 Pine Lake Road, Suite 100
Lincoln, NE 68512
www.iuniverse.com

ISBN: 0-595-28305-5

Printed in the United States of America

Contents

CHAPTER 1

Mystery Shrouds Appointment Situation

"Of course it's a prank," said Lars Paulsen's wife Marian after he told her about his just concluded phone conversation.

"I really couldn't tell," Lars responded as he stared thoughtfully out the living room window at the mid-summer sunshine reflecting off the surface of Lake Michigan.

"If it really were an offer to be a member of the board," Marian said with some sharpness in her voice, "you wouldn't do it, would you?"

Lars continued studying the lake some moments before he answered, "I don't know." Lars surprised himself with his answer, for he had never been conscious of any interest on his part of serving on the state university system board of trustees.

"God, some people don't know when they're well off," Marian said tartly.

"I didn't say I wanted to do it," Lars responded with an irritation that matched Marian's. He knew that his defensiveness betrayed an attraction toward the possibility raised by the peculiar call.

The caller had identified himself as a member of the staff of the governor of the state and—after stressing that his call was off the record—inquired whether Lars, a professor of political science at North Shore State University, would accept appointment to the faculty seat on the state university system board of trustees if the governor were to offer it.

The question was not merely surprising, it was improbable, reflected Lars as he recollected the event. He had lowered the phone from his ear and eyed it suspiciously until he could decide what to say. It seemed unlikely that his caller was who he claimed to be and that the question that he asked should be taken seriously. Initially feeling that the call was a prank, Lars had to suppress the temptation to say flippantly that the caller should put on Ole Barry, as the governor whom Lars had never met was popularly known, so that they could chew the fat for a little before they got down to business. Lars's silence prompted the caller to assure him that the call was genuine and identified himself as Craig Berg, which was a name that Lars was familiar with as the governor's chief of staff. Of course, the name was common knowledge, so Lars had to decide whether to hang up on a prankster or play along until the caller said something to reveal that the call was a phony.

"Would you repeat your confidential question?" Lars had asked, trying not to sound sarcastic.

"Again, Dr. Paulsen," said the serious voice, "and I stress the off-the-record nature of my question, the governor is interested to know whether you would be willing to serve if you were to be considered for the now vacant faculty seat on the board of trustees of the state university system."

Lars's common sense argued that the call was a prank. The single faculty seat on the twelve member state university system board of trustees was an intensely brokered assignment that usually showed faculty politics to have a maneuverability that made the competitiveness of electoral politics seem crude and unsophisticated by comparison. There were three universities in the state system, North Shore State, an institution of substantial quality but only modest prestige where Paulsen served in the political science department; Beau Prairie State, a predominantly undergraduate liberal arts institution in the rural southwest corner of the state with about one-fourth the enrollment of North Shore's ten thousand; and Pauliapolis State, the large multiversity in the state's single metropolitan area where the twenty-five thousand undergraduate students shared a sprawling campus with twelve thousand graduate students who pursued a variety of first rate professional programs ranging from medicine and other applied sciences through the fine arts.

Without exception, the faculty seat on the board had been occupied by a distinguished member of the Pauliapolis faculty who was proposed and supported without dissent by the faculty senate at the Pauliapolis campus on the basis of two criteria. One was that the person would be someone with so impressive a scholarly record that his or her fellow trustees would recognize the person as an ornament of the university to be accorded the sort of deference that all faculty deemed themselves entitled to. The second was that the person would express about all the board's business the self-interest of the academic community at large, which could be summarized by the faculty's unqualified belief that what was good for the faculty was unquestionably good for the university and its students. The support of the faculty political structure had never deviated from endorsement of the single name it proposed, and the central administration of the university customarily remained mute in the face of this apparent unanimity, it never having occurred to them to explore whether the faculties of the two less prestigious universities concurred in the name proposed by the Pauliapolis senate for the governor's decision.

With knowledge of this history, Lars concluded that he was the recipient of a prank call coming from some member of the North Shore State faculty who still harbored some ill will toward him for some action he had taken during his eight years as NSSU's academic vice president prior to his return to teaching duties three years ago. Lars weighed several sarcastic responses to his caller's malicious little game; however, he managed to curb his blossoming wrath and decided on a response that carried neither the hostility that the childish prank deserved nor the ingratiating and eager affirmative that the caller hoped for so that he could prick an expanding balloon.

"You may tell the governor," Lars began, "and I hasten to say that I respect his desire for confidentiality, that I would be willing to serve on two conditions: that he would always be available to consult when I wished to discuss matters before the board, and that he would have no expectation of being able to control my vote on any matter before the board."

The silence at the other end of the line convinced Lars that he had denied his caller the opportunity for a snide retort to end his call. Eventually, the voice said, "I think I have that, sir. Thank you very much for your time." A click ending the call followed momentarily

Lars chuckled a hearty, "No trouble at all," into the dead line, satisfied with his successful parrying of the tasteless attempt to score a laugh at his expense.

When Lars related the tale of the call to his wife Marian, he omitted his response to the inquiry, which, taken at face value, was a conditional expression of interest in the appointment. He emphasized the unlikelihood that such business would be conducted by phone. That analysis gave Marian a chance to reiterate a point that she liked to keep fresh in her husband's mind. Marian, who was a university faculty member herself, had never liked Lars's being in university administration for two reasons. The work claimed a much greater share of his time than when he taught, and administrative work kept Lars continuously in conflict and controversy which upset her as much as it did Lars. Hence she relished every opportunity to remind her husband what wrenching difficulties he had left behind by returning to the classroom, and how foolish he would be to undertake any assignment which would lead to renewed embroilment. Lars was never slow to concede her point because he did enjoy the tranquil tenor of their lives and the re-focusing of his attention on teaching and research. He was pleased that he had parried what was most likely a prank call and had expressed his interest in the trusteeship in unacceptable terms that denied the small-minded caller the chance to enjoy Lars's discomfiture when the offer he had treated seriously was revealed to be a hoax.

Of course, serving as the faculty trustee was an assignment that most faculty would be interested in performing. The possibility of such service had never crossed Lars's mind. As a former administrator, he was never accepted at the emotional level as a full-fledged member of the faculty. He might have overcome this if he had been one of those rare former administrators who rapidly became union activists after leaving the administrative ranks. Though Lars was more sympathetic than antagonistic toward unionization, he could not bring himself to become involved in union activity. It somehow seemed too nimble and too desirous of peer acceptance to leap from being a major participant on one side of the table to being the technically loyal but ardent opposition on the other side.

The phone call had claimed no further attention from Lars after his discussing it with Marian. Thus, he was surprised to be greeted by the same voice when he answered the phone in mid morning of the next day. Lars barely allowed the caller time to identify himself when he began to vent the irritation that he felt at what now appeared to be the beginning of a campaign that would intrude on his tranquility.

His caller interrupted Lars before he got very far in the expression of his irritation. "Dr. Paulsen," the voice that in the earlier call had identified itself as Craig Berg began in a conciliatory tone, "perhaps you will accept this call as legitimate if I explain the situation that the governor is trying to handle and why our approach to you is happening in this oblique, secretive fashion."

"You are no doubt familiar," the voice continued, "with the advisory process that has been customary through which the governor appoints a faculty member to the state university board."

"It is my understanding that the choice is totally at the governor's discretion," Lars said, choosing to be simplistic.

"Yes, sir, but traditionally the suggestion of the academic senate at the main U has been most influential," the caller said.

Lars suppressed his irritation at his caller's use of the traditional label for Pauliapolis State's preeminence over its sister institution on the north shore of the lake. Lars believed that NSSU was a peer to the urban campus in everything but size. "I am aware of the tradition," said Lars.

"You are no doubt aware that the faculty union at North Shore, an organization that does not exist at the main U, has for the first time proposed its own appointee to the faculty trusteeship."

"I was not aware of that," Lars said with a modicum of surprise, "but I would not imagine that to be greatly persuasive, political realities being what they are." Lars was recognizing that the non-unionized Pauliapolis campus, with its traditional faculty senate, had always had more influence with state officialdom and the board of trustees than did the faculty union at NSSU, which had the only unionized faculty in the university system.

"Frankly, Dr. Paulsen, certain legislators with close ties to organized labor have made known to the governor their support for the faculty union's suggestion."

"That changes political reality a bit," Lars volunteered.

"Indeed, sir, it has become more than a bit of a change now that the Pauliapolis campus senate has marshaled support for its own position among legislators who are also lobbying the governor for the senate's choice. In addition, other legislators have taken the situation as an opportunity to suggest additional names that have some political dividend for them personally," the voice said as it betrayed a hint of exasperation.

Lars could not decide on a response. The governor did not need his sympathy. These tensions were certainly not a novel experience for a high level politician.

"Do you follow me, sir?" the voice asked and added before Lars responded, "the governor is interested in considering an able alternative to all of the competing possibilities. Your background, Dr. Paulsen, which includes administrative experience as well as teaching and scholarship in political science—certainly a relevant specialization—constitutes a broader background than that of the suggestions being lobbied for. In addition, your knowledge of university fiscal matters is a desirable background for the assignment. Frankly, sir, while the governor's interest in your serving does contain an element of political pragmatism, it is more importantly based on the conviction that you are a worthy choice for the trusteeship."

Lars could not fully escape the feeling that he was being hoaxed, yet he had to admit to being intrigued that an assignment that many of his colleagues in the university system would have pursued ardently was being offered to him, who had never entertained an interest in it. He decided that if he were exposing himself to be the butt of an elaborate joke, he would endure it for the possibility of doing something that now seemed attractive. "Mr. Berg," Lars began, "I would be honored to serve as a trustee of the state university system, but my conditions remain as I previously stated them."

"With regard to those, Dr. Paulsen," said the voice, "the governor finds them not only acceptable but desirable. Your willingness is good news, sir. I must ask you to please continue to keep this matter confidential. You can expect a formal letter offering the appointment shortly. And on receipt of your acceptance, we will make a public announcement. The governor will be pleased, Dr. Paulsen. Goodbye."

Lars was slow to put down the phone. A consciousness of having been impetuous dawned in him. He should have asked for time to talk to Marian before he accepted. He doubted she would be pleased to learn what he had done. Maybe now he should hope that it all had been a hoax. Of course, if the offer letter came, he still could respond negatively. He began to rehearse the arguments he would use with Marian to overcome her misgivings. He had to admit that he now felt that he wanted to do the trusteeship.

CHAPTER 2

U Trustees Oust Sportsmen From Little Moose Lake

Lars Paulsen could think of only two theories of how the persons who wrote headlines in newspapers were selected. One possibility was that editors carefully screened to find the person who was absolutely certain to miss the main point of the article being headlined. This would be someone who would headline an account of Jesus' actions at the wedding in Canna with: WEDDING HOSTS BUNGLE WINE SERVICE. A second possibility was that the newspaper management made an industrious effort to secure a person who could come up with a way to make any action being reported appear suspicious. This would be someone who would characterize Jesus' actions at the wedding with the headline: CARPENTER SUSPECTED IN WINE MYSTERY.

He could not be certain which of the two approaches had been used to select the person who had written the headline in this morning's Pauliapolis paper about yesterday's meeting of the state university's board of trustees, but it was someone who would have qualified on either criterion. Of course, he was not surprised at the outrageous headline, which make a decision motivated by concern for public safety seem like arbitrary small mindedness. He was convinced that headline writers nationwide, whether for small town dailies like the one in his hometown of St. Claude or in a major metropolitan location like Pauliapolis, were selected for their talent to misconstrue or to give every event a sinister cast.

He took another bite of his breakfast muffin and glanced again at the headline: U TRUSTEES OUST SPORTSMEN FROM LITTLE MOOSE LAKE. The article reported yesterday's decision by the university trustees about the toxic waste seepage from university property into Little Moose Lake, a body of water contained within the property. The headline misled the reader about the article, a piece which would have been a good account of the complex discussion if the reporter had been able to resist the temptation to treat the subject in an inflammatory manner.

Lars had sat in on that discussion, having been installed in the faculty seat on the university system board of trustees at the start of the meeting. The problem was a thorny one. Over thirty years ago, the university arranged to dispose of the hazardous waste produced by its hospital operations and its research laboratories in accord with both state and federal regulations then in force for handling such material. The waste was buried in sealed metal drums in a remote corner of a four thousand acre agricultural experiment station. At the time, the arrangement was considered so responsible and effective a means of disposal that the university invited other public entities such as state agencies and public schools to use the site if they would do so in strict accord with the disposal regulations. Recently, more than a decade after the site was no longer used for waste burial, it was discovered that seepage from the drums was finding its way into a sizeable lake on the same university property. The previously thriving fish population in the lake and the ducks that fed along its shores had begun to diminish in what was formerly a very friendly environment. This outraged the sportsmen who, with the university's permission, had regularly fished and hunted waterfowl on the lake. They had written to the university administration demanding an immediate cleanup of the problem. The previous day, a group of them had appeared at the trustee meeting to vent their outrage and to underscore their demands for an immediate elimination of the problem.

After the sportsmen's impassioned presentation, the university central administration explained to the trustees that elimination of the problem would require digging up the entire disposal site and removal and disposal of the toxic material in accord with recent more stringent regulations. Preliminary estimates indicated that the cleanup and re-disposal would cost more than twenty-five million dollars. While this action would inevitably have to be taken, funds could not be made available during the current budget period, which still had almost two years to run. Therefore, the central administration recommended to the trustees that Little Moose Lake be declared off limits for hunting and fishing in the interests of safety until funding for a clean up could be secured and the work was completed. The sportsmen were vigorous in asserting this plan to be unacceptable and urged the trustees to take immediate action to begin the clean up.

Lars was no stranger to the dialogue in trustee meetings, since he frequently was part of the audience for them during his years as the academic vice president at North Shore State University. He recognized very early in the discussion the familiar pattern that statements and questions took when the exploration of a matter by the trustees did not reveal to the board members a course of action that was affordable and readily implementable without displeasing some vociferous faction. One after another, trustees would make extended statements which began by affirming that their convictions were unswervingly on the side of the public interest and in accord with the values that all right thinking people hold dear—in this case preservation of the environment and the right of the citizens of the state to wield fishing rods and fire arms with a devotion equal to their regard for their families and religion. Then each speaker concluded by deploring with restrained passion the stringent financial plight of the university in recent years as legislative funding had diminished and tuition increases had grown increasingly more burdensome for the students. Each of these verbal pirouettes left the audience unable to discern how the speaker would vote when the issue under discussion came to a vote. The purpose of these monologues was to impress on the press gallery the speaker's support of the values required for political survival. Of equal importance, recitation of these verities signaled to the other members of the board that the speaker desired a course of action that would not leave the board vulnerable to criticism.

After all the board members who desired to had been duly recorded on the side of the angels, someone usually came up with an innocuous, often evasive, course of action that was quickly put to a vote and passed unanimously. That was what occurred in the case of the toxic waste problem affecting Little Moose Lake. It was moved that the clean up and proper disposal of the waste buried at the agricultural experiment station begin immediately once funds to accomplish the task had been identified by the central administration; and, that until the cleanup was accomplished, Little Moose Lake would be off limits to everyone to protect persons from the dangers of drinking hazardous water or the eating of contaminated fish or fowl. The sportsmen, who expressed the hope that funding would be identified quickly, accepted their meaningless victory and left with no real hope that the university administration would find the clean up funding in a budget that had been fully committed at the beginning of a biennium that had begun only two months before. The trustees, on their part, dodged another insoluble dilemma, except for the inflammatory characterization of their action by the Pauliapolis Press Leader.

CHAPTER 3

Student Lobbying Proposal Causes Split

Lars put aside the paper to devote himself to the remainder of his muffin, diced fruit and coffee. As he speared a cube of watermelon, a voice nearby and above said, "I thought a new state university trustee would be eating something fancier than the hotel's free continental breakfast." Lars looked up at the broadly smiling young face of Butch Kirk, one of the two student representatives to the board from his home campus. Lars smiled in return. He knew and liked Butch, with whom he had had considerable contact during his last year of service four years ago as North Shore State's academic vice president while Butch was a member of the executive committee on the campus student government. They had occasionally run into one another on campus since. Lars always enjoyed Butch's casually pragmatic approach to campus politics. Butch was not burdened with the adversariness and rhetorical self-righteousness that afflicted so many of the student politicians with whom Lars had dealt. In fact, if Butch had a weakness, it was his constant readiness to make a deal, even if the result was not entirely principled. Yet the handsome youngster was universally popular with faculty, administrators and his fellow students for his good humor, intelligence and his absolute willingness to show himself as exactly what he was—a young man who believed that life was a game with highly flexible rules which he had learned early to use to advantage very well.

"Now how would it look if I began loading up at meals just because I could put it all on the university's tab?" Lars asked with mock seriousness.

Butch slipped into the chair opposite Lars and said, "You might as well take advantage of the little perks that go along with being a university trustee. There isn't any salary with the job."

"Ah, but think of the honor," said Lars sarcastically.

"Surprisingly," said Kirk with a shake of his rosy-cheeked head, "the other trustees do think it an honor to be on the board."

"There isn't another assignment in the state that lets one volunteer his or her time for the chance to be constantly misrepresented in news stories, second-guessed on the editorial page, criticized by legislators, lectured by the faculty and conned by administrators," Lars grinned wryly.

"Why are you doing it?" Butch asked as he relaxed in the chair opposite Lars.

"A misguided sense of responsibility and the opportunity to associate with high-class student politicians like yourself."

"As a matter of fact," Butch admitted with the earnest look that signaled his adoption of his persuasive demeanor, "I wanted to talk a bit of business with you if I could."

"I hope you don't think that surprises me," Lars smiled. "When did you ever look me up that you didn't want something?"

"But never for myself," Butch hastened to inject, flashing the smile that disarmed fellow student politicians and unwary maidens alike.

"Or at least rarely for yourself," Lars corrected. "What is it this time? What boon to the students of the university are you espousing this fine fall morning?"

"I'm glad you asked."

"I'm only trying to save myself from one of your stealthy approaches," Lars jabbed. The truth was that he admired Butch's wily ways, though he frequently chided the young man for his maneuvering. He waited for Butch to adjust to the rare attempt to be straightforward.

"As you know, the students include in the activity fee that they pay each term five dollars to pay for their own lobbyists at the legislature."

"But it's refundable if a student doesn't want to support the lobbying," Lars recalled.

"Right," said Butch, "But now the Beau Prairie campus has proposed that the refund provision be eliminated. The system wide reps to the board each consulted with their campus organizations on whether or not to request the policy change of the trustees."

"And what position did your colleagues in the student senate at North Shore take?" Lars asked, noting that Butch was struggling with the concept of directness.

"They voted to keep the refund policy."

"So that was the position that you and—who's the other North Shore rep, Grace Hytonnen—took to the meeting of the system wide reps yesterday," Lars inferred.

"Sort of," Butch said with a facial expression that pleaded not to be pressed.

"It's hard for me to imagine that you, of all people, couldn't clearly convey such an uncomplicated position," Lars chided, seeing that the story was beginning to drift toward the usual complexity of situations Butch was involved in.

"The truth is," Butch began, "that I was swayed briefly by some of the arguments for having everyone pay the fee."

"Did this brief moment of your being swayed last through the vote on taking the proposal to the board?"

"Unfortunately, it did," admitted the young man, though he showed amusement rather than contrition.

"And the motion to take it to the board passed."

"Very narrowly."

"So now," Lars concluded, "you'd like the board to reject the proposal so that you can avoid the awkwardness of explaining to the student government at home why you didn't support their position."

"You know, Dr. Paulsen, you've got a real knack for grasping these things, if I may say so."

"It's kind of you to say so, but," Lars paused in preparation for returning his young friend's intentionally transparent flattery, "I have, after all, been observing your knack for these matters since you were a freshman."

Butch smiled impishly. With confidence that he could take occasional liberties with his elder, he asked, "Well then, in gratitude for all I've taught you, do you think that you will be able to vote against the proposal that would make the lobbying fee required."

"As it happens, my young and foolish friend," Lars answered, "it happens to be my independently arrived at position that the refund option should continue to be available."

"Terrific."

"I'm sorry that you can't chalk up another victory for your persuasive powers," Lars added. "Of course, if it reaches me that you are claiming such a victory, I will be diligent in seeking a means to make you suffer for it."

"Heaven forbid I should do such a thing," Butch offered as he rose from his chair and pressed his hands feelingly to his chest. "Will it be all right if I made an occasional comment on your superior judgment—very low key, of course."

"I think I can tolerate that," admitted Lars as he turned to finishing his coffee. Butch Kirk offered a broad grin and a casual salute before he walked away.

Shortly before the trustees meeting was to be called to order at 9:00 a.m., Lars was walking down the hall toward the meeting room when he recognized Grace Hytonnen walking toward him. She was a familiar face despite the difficulty Lars sometimes had mustering her name between the times when they met. As she neared, Lars said, "Don't worry, Grace, I've received my instructions."

The pleasant young woman looked at Lars rather distractedly. "Dr. Paulsen, good morning." Grace's face lost its distant look and brightened into the genuine smile that Lars always expected that the young woman would have no matter how long it had been since he'd seen her. "It's nice to see you."

"You look like you have things on your mind, Grace," Lars said as he and Butch Kirk's colleague as student representative to the board from the North Shore State campus stopped to talk. "If you're thinking about the vote on the student lobbying fee proposal, you needn't worry about me. Your ever active partner has already talked to me and been assured I will not vote to eliminate the refund policy."

"Butch? Butch is working to get votes against the mandatory fee proposal? The creep. There's no limit to his brass." Grace spoke with uncharacteristic vehemence. Her epithet describing Butch was a surprise. If Lars had been asked for an opinion, he would have said that Butch's good looks and ingratiating manner had not gone unnoticed by Grace. In fact, many people Lars's age would have detected a bit of chemistry between Grace and Butch and described them as an attractive couple.

"I don't understand," Lars queried. "Why wouldn't Butch be soliciting votes against the proposal? That's what the NSSU student senate instructed its representatives to do, isn't it?"

"Yes," Grace affirmed, "but did Butch tell you that in the meeting he supplied the vote that got the proposal moved out of our group to the board agenda?"

"He told me that he was for a while swayed by the arguments for the proposal."

"Well," Grace said, twisting her normally pleasant face into a wry mask, "if you look behind you, you can see the argument that swayed him coming down the hall."

Lars turned and saw approaching a stunningly beautiful young woman. She was almost six feet in height and walked with an erect and easy stride. Without the exaggeration of a fashion model's runway strut, she achieved the same effect. Her long blonde hair ended in a disciplined curl just off her shoulders. Her well-proportioned figure looked lean and curvaceous. Everything about her from her oval, fine featured face to her enticing body and the proud carriage of her walk seemed certain to give any male between sixteen and sixty the urge to bring home his kill, strip off the hide and chew it himself to be certain that it would be comfortable as well as warm for her to wear.

"Oh, my," breathed Lars, playing at astonishment, "do you mean that our young Mr. Kirk was so taken with the shallow but admittedly quite visible charms of that blonde that he voted against the wishes of the North Shore State Student Senate?"

"It wasn't the logic of what she said that swayed him, I assure you," Grace said, the disgust heavy in her voice.

"Who is she?" Lars asked.

"She's one of the student reps from the Beau Prairie campus," Grace reported with a tone that offered the information as an indictment.

"Well, Grace, at least he's come to his senses."

"What he's come to is a desire for revenge," Grace grumbled in a half whisper as the gorgeous creature walked by and smiled. Lars noted that the possibly ten pounds that would have disqualified her as a model increased her allure to any male who preferred women with curves rather than the structure of a clothes hanger.

"Why would our Butch be interested in revenge? It's not like him."

"Your Butch," Grace reported, showing amusement for the first time, "and please note that's 'your' and not 'our'—your Butch thought his vote for the proposal from the Beau Prairie campus would assure him a date with Miss Bliss Wetmore, but she turned him down to play tennis with Trustee Cartwright. She was shopping for votes on the board, not for what Butch was selling. He was so annoyed at being turned down for a date that he's been working since dawn to get the trustees to vote down the proposal to kill the refund policy, which, by the way, wouldn't even have made it to the board agenda if he hadn't voted for it."

"Our boy's not used to that kind of treatment from women, is he?" Lars chuckled. "He'll have to learn to take rejection better."

"Maybe he needs a lot more practice."

"I hope you won't make that your assignment, Grace. Butch is really very nice when he's not trying to demonstrate what a power he is with the ladies."

"I'm really much too busy to wait until he gets around to me. And speaking of being busy, I'd better get after some votes against that proposal. I'm glad you're going to vote against it, even if it does help rescue our favorite little creep."

Lars laughed heartily as Grace walked away. Much of his amusement derived from hearing Grace belittle what he suspected she held dear, whether she'd come to recognize it or not.

Lars took his seat at the large table around which the trustees sat for their deliberations on university business. Being among the first to take his chair, he examined the familiar room from his new perspective of a seat at the official place of business. Eleven chairs for the members of the board other than its chair were along three sides of the long rectangular table. At the narrow end to his left and farthest from him were three additional chairs. The center one would be occupied by the chair of the board, its twelfth official member. The seat to the board chair's right was reserved for the chancellor of the university system, who was the supervisor of the three campus presidents. As the administrative head of the entire system, he participated throughout the board's deliberations. The seat to the board chair's left was occupied by whatever person, whether administrator, student, instructor or private citizen, who happened to be presenting a matter to the board at the moment.

The board's meeting area was actually to one side of the front portion of the room. Beside the board seating area were several rows of tiered seats reserved for reporters of the print and electronic media. This section would always be completely filled, since activities at the university—be they scandalous or merely capable of being misrepresented as such—were of constant attention by the media. Occasionally, the television stations deemed the discussion of some topic worthy of the presence of a camera crew and reporter. These champions of the public's right to be told all things through twenty seconds of film and a voice over that reduced all complexities to a few hundred questionably chosen words would set up at either end of the tiered seats. The two thirds of the room beyond its forward portion was a seating area with approximately eighty seats. The audience that filled these seats from hour-to-hour would be variously composed depending on who was interested in the subject of the moment that the trustees were discussing for a portion of the two-day meeting that occurred each month of the year.

Lars felt like one of the animals in the zoo looking at the patrons. He turned from his casual study of the media gallery and opened the notebook that had been laid at his place before his arrival. He found the material on the day's first agenda item as his fellow trustees began to find their seats and prepared, as he, to begin the session.

Lars returned their nods, smiles and brief greetings. He inventoried the group as they settled in. At the narrow side of the rectangular table to his immediate left were three chairs now occupied by three members with long terms of service on the board. They sat together because they consulted with each other regularly during the board's discussion of all sensitive matters and worked out a unified position and vote on the topic at hand. Their home districts were contiguous in the northwest, largely rural portion of the state. The three of them, Bensweiger, Talbot and Ugstad, saw themselves as needing to represent the interests of their less populous, economically depressed region against the frequently contrary interests of the dominating single metropolitan area of the state consisting of the city of Pauliapolis and its suburbs. Lars thought of them collectively as BUT, using the first letter of their last names. The appropriateness of the term referred to their beginning the statement of their positions with the phrases "on the other hand," "however," or the word "but" itself.

Directly across from Lars sat the student member of the board, Henry Amberson. The young man had been appointed a trustee as an undergraduate senior two years ago and was continuing to serve the six-year term as he attended law school. As might be expected, his positions on university matters were always consistent with what the student representatives to the board desired. On matters that were not of interest to the students directly, he could generally be counted on to position himself in accord with what would best serve the interests of someone pointed to a career in elected office in the near future. His expressed positions, it seemed to Lars, always seemed to be made with a consciousness that the media were in attendance.

Unlike the three trustees from the northwest portion of the state, the three trustees who represented the Pauliapolis metropolitan area, which qualified for a fourth of the board positions just as it did for seats in the state senate by virtue of its being the locus of such a large portion of the state's population, neither sat together nor voted as a bloc. They were as diverse in temperament as they were in their perceptions of the role of the board in overseeing the management of the university system. Marsha Brandwyn was in her second term on the board and currently served as its vice chair. She held the position of director of personnel in a manufacturing company on the eastern edge of the city. By a combination of temperament, philosophical outlook, and profession, she looked at every situation in terms of its impact on people. She was so sensitive to who might be affected by any decision that it was difficult at times to tell whether she was motivated by compassion or her internal need to be viewed as compassionate. Lars respected her concern for people's welfare in many instances; however, there were times when her speculation of negative consequences to all the possible courses of action left one thinking that there was no desirable course of action to be had, no matter how injurious the status quo was. Consequently, her fellow board members were often impatient with her. Were it not for her exceptional persistence and willingness to speak often and extensively, her colleagues often would have ignored her.

To the governor who had appointed him, Harlan Cartwright was the one member of the board who was certain to be the member whose service would benefit the university. The governor believed that the operation of the university greatly needed what he and the most influential members of the Pauliapolis corporate leadership customarily termed "a sound business approach." Lars had heard some wag among his faculty acquaintance explain that "a sound business approach" meant that "if you don't agree, don't make a sound or you'll get the business." Cartwright had, in fact, a background that amply qualified him to provide whatever wisdom that success in business could bring to overseeing the operation of a public university system. Cartwright was too recently appointed for Lars to have observed his contributions to the board's deliberations first hand. However, Lars had read in the newspapers, both in Pauliapolis and St. Claude, statements by Cartwright made during the discussion of significant matters. He did make sense when discussing the fiscal aspects of a university policy or budget issue. Yet his understanding of why a university existed at all and what moved and motivated those mysterious entities called teachers and researchers was dim, to characterize it most charitably. Cartwright's most memorable statement, in Lars's mind, was, "Compared to a manufacturing company, a university is really a very simple thing." Since then, he was always thought of by Lars as Half-right Cartwright, though the former NSSU administrator, current faculty member and now fellow board member with Cartwright had never had the courage to utter the epithet aloud.

The third of the Pauliapolis area members of the board was Dr. James Middlebrook, who was a Professor at one of the prestigious private colleges within the city. This was the appointment to the board that Lars harbored the greatest misgivings about, though Middlebrook more often than any other member of the board expressed views that Lars found agreeable. When, however, the private college humanities professor occasionally betrayed his attitude about public higher education as qualitatively inferior to education in a private college—any private college, was the implication—Lars fumed indignantly. Lars' entire academic career had been spent, as student, instructor and administrator, in public educational institutions. He firmly believed that his current professional home, North Shore State University, had an able faculty and an intellectually talented student body. In fact, Lars knew he could readily show NSSU's intellectual superiority over many an intellectually poverty-stricken private college whose reputation was largely a product of the untested assumption in the nation that the word "private" in the status of an educational institution automatically meant qualitatively superior. Because the part of Lars's career served in administration inevitably required him to deal in objective data, Lars knew his annoyance with the assumption of superior quality in private education was neither defensiveness or bias. Thus when Middlebrook offered a solution and explained its wisdom simply by pointing out that that was how it was done in the private sector, Lars seethed at the reasoning that had placed a private college faculty member on the governing board of the major public university system in the state.

The trustee from the area which included the town of St. Claude and its university, North Shore State, came from an even smaller town than St. Claude. Blue Rock Ridge was situated fifty miles northeast of St. Claude on the shore of Lake Michigan in what was once a prosperous copper mining region. Stanley Konjeski, an attorney from "The Ridge," as the town's residents called it, fulfilled a role on the board in exactly the manner that people from his region wished him to. Since the mining economy of that part of the state had deteriorated and the population had declined, the remaining citizens had developed a combative attitude by which they were henceforth identified by their fellow citizens in the state. Their real economic difficulties had generated a persecuted state of mind that saw evil intent in what was merely the result of circumstance. They perpetually saw themselves as short changed in everything from health care and infrastructure support through educational opportunity.

That population decline had led to a real decline in the region's power in the state government. Now of their actual marginalization had intensified their collective feelings of persecution. Hence, the citizenry of the region constantly demanded educational services within their area beyond what could be justified by the need. While they occasionally offered support for NSSU's needs because St. Claude was a manageable but arduous commute from the ridge—even in the winter months—they maintained a constant displeasure with the institution in St. Claude because they deemed it lax in bringing degree bearing programs into each of the towns scattered throughout the region northeast of St. Claude. Stanley Konjeski carried the defensive attitude of his region to the state university board and made it his lens for scrutinizing every subject which appeared on the agenda. Consequently, while there was ample reason for Konjeski and the faculty trustee, particularly one employed at NSSU, to discuss matters and seek to cooperate, Konjeski had politely but coolly sidestepped Lars's suggestion that they regularly keep in touch.

Continuing his survey of his board colleagues, Lars's eyes fell on Martha Collins, who was the member of the board who was the object of continuous courting by the male members. This attention did not result from any sexual interest, although the woman with the ready smile and Rubenesque figure did not lack for charm. Mrs. Collins was the one member of the board who approached her job with complete detachment. She took with uncomplicated seriousness her obligation to oversee in the public interest the state's largest best teaching and research institutions. Consequently her initial examination of every agenda item that appeared on the board's calendar was not hampered by personal loyalty or self-interest. By the same token, that made her a target for every other member of the board who wanted to have a matter looked at from the particular slant that that person brought to the issue. Constantly being lobbied did not seem to bother Mrs. Collins, Lars had noted during the time he had been an observer of the board's monthly meetings. She stood attentively through each of the monologues to which she was subjected in the hallways and the whispered Niagara of words that was poured down on her between sessions when she had not left her seat. But when the time came to vote, it seemed from all Lars could tell that she voted in accord with her own judgment, even if it produced a visibly frustrated reaction at some spots around the table.

The last to come to the table in the few minutes left before the session would be called to order was Pete Henderson, who insisted on the informal version of his first name as a declaration of his being a farmer and damn proud of it, as he frequently affirmed. Of course, everyone knew that in Henderson's case the word "farmer" did not mean one who worked his land to feed his family and sell a bit of surplus crops to generate what cash the family might need to get by. Henderson was one of the largest swine producers in the Midwest.

He was in reality a corporate head who supervised thousands of acres of cultivation and livestock production. His fortune from these operations was largely from his own business sense. He had taken the small family farm left him by his father and built the multi-million dollar operation that Henderson operated today. Henderson's being on the board was not the act of a millionaire who now felt he had time to devote to disinterested public service. He was on the board to promote and protect the interests of the agricultural industry in the state, which consequently placed his own interests paramount in his approach to the board's dealings. His willingness to serve stemmed from the circumstance that agriculture had slipped from the first to the second largest industry in the state in terms of economic impact. Since it was speculated that the university might de-emphasize its agricultural programs and the state extension service that the university operated as an important resource to the state's farmers, the industry wanted a vigorous spokesperson on the board. For vociferousness and singlemindedness they could not have wanted anyone more appropriate than Pete Henderson.

Lars looked down to the head of the table and saw that Dr. Walter Appleby, the chair of the board, was making his final preparations before calling the meeting to order. Appleby was generally considered to be the board member who was making the greatest personal sacrifice to serve. He was a highly respected surgeon in a well-known clinic in Pauliapolis. Consequently, the two days each month when he was unavailable to practice were a sacrifice on his part. In addition, the chair of the board spent much more time on university affairs between meetings than did other members of the board. Because the university system chancellor, Ivor Brown, was ultra-sensitive to knowing in advance of the meetings what board leadership sentiment was likely to be, Appleby was often in dialogue with Chancellor Brown between meetings. Appleby, Lars judged from what turned up in print and on the air, was not irritated by constant dialogue with Brown. It meant that he was almost as frequently interviewed and quoted by the media as was Brown himself. The expansiveness with which he ran the meetings seemed to confirm that he enjoyed the visibility that chairing the board gave him.

With a tap of his gavel and a brief greeting, Dr. Appleby displayed the usual flourish with which he called the meeting to order. He announced that a policy change proposal from the student representatives to the board to make the student lobbying fee mandatory was the first item on the agenda. The student board member, Henry Amberson, immediately asked to speak to the matter. His remarks, delivered in an almost judicial tone, showed that he had learned well from his elders on the board the art of inoffensiveness. The young man noted that the proposal to eliminate the refund option had been forwarded by a majority of the student representatives to the board, who no doubt had made known to themselves the sentiments of their constituencies on their respective campuses. He recognized the cogency of their argument that successful lobbying efforts benefited the entire student body of the university system. The presence of recent construction at the various campuses—often garnered in a different priority order than the board itself had proposed to the legislature—underscored the effectiveness of the student lobbying effort. Undeniably, Amberson added, student funded lobbying efforts had also kept tuition increases down by urging increases in legislative funding. Therefore, Amberson reasoned, there was cogency to the argument that all students should share the cost of the effort from which they benefited. On the other hand, Amberson continued, the increase in the number of fees and their amounts had been substantial in recent years, and the students who opposed any addition to this burden certainly had a relevant point. Finally, Amberson recognized, there were students who felt that lobbying was a political activity rather than an educational one and hence should be left to the board. He admitted that the refund option let them excuse themselves from what they considered an inappropriate expense as part of their education. Nevertheless, Amberson concluded, he felt duty bound to vote for the proposal which had been forwarded as the majority position of the student representatives to the board.

Lars soon could tell that various members of the board had been worked on energetically by the almost evenly divided student representatives. One after another board member spoke cautiously with regard for every argument that had been advanced for or against the proposal. Of course, the proposal was more a matter of great sensitivity rather than great financial significance, since the fee was only five dollars a semester. Therefore, all the members of the board except Lars and the chair, anxious to demonstrate concern for a student issue, were eventually heard from on the matter. Lars kept a careful tally of his perception of the inclination to vote that was revealed by each speaker; however, that assessment was highly inferential because of the caution of each speaker. On the basis of that count, Lars remained silent when a voice vote was taken, in the hope that an opportunity would emerge for a course of action he had in mind that has some long-range value for his campus.

The chair said that he discerned no majority either of yeas or nays from the voice vote and requested a show of hands. Lars speculated that there was some hope for his plan and abstained in the raised hand yeas and nays. The tally showed that he had interpreted the discussion of the motion correctly when the vote turned out deadlocked at five for and five against the proposal. The chair, recognizing that the burden of decision had come to rest squarely on his shoulders, asked Lars if he had correctly observed that Lars had not voted. Lars replied that he had abstained. Consternation showed at more than one spot around the table in addition to that being shown by Dr. Appleby. Lars could see that the chair thought the new faculty board member was off to an inauspicious term of service if he would produce an unwanted complexity with his very first vote. Dr. Appleby called a five-minute recess after which he would cast his tie-breaking vote on the matter. As he rose from his chair he motioned Lars toward the hall.

When Lars reached the hall, Appleby led him by the elbow down the corridor away from the noisy audience that had spilled out into the hall to stretch itself and chat about this unexpected complication in what would normally be a matter quickly disposed of.

When he and Appleby had reached some distance from the crowd, the lean and craggy-faced surgeon asked Lars, "You really can't make up you mind about this fee business?"

"Oh, no," Lars responded, "my mind is made up, but I was hoping for a deadlock because I have an idea that I'd like to propose instead."

"Why didn't you just vote against the proposal, then?" Appleby asked with a bit of impatience showing.

"That would result in keeping the policy as it is, and I don't think that's the best way to go either."

"What do you have in mind?"

"I think that we ought to let each campus decide for itself if it will have a refund option or not. Obviously the Beau Prairie campus wants to go one way and my students at North Shore seem to want to go the other. And the Pauliapolis group are split. Why not let each campus go its own way on the matter?"

"We've always had a system wide policies on things like this," Appleby stated.

"I don't see why it has to be. I think that we ought to have more campus-by-campus autonomy in matters like this. Maybe this is a good place to start." Lars could tell that Appleby was struggling with the idea. In fact, the situation had developed exactly as Lars had hoped. He wanted to make it a constant refrain of his service on the board to express the idea of each campus having the freedom to set its own policies rather than having to adopt a system wide rule.

Appleby studied Lars briefly. "You're probably aware that the central administration of the university has always discouraged the board from permitting campus-by-campus variations in policy."

"I know it well," Lars affirmed, "and I find it unfortunate. Maybe doing it on a small matter like this will start them getting used to the idea."

Appleby smiled, "Or start them making your life somewhat less pleasant."

"I'm not worried," Lars smiled.

Appleby thought a moment longer. "All right," he said. "I'll report myself abstaining as well, which keeps the proposal from being adopted. Then I'll recognize you, and you can move the campus-by-campus choice of having a refund policy." Appleby cautioned Lars with a pointing stab of his hand. "Maybe there won't be a second."

"Maybe," Lars agreed, fairly certain that would not be the case.

"Well, let's see what happens," Appleby said and turned back toward the meeting room. Lars followed him, feeling hopeful of the possibilities. As he neared the door of the meeting room, he saw Butch Kirk and Grace Hytonnen standing nearby looking at him with puzzled expressions. He gestured with his hands slightly extended with palms downward, hoping that the sign would convey the message to relax.

Dr. Walter Appleby called the meeting of the state university trustees back to order and announced that his vote on the proposal to eliminate the refund option to the student lobbying fee would also be recorded as an abstention, and the proposal, having failed to achieve a majority vote, was not adopted. He then recognized Lars, who moved the adoption of a policy that the students at each campus of the university system would be permitted to decide, through their campus student government organization, whether or not to have a refund option of the student lobbying fee. There was a brief silence around the table and the heads of his fellow trustees turned toward Lars.

"Mr. Chairman," began Martha Collins, "I'm not sure what's going on. Could you explain?"

"Of course," Appleby said, smiling at his colleague. "With the defeat of the previous motion, the floor is open to additional consideration of the matter before the board. However, Dr. Paulsen's motion is not open to discussion unless it is seconded."

"I will second it," said the student member of the board, Henry Amberson, his face showing immediate interest in the possibility of pleasing a larger number of his constituents than he had thought likely.

"Would anyone care to speak to the motion?" Dr. Appleby offered.

The extended silence was unusual for a group which usually was quick to assess the direction of the wind and align with it quickly if not too blatantly.

"Mr. Chairman," began the chancellor of the university, Ivor Brown, with the deliberateness and restrained tone in his voice that was both characteristic of him and a concession to his being seated at the board chair's right elbow. "I should like to point out to the board that adoption of this motion would institute a significant departure from a long tradition in university policy. It has consistently been the administrative approach of the university to have policies applicable to all campuses applied consistently to all the campuses. This approach has maintained a simplicity and an equity that has served the university well. I caution against eroding this longstanding tradition by permitting campus-by-campus variation in the student lobbying fee policy."

Lars, with some difficulty, restrained himself from immediately responding to President Brown's opposition. Brown's position had not been unexpected, and Lars's rebuttal was long since rehearsed; however, he knew he should avoid seeming anxious to clash directly with the chancellor. When the silence endured sufficiently that it appeared no one would speak to the motion or explore Chancellor Brown's objection, Lars said, "Mr. Chairman, perhaps I should try to ally Chancellor Brown's concern. First of all, I would point out that the fee in question is not for any educational purpose; hence the need to apply it identically on all of the campuses seems less compelling than for fees such as computing fees, lab fees, consumable materials fees and the like which are connected with academic programs. It also seems relevant to point out that while a fee for the sort of activities just mentioned are the case uniformly throughout the university system, the amounts vary from place to place. Finally, since the refund option already exists, the elimination of it which failed to pass this body would have been more of a change that what is intended by my motion."

Lars thought that his defense of his motion had been as non-adversarial as one could make it; however, he could see that the expression on Brown's face indicated irritation. Lars had prior experience with Brown's feeling that anything less than full support in public was an affront on the part of a university employee—and a university employee was what Brown no doubt deemed Lars to be, be he trustee or not. During Lars's administrative days, he had been cautioned several times against disagreeing with the chancellor in public by way of Brown's having the North Shore State president lecture Lars on loyalty. Of course, Lars felt he was free of such restraint now, and while he did not intend to be openly adversarial, he did intend to work toward changes that he thought made sense.

Walter Appleby briefly surveyed the silence that was re-newed after Lars's statement and called for a vote on the motion. There were few audible "ayes," but no "nays" were expressed and Appleby announced that the motion had carried.

Lars sat through the rest of the morning's meeting in a state of satisfied silence. He did not contribute to the discussion on the other agenda items, not simply because they were routine and non-controversial but because he felt he had had enough visibility for his initial meeting as a trustee. His successful initial foray had earned him an occasional look of poorly veiled irritation from members of the central administration in the audience when casual eye contact occurred. Chancellor Brown, who was by nature too circumspect to show irritation at anything or anyone in the course of a board meeting, carefully avoided eye contact with Lars. He adopted the behavior that he resorted to with all the trustees when the board had been unresponsive to his preferred course of action. His politeness and deference exceeded its usual high degree of refinement.

At the adjournment which occurred shortly after noon, however, two of his new colleagues, Mrs. Collins and Henry Amberson, commended him on his suggestion on the lobbying fee policy and offered the prediction that he would be a genuine asset to the board. That put him in the right frame of mind for his brief hallway encounter with Butch Kirk. The relieved student advocate allowed that he was surprised that Lars, in his choice of strategy, would walk so close to the edge of the cliff, but he conceded that the outcome had been a stroke worthy of himself.

Lars said that he could think of no higher compliment that he had received in recent memory. A few steps behind Butch, Grace Hytonnen wore an expression of the tolerance that mature women have always shown for masculine chest pounding.

CHAPTER 4

U Trustee Selection Unpopular at Home

Lars enjoyed the drive from Pauliapolis north along the shore of the lake to St. Claude during the fall afternoon after the adjournment of his first trustee meeting. Once he left the city of Pauliapolis behind, the highway was lined with a stunning mixture of gold, red and green foliage. The oaks, maples, pines and spruce combined in a festival celebrating the end of summer. Surely, thought Lars, such splendor was not intended solely to announce the advent of the North Country's long and rigorous winter. Whatever its message, Lars enjoyed every moment of it. Fortunately, traffic was light, so he could pay more attention to the countryside than he did his driving. From minute-to-minute, each new cluster of trees outdid the brilliance of the previous one. He regretted that Marian was not along to enjoy it with him, but her scheduled class activities were not of a nature that she could accept a colleague's offer to fill in for her so that she could spend the two days in accompanying Lars to his first monthly meeting of the trustees. Of course, had she been along, he would have had to restrain himself from saying something about particular glories that caught his eye, for she would urge him to keep his eyes on the road. Though her appreciation of natural beauty was equal to his own, her regard for Lars's driving skills was not on the list of things that she admired.

While he was still an hour's drive south of St. Claude, the color scheme changed. Red was less frequent, for the oaks that were so plentiful in the Pauliapolis area were rare this far north. The maples continued to contribute their crimson and gold, but did so less frequently, as birch and aspen now predominated among the pines in the woodland through which he now drove. The farmland, which was more extensive than forest to the south, was replaced by the continuous woodland that supplied the region's paper mills with their raw material. It was no sacrifice, however, to have the bright yellow of the birch and aspen leaves prevail except where they were punctuated for emphasis by the white trunks of the birch and the increasing frequent green of the pines and spruce. Still, an occasional splash of red maple leaves shouted that they would not be left out of the glorious riot.

Lars had still not had his fill of fall colors when he reached the crest of the hill that began the drop down to the lakeshore and the town of St Claude, which sat there below the ridges that bound the inland sea. The wooded ridges that ran uninterrupted west and east from the town crowned the habitation that strung out along the lakeshore with a flamboyance that would soon be replaced with a relentless whiteness that had its own kind of beauty, like a gorgeous woman that one might admire but not get too close to. At the bottom of the hill, he slowed for his first encounter with local traffic. It was an effort to slow down to stop-and-go driving on residential streets. At the bottom of the hill that began the drive up to the home he and Marian had lived in for eleven years since coming to St. Claude, he stopped for the light at the end of a column of eight or nine cars. He smiled as he did when there was a short line of cars in front of him at a stoplight. "Rush hour in St. Claude," he would think at such times. In fact, the normal flow of traffic in town was light enough compared to the congestion of large city driving, that more than a few cars at a stop light in St. Claude was considered by locals a major tie up. People grumbled about rush hour traffic in St. Claude at a flow rate that, in a city of great size would be the two A.M. flow on Saturday night of a three-day weekend in the midst of the worst weather of the year.

In fact, the rarity of congestion was for Lars one of the joys of living in St. Claude. Another was the house in which he and Marian lived, he reflected as he neared the one story brick house on a street where mature trees sentineled the green spaces between long, low dwellings, each with its attached two-car garage at one end. Though their two children had left home before the Paulsens had moved to St. Claude, Lars and Marian had bought the spacious place because it had enough rooms that they could, for the first time, each have their own study and still have rooms for their son and daughter when they visited on holidays.

Lars entered the house from the garage into the kitchen and heard Marian's greeting from the living room, "Pour the wine, please." The request was the cue that had been established between them by custom for declaring the end to a taxing workday and the beginning of an evening of relaxation. Lars knew that a bottle of wine, Marian's favorite medium dry white, would be chilling in the refrigerator, and he soon was carrying a glassful in each hand into the living room. Marian smiled as she looked up from her book. Lars set her wine on the table at her elbow and managed to bend down and give Marian a brief kiss without spilling his own glassful. When he had set his glass on the coffee table and settled himself on the couch, Marian asked, "Well, Trustee Paulsen, how was your meeting?"

The question, Lars could tell, was asked more in apprehension than curiosity. Marian had not wanted him to accept the faculty trustee seat. She had enjoyed the tranquility and anonymity that they had enjoyed since his leaving his vice presidential assignment and returning to the classroom. She was concerned that his being a trustee of the university would bring controversy and complication into their lives just as his being a senior university administrator had done.

Lars finished a first satisfying sip of his wine and said, "The trip itself would have been much more fun if you had been along. There was a highly regarded production of an original play at that little theatre near the hotel. You might have enjoyed it."

"How did you like it?"

"I didn't go," Lars confessed.

"Why not?"

"Too much of an effort to go alone, I guess," Lars said having finished his second swallow of wine and reminding himself to slow down. The comfort of home and the release from the stress of driving, like that of teaching, made him intensely indulgent, as though he urgently needed to remove the tension and sense of urgency with a rapidly administered antidote of pleasure without delay. "Did you have a pleasant evening yesterday?"

"Quiet," Marian offered. After a moment's pause, she added, "I brought you something from campus."

"What?"

"The latest union newsletter," Marian answered, her terseness now telling Lars more than her words.

When she did not volunteer the newsletter's location, Lars solicited it and soon returned to the sofa and settled himself to read it. The piece that had prompted Marian to bring it home was not difficult to discern. What had no doubt drawn Marian's attention was the opinion piece by the president of the faculty union, Harriet Avery, on the very first page. Lars did not have to get very far into the Avery's subject before he identified the reason for the brevity that was always a feature of Marian's conversation when she was feeling some distress.

The substance of Harriet Avery's essay was that Lars should not have been appointed to the university's board of trustees in the faculty seat. The union had proposed a veteran professor of history from the NSSU faculty for the assignment. He, Avery stated, would have been a worthy choice because he not only was a distinguished scholar but had been a member of the North Shore faculty for over twenty-five years. Furthermore, he had served on the campus academic freedom committee for twelve years. Lars Paulsen, Avery wrote, had only been in the university system for a little over a decade, during which seven of those years had been served in administration. In addition, Avery had commented, while Paulsen had a respectable record of scholarship before his fifteen year career in administration at NSSU and elsewhere, he had not been an active scholar for a long time. Besides, Avery had asserted Lars' scholarship was not as widely known and respected as was that of the professor supported by the NSSU union. It was clear, Avery had concluded, that Paulsen had been appointed because the state government wanted the faculty seat on the board occupied by someone with an administrator's point of view rather than someone who would be a strong faculty advocate.

"Rubbish," Lars said as he tossed the union newsletter on the coffee table. "And quite predictable, isn't it?"

"It isn't a surprise," Marian answered, and, after a brief pause added, "And makes it all the more puzzling why you were willing to accept that thankless assignment."

Lars sighed and said, "As I've said before, I think that I can do some good."

"For whom?" Marian asked, setting down her wine glass and clasping her hands in her lap as though she needed to concentrate her body into a defensive posture.

"Surely not for me," Lars answered. "I understand that. But I don't expect it will do us any harm either."

"You just can't stand peace, can you?" Marian offered. She got up from her chair and took up her glass again. "Dinner's ready," she stated flatly. She started toward the dining room without further comment. There had been, however, a message. Usually Marian asked him if he were ready to eat. When she was displeased with him, his readiness was not a factor. Lars knew not to worsen the situation by telling her that he was not especially hungry at the moment.

The tension in the air and the terseness of the conversation was mitigated considerably by the flavor of the meal. Whether Marian served simple or elaborate fare, it was always delicious. Lars genuinely enjoyed Marian's cooking skills. He had a difficult time not smiling too broadly when some of his academic colleagues whose wives were university faculty as well bemoaned that their spouses' cooking skills were not the equal of their intellectual prowess. Marian proved that the two attributes were not exclusive to the same person. This evening, however, Lars's compliments could not produce a warming of the atmosphere. After a chilly evening, they went off to bed to demonstrate how many miles apart two people could be while lying in such close proximity.

CHAPTER 5

Students Outraged at Dismissal of Popular Prof

Lars found that the Monday after the trustees meeting called for conducting his classes in a mild frenzy. Because the trustees meeting required him to miss the Friday session of his Monday-Wednesday-Friday teaching schedule, he had given his two classes some library research questions related to the material he would have lectured on in the cancelled classes. However, in an attempt to encapsulate what he had not presented on Friday, he lectured at a pace just short of the speed of an audio tape being run at fast-forward speed. It was a mode he disliked because he treated the students' questions, which he normally considered much too rare, with a brevity that might be confused with irritation. Nevertheless, he fulfilled the semi-religious professorial obligation to "cover" the material to which the missed classes were to have been devoted.

He sat virtuously and limply in his office at the end of the non-stop morning when the sound of a knock on his half-open office door caused him to look up and see several youthful figures in the contemporary uniforms of university students—blue jeans, in one case with the highly fashionable tears at the knees, sweat shirts with the logos of various colleges and professional athletic teams, and billed caps which had probably been put in place at the moment of arising and would not be removed, come class time, mealtime or romance, until bedtime.

"Yes?" Lars asked of his visitors.

"Dr. Paulsen?" asked a tall blond-haired and milky-complexioned lad whose appearance typified a large segment of the young male population of both the region and the university's student body. "Could we speak with you?"

Lars motioned the four of them into his small office. The two women took the two available chairs after some urging from Lars and the pair of males stood beside the seated women, their bulk ample enough that the four made a solid wall facing Lars. They seemed to need an invitation to speak, so Lars offered one.

Their broad-shouldered blond spokesperson began, "We are here to present a petition requesting that you look into the firing of our theatre arts professor, Eric Gonzales." With this information, the young woman with chestnut hair that dropped straight to her elbows leaned forward in her chair toward Lars and offered to him a sheaf of sheets curled at the edges and somewhat the worse from handling. A glance was all Lars needed to see the top page was a double column of signatures and to infer that the pages underneath were undoubtedly the same.

Lars was puzzled on two counts. The fall, with the university year just under way, was not the usual time that employment decisions regarding faculty were made. Secondly, he wondered why the students were under the misapprehension that he still had some administrative role at the campus. His duties as academic vice president had ended over three years ago. "I'm not the person that you should present your petition to," explained Lars. "You should take it the academic vice president or, if he has already made that stage of the decision, to the president, Dr. Haskell."

"But," began the blond spokesman, "we were told that you were the only person on campus who could look into this. Mr. Gonzales is really a good teacher. We've all had classes from him. The theatre department shouldn't be losing such a good teacher. We have over three hundred names on that petition."

Lars struggled to keep from smiling, the intensity in the student's voice had the kind of passion that he had not heard since he left administration, where the handling of student complaints was a frequent part of the routine. The part of administrative work that Lars was glad to be free from was matters that had became a public concern of a group. Such situations were inevitably convoluted and consumed an administrator's attention and energy for weeks, yet always ended with bitterness for one group or another despite one's most judicious efforts. Lars studied the earnest faces before him and said with relief, "I'm a professor of political science. I don't have anything to do with firing people. You need to take your concern to one of the two top officials on campus. The academic vice president has assigned to him by the president the responsibility for hiring and firing faculty. If you think that he's made a mistake, then you should take your concern to the president."

The young woman who had handed him the petition asked him with evident anguish in her voice, "You mean that you won't do anything?"

"I don't have the authority to do anything," Lars said to her. "The academic vice president and president are both reasonable men, I assure you. I'm sure that they'll be happy to talk to you about this."

The young woman who had not yet spoken reacted with irritation. "We were told that you were more important than the president because you are a—" When the word she wanted did not come, she looked up at the blond standing behind her.

The Nordic face held his guileless expression and spoke the one word, "Trustee."

Now all was clear to Lars. A favorite instructor of these students had some how landed in a predicament that may or may not have been of his making, and he was now in jeopardy of losing his job. In such cases, if the instructor is a favorite with students and is acceptable to his colleagues, a campaign is launched by interested parties the moment that it appears that the administration will terminate the person. What the instructor in question may or may not have done, or whether there may be some legitimate reason for the action is irrelevant. An effort will be made to save this person who has now become, in the view of his or her supporters, the single essential ingredient to preserve the viability and quality of the program in which he or she is teaching. Possibly, the person may be an asset to the university and the removal is based on some fiscal reason rather than the person's performance. On the other hand, the person may have, by his or her own actions, merited being in the predicament. In any case, if the person is popular, a grass roots campaign spearheaded by students who were motivated and managed by the person's faculty colleagues occurs.

In this instance, Lars could guess that the campus administration had already made its decision and the faculty managers of the sincere group of young people who faced him now had been told that Lars, as a member of the university's board of trustees, could challenge the administration's decision.

"Let's see if I have the situation straight," Lars offered. "An instructor you're found very effective—what's his name, Gonzales?" The big blond nodded. "Has been fired by the campus administration, right?" There were several nods. "The next thing that would happen is that the campus decision is either rejected of accepted by the administration in Pauliapolis. If the central administration accepts the decision to fire, it goes on to the board for final approval. And you're here because I'm a member of the board. Is that about it?"

The young woman seated to Lars's right leaned forward and said, "And it's not just us who support Mr. Gonzales. The petition has over three hundred names on it."

"I recognize that," Lars said, searching for the eyes under the bill of the woman's baseball cap that was worn low so that her hair could be pulled through the opening at the back where the size could be adjusted.

"But I can assure you that you'd be taken just as seriously if you were speaking for yourselves alone."

"Most of the people who signed that petition have either had Mr. Gonzales for a class or worked in a play he's directed," the student stressed. "Every one of them will tell you how much they've learned from him."

"I've gotten your message about your regard for Mr. Gonzales's skills very clearly," Lars answered with equal earnestness. He studied the sincere and concerned young faces for a moment. He felt fortunate that they had been neither hostile nor arbitrary. Such confrontational behavior aroused the warrior in him too quickly. "Let me tell you where Mr. Gonzales's situation is in terms of university policy. That way I can make clear what I can and cannot do. Any personnel matter, like this one or a hiring and so on, goes through a number of steps before it reaches the board. At that time, the board considers the matter as a group, not as individuals. One member wouldn't conduct his or her own separate investigation, for example. I can promise you that if or when this case goes before the board, I will see that your petition is considered with regard to the matter."

Lars could see the doubt creeping onto the four faces. He smiled. "You look like you think you're being conned."

"You said it, not us," snorted the young man who had not spoken until now.

"You'll know if I don't carry your position to the trustees' meeting," Lars offered. "The meetings are open to the public."

"Why don't you just investigate it now?" asked the tall blond. "Then, when it comes before the board, you'll be able to explain all the facts to them."

Lars smiled at the student's assumption that a grasp of the facts would work to the advantage of his cherished instructor. "It would be inappropriate for me to involve myself in such a matter before the usual university procedures prior to trustee consideration have been followed. However, you must not think that

Mr. Gonzales will be without anyone to look after his interests before his case reaches the trustee level. The faculty union will surely hear Mr. Gonzales's side of it and explore all aspects of the situation thoroughly. If some improper action has been taken, the union will vigorously represent his case. I hope you will just wait to see what happens."

"We want to do everything to help Mr. Gonzales that we can," emphasized the young woman in the billed cap.

"I think you have," Lars assured. "Really. If you think after some time that there's more for you to do, you're welcome to come back." Lars looked in turn into the faces of each of his visitors. He could read no satisfaction there, but the expressions indicated a perplexity about what more to do or say. Lars began to feel relieved. During his administrative days, the most disastrous of meetings of this kind for him were those in which his visitors persisted long after he had said and promised everything relevant and constructive that he could but could not bring the meeting to a conclusion. At such times he was in danger of his frustration growing to the point that he would say something regrettable in a hostile fashion. In those situations, he felt like a cornered animal with no recourse but to strike out. His aggression would be generated by a feeling that the situation would never end, or not end until he had made some concession contrary to his integrity and common sense.

Lars rose from his chair to encourage closure and started around the desk to shake each of his visitor's hands. "Please feel free to come back any time," he said as he offered his hand to each one. They filed out without further comment, and Lars closed the door behind them with great relief.

Though Lars had properly told the students that it would have been untimely for him to investigate the firing of their theatre arts instructor, he recognized that it would prudent to inform himself about the case in an unofficial fashion. In that way he would avoid developing an uninformed view of a case that appeared likely to become a public controversy. Lars's experience had taught him the paradox that it was easier to decline comment to the zealous, the curious and the media when one was informed about what one was declining to comment on. He considered whom he could he call for information who would provide him accurate information and keep his inquiry off the record. If he called Everett Lawlor, the faculty union grievance officer, he was likely to get a version of the truth that was less than objective; nor would he get confidentiality. Besides, as one who now as a trustee technically had a management relationship with the union, his discussion with Lawlor would be indiscrete. If he called his successor of several year's standing as academic vice president, Andrew Weaver, he was likely to get a version of the truth colored to defend an administrative decision that had already been made and would eventually be reviewed by the trustee body of which Lars was now a member. His best chance for information that was accurate with the likelihood that his inquiry would also be kept confidential was to speak to Preston Selkirk, the dean of the college of fine arts. Selkirk had been dean for over ten years and had worked with Lars as an administrative colleague. Lars knew him to be capable and wise in the ways of the academic world.

Lars managed to reached Selkirk by phone, itself a mild surprise, since administrators spent so much time in meetings or otherwise out of their offices. In response to the dean's greeting, Lars began without identifying himself. "I hear that the lunchtime taco fillings at the Casa Caliente are ready and waiting." As Lars expected, Selkirk knew who his caller was, for the restaurant Lars referred to was a place where he and Selkirk had occasionally lunched when Lars wanted to escape from the pressures of his job, something that was impossible if he lunched at the faculty club, where he would be approached by a series of people who needed to speak to him "just for a minute." They invariably brought him a request or dilemma that could not be decided in days, let alone a moment's interruption of a half-eaten lunch that soon turned to stone in Lars's suddenly tense digestive tract. Selkirk, Lars had always found, had a good perception of what was a reasonable business dialogue to accompany lunch and what was not.

Lars had not expected Selkirk to be available to meet on such short notice, but he was. When the dean agreed to meet for lunch, Lars felt a twinge of guilt. "I hope I'm not taking you away from your midday volleyball game." Selkirk assured him that this activity, to which he was devoted for what appeared to Lars as social as much as fitness reasons, had not been scheduled for that day.

Lars found that Preston Selkirk had preceded him to the restaurant. Selkirk waved to him from a booth near the back of the plain and well-worn room. Lars smiled in anticipation of his lunch as he moved through the room. The Casa Caliente was something of an anomaly in the extreme northern U.S., where the preference for steaks and potatoes was moderated only by the ready availability of fresh lake trout, pike and salmon. The room made little pretense at Mexican decor or atmosphere, but had become a fixture in St. Claude from the tastiness of its fare. If one wanted faux Mexican, one had it available in Pauliapolis, but if one wanted genuine Mexican taste, one had to come to St. Claude, despite its being called the Norwegian Riviera by wags in Pauliapolis.

Selkirk was ready with a smile and a handshake when Lars reached the booth. "Trustee Paulsen," the dean said with mock gravity, "what an honor to see you."

"Now, dean," Lars returned as he made himself comfortable, "sarcasm is inappropriate toward one of my august station."

"I forgot," Selkirk. "Trustees are supposed to be fawned over. I didn't realize that you'd acculturated so quickly."

"I'm totally acculturated, as you'll realize momentarily, when I engage in another longstanding trustee tradition by asking you to fill me in off the record on this Gonzales firing. After we order, of course," added Lars, showing that he retained the proper perspective by putting food before business. Shortly, his usual quesadilla had been ordered and he waited as Pres gave the waitress his considerably more complex request that showed his genuine appreciation of Mexican food. Lars knew that Pres never tired of the pleasure of being able to get tasty and authentic versions of his favorite fare in this one exception which was surrounded with restaurants offering beef or battered fish accompanied by one of the several ways to destroy the natural healthfulness of potatoes and vegetables.

His ordering completed, Pres rested back in his chair and playfully chastised Lars for calling him for a social meeting only when he had business to discuss. "It's worse than that," Lars admitted. "I shouldn't even be asking you about what I want to know about."

"That never stopped you before," Pres answered, confident that the relationship that had permitted them as administrative colleagues to discuss matters off the record when necessary continued though Lars was no longer the dean's administrative superior. "However, if the subject is what I think it is, I doubt that I can tell you anything that is not already the topic of rather energetic campus gossip at the moment."

"Actually, the only nugget of current gossip that's reached me is that one of your theatre instructors has been fired."

"Eric Gonzales," Pres confirmed. "That's the hot topic at the moment."

"And of advocacy as well," Lars said. "I was visited by some students with a petition."

"I heard," Pres nodded. "I guess you'll be getting a lot of that from now on."

"I'll be able to handle it if I don't make statements and commitments before I know the real story," Lars explained. "That's why I wanted to talk to you."

"Nothing very complicated about this one, Lars. There was nothing we could do but fire the guy." Pres looked dismayed as he said it, then shook his head thoughtfully and took a sip of water.

"Can you tell me what the problem was, or is it something so personal that you'd rather not?"

"No way it's not going to be known. Haskell will probably have his staff leak it in self-defense when there's an outrage over the firing of such a popular and talented instructor," the unhappy looking dean of fine arts muttered.

He studied Lars resolutely before he continued. "One of Gonzales's assignments has been managing the summer theatre. When we looked over the financial records this fall, there are thirteen thousand dollars unaccounted for. Gonzales doesn't have any explanation that's even close to being plausible."

"It appears, then, that no one's going to be able to mount any serious campaign against the decision when the facts become known," concluded Lars. "I take it that the students who visited me are unaware of the reason that they're losing their beloved instructor."

"They aren't," said Selkirk. "I'm not even sure that they'll believe it when the word does reach them. He's a real talent, Lars, and he relates to kids exceptionally well. He's a damn fine director and seemed to be a capable manager until this problem came up. He made some real improvement in the summer theatre program." Pres continued with an enthusiasm that was typical of him when he spoke of theatrical matters. "Gonzales is the one who convinced me that we ought to bring in professional level lighting and design talent to work the entire summer season. It made a big difference in all the productions last summer. The designer Gonzales brought in was terrific."

Lars knew that Selkirk's assessment of the sets and lighting of the summer shows was meaningful. They were Pres's own area of specialization and he deferred to no one where his professional skills were concerned. "Do you think that Gonzales pocketed the thirteen thousand?" asked Lars.

"I don't know," Selkirk sighed unhappily. "He says that the money went for promotion and production costs, but he doesn't have a single receipt. The bills for materials don't add up and he says he can't remember who he dealt with in arranging the additional ads and other promotional activity."

"Sounds like he's not even a very good storyteller."

"Yeh," said Selkirk, "but he sure has a lot of other talents that we've needed."

"Oh, well," Lars said, "I'm sure you learned long ago that talent and scruples frequently don't go together." With that, the pair spent no further time on the subject during their lunch.

CHAPTER 6

Peace Talks Fail: Hostilities not Anticipated

Lars returned from lunch to find a message from President Jim Haskell's secretary asking that Lars call at his convenience to make arrangements for a meeting with the president. Lars's immediate reaction was that what might be convenient was not necessarily desirable. A meeting with Haskell would undoubtedly be awkward, despite the length of time since Lars had left his assignment as Haskell's chief subordinate under pressure from his superior. The truth was that he harbored no resentment toward Haskell despite the president's having forced his resignation as academic vice president over three years ago. He had enjoyed life too much in the past three years to have regrets over the loss of an assignment that had become more burdensome than satisfying. Besides, he felt no loss from not having the status that came with a leadership post. He could take no credit for this as a conclusion drawn from wisdom. Status had simply never been something in which he took pride.

The principal factor in his reluctance to meet with Haskell, with whom he had passed no more than a nod since Lars had handed him a resignation, was that he anticipated that Haskell would want to re-establish some air of amiability between them because Lars now was the faculty member on the university's governing board. Because Lars took it as a given that Haskell was entitled to his good will, he did not look forward to an awkward meeting where the subject of an amiable working relationship was the topic of conversation. However, there being no legitimate way to avoid a meeting that had to come sooner or later, Lars called and made the appointment for the following day.

When Lars arrived for that appointment, he was treated with great friendliness by the president's office staff. Since they had been equally friendly during his days as academic vice president, he avoided concluding that his new role as trustee, which Lars had noted had a sweetening effect on dispositions around him on campus, was the cause of their pleasantry. The deferential impact of his new role was evident, however, in the case of President Haskell, with whom he had parted under strained circumstances when he left his administrative post. With a broad smile and a firm handshake, Haskell greeted him and urged him toward the couch which made possible the seating arrangement Haskell used when he did not want his desk as a barrier between him and his visitor. Taking the chair that put the low coffee table between them, Haskell smiled disarmingly and said, "It's good to see you, Lars. It's been a long time. How have you been?"

Lars rejected a series of sarcastic responses that could have fit the context and answered, "Just fine. I'm enjoying teaching."

"I hear you're doing a wonderful job," Haskell reported. Lars was tempted to ask how Haskell knew that but settled for looking complacent.

"And now you've taken on some additional interesting responsibilities," Haskell said.

"Yes, It should be interesting," Lars nodded.

"Well," Haskell began, "I apologize in taking so long to offer congratulations on your selection. Of course, it is the rest of us who should be congratulated. Higher education has gained a valuable asset on the board."

"That's kind of you to say," Lars responded. He wished Haskell were not working so hard at being conciliatory. "I'll try to do a good job."

"And of course you will," Haskell said enthusiastically before he entered a dramatic pause. "I suggested you for the faculty trustee seat, you know. I have great respect for your judgment, Lars."

Lars was mildly curious at what point Haskell had made his suggestion, if, indeed, he had. He thought it better not to explore the matter. "I can't tell you what that means to me," Lars said, uncertain in which of several ways he meant for the statement to be taken.

"I'm looking forward to working with you again." Haskell exhibited some unaccustomed awkwardness momentarily before proceeding. "I've been concerned that you have been harboring some ill feeling over the severing of our previous association."

Lars had difficulty restraining a laugh over the vague terminology for describing his quiet but forceful removal from his position as Haskell's chief subordinate. "I've long since come to terms with the fact that you did what the circumstances required you to do. Let's not say any more about that. But as to our current working relationship, I'm sure that you understand that I must view matters from a perspective of the university has a whole, so it will sometimes not be possible to be guided by your arguments of behalf of this campus."

"Oh, of course," Haskell hastened to assure. "You have a certain role to play as a member of the governing board of the entire university system."

"Exactly," Lars smiled at his former supervisor, "I knew that you'd understand. Like you, I too will be subject to circumstances." Lars thought that note might be a good one on which to end a dialogue that had so far avoided any serious awkwardness. He began to rise from his chair, but Haskell asked if he might keep him a bit longer to discuss a matter of some sensitivity and immediacy. Lars settled back and waited for Haskell to address his subject.

Haskell looked his most earnest. "I imagine that you have been approached about a controversy that has been the subject of much campus gossip in the last few days."

Lars resisted saying that Haskell had no need to imagine anything because it was probably the topic that students had approached him about. "The dismissal of the theatre arts professor?" Lars offered tersely.

"Yes," said Haskell. "I'd like to give you the accurate story. There are so many distortions abroad that I'm afraid that you may be hearing some serious misinformation."

"Please don't bother yourself to go into it, Jim. It's far from being a trustee matter at this point." Lars did stand in preparation of a speedy exit now. "I'm confident that you're handling the matter as it should be dealt with."

Haskell looked relieved. It seemed strange to Lars to see it, in view of his having lived with the necessity of Haskell's approval for seven years as a member of his staff. "It's very comforting to know that I have your confidence," said Lars's former supervisor.

"Why shouldn't you have my confidence?" said Lars as he moved toward the door. "That didn't stop three years ago, no matter what else changed." Lars closed the door behind him while smiling toward a thoughtful looking university president. He had to admit that he probably felt better than he ought to feel as he left his former supervisor's office.

CHAPTER 7

Local Man is Surprise Winner

Lars made the short drive from the campus home in high spirits that afternoon. Such was unfailingly his mood when he had had a successful afternoon in the classroom. He had had two demanding classes—both large, both requiring some delicacy in getting the students to engage the material. However, when the sessions went well, the result was never fatigue but rather the energizing effect that success had. He would not feel tired from the effort until much later. Even then, it would be a different kind of fatigue than the one he felt when the classes had not gone well.

Marian's car in the garage signaled that she had already arrived as well, and Lars entered from the garage into the kitchen calling her name. In response, she announced that his wine was on the counter. He dropped his briefcase, took up the glass and carried it into the living room where Marian sat against one arm of the couch with her feet stretched out before her and her arms holding the evening paper. A half-filled glass of wine was on the coffee table at her side. Lars smiled a greeting and lowered himself into his favorite reclining chair, set his wine glass on the nearby book table and put up the footrest of the chair.

Marian returned Lars's smile and without further preliminary began the most invariable and mutually meaningful interlude of their day. Lars and Marian not only shared a marriage of more than twenty-five years and the usual things that went with it—children, financial struggles, good times and bad stemming from both recognizable reasons and causes unrecognized to this day—but a profession as well. As any couple that shared such a dominant portion of their separate existences and had always easily talked to each other about their work, they devoted some portion of each day to reporting the day's activities to each other. But more important, each felt secure that the implications and professional aspects of their work could be dwelt on without the listener showing impatience and boredom. And so what was known to them commonly as the daily report, a name chosen even though it seemed to diminish the importance of something that was truly of major importance to each of them, was recited by both parties in full.

The report completed to the mutual satisfaction of both parties, Lars looked at his now empty wine glass and sought a refill. When Marian answered his inquiry by saying that she would have more wine, Lars brought the bottle in and re-filled her near empty glass. He set the bottle down and kissed Marian lightly on the mouth and then on the forehead. She put her arms around his neck and kissed him more earnestly than he had her. "Are you in a hurry for dinner?" Marian asked.

"No," Lars said, "Why?" suspecting that he knew the answer to his question. He was pleased to think that he might be about to be given the gift that required no thanks, that of recent times came unasked and always unexpectedly, and never the same, but never disappointing.

"I thought we might play a bit," Marian said. It was her way of inviting Lars to make love. It was an invitation that was never declined. It was not frequently given and she knew Lars wished it would occur more often. But it had become their only pattern for initiating sex. Lars had stopped asking sometime ago. Marian almost never responded to his initiatives, so Lars had become accustomed to waiting for her need to signal that he could begin to kiss and caress her without being rejected. Once he sensed his welcome, he could still make Marian respond with increasing intensity in anticipation of what had yet to come, and they both would soon be amply satisfied.

If Lars resented that their lovemaking was totally under her control, he never mentioned it to Marian. He wondered if it occurred to her that he was bothered by it. Years ago, she had often given when she was not needful. Now she made love only when the urge was strongly with her. Now if she wanted it and Lars was not being affectionately exploratory, she simply asked for it. They joked about the unfailing way in which he responded to these opportunities. Perhaps Marian believed it a positive situation that she controlled their sex life. Lars would have had to admit that he did not suffer the disappointment that had been frequent for him when both the mutual passion of youth and Marian's patience with his unshared urgency were gone. It was rare that his physical or verbal exploration was shunted by gentle words or passivity, but this was because he had learned better than to make advances. Yet that less compelling urge that occurred within him more often than it did in Marian left him with a small disquiet at pleasure denied.

Marian was by nature too private a person to have discussed something so intimate as her marital lovemaking with anyone, even Lars. However, one discussion she had had in the course of her scholarly writing had caused her to think about the lovemaking pattern that had evolved between her and Lars.

She was having a discussion with her fellow researcher and co-author Emma Hardesty about teaching techniques they would recommend in their book on the methods of teaching social studies in high school. Marian could not agree with Emma's proposal that they recommend the use of role-playing and simulation activities as a teaching technique. Marian did not believe it was an effective technique. She asserted that students already experienced vicarious involvement with past events or future possibilities through the reading of literature. In that context, they were learning that such imitation of reality is subject to imaginative manipulation to create drama or espouse a viewpoint. Vicarious identification with fictional characters and situations, therefore, showed role-playing was a means to avoid the inescapable realities of the actual world rather than addressing those realities. How then, reasoned Marian, could it be a device for prompting thinking about hard reality, as one wanted students to do in a social studies class?

Emma was quick to respond, "We'd be shortchanging the young, Marian, by depriving them of practicing one of life's valuable skills."

"What skill is that?"

"Role-playing is essentially a game and students might as well get good at games because they'll be playing them all their lives," Marian asserted.

"Surely," Marian asked with some surprise, "you're not talking about game playing as a means of relating to other people?"

Emma looked amused. "Oh, come on, Marian, don't you have any games you play with Lars?"

"No," Marian said with a confidence that permitted a quick response. "Not the kind you're talking about."

"I can't believe it," Emma asserted emphatically. "Surely any couple that's been married for a long time has some game playing by one or both partners in their relationship. Don't you have any control games that you play with Lars?"

Marian rebelled at the very thought. She and Lars had always prided themselves on the candor of their relationship. Her denial to Emma was just as emphatic as the other woman's assertion.

"I wouldn't be surprised," Emma began archly, "if you used something like my favorite ploy for managing my Harry."

"I don't think so. Besides, even if I were inclined, Lars isn't susceptible to manipulation."

"Does Lars ever rub your back?" asked Emma with an air of innocence.

"Yes, once in a while," Marian said.

"I ask Harry to rub my back at some point in just about every evening when we've settled down to read or watch television." Marian smiled and said that Lars was nearly impossible to move from his chair once he had begun his evening. "Oh, my," continued Emma, "Harry often grumbles when I first ask, but I just coax until he gives in."

Marian felt some self-consciousness but confessed in the light of her long working relationship with Emma. "If I did much coaxing of Lars to rub my back, I'd be likely to get more than a back rub, whether I'd intended that or not."

"That's my point, Marian," Emma said, looking a bit smug. "No normal male needs much encouragement, do they? But whether or not the back rub leads to anything beyond that is in our hands, isn't it?"

"It's a bit hard to say 'no' when one has stirred things up, isn't it?" said Marian.

Emma gave Marian her best look of the instructor leading the uncomprehending student. "But saying 'no' occasionally after one has stirred things up is exactly how one establishes control, my dear. Sometimes I stop the progress of activity even when I am feeling a bit up for it myself. It keeps him interested and conscious that he's only going to be satisfied when I let him."

"Sounds like plain, old teasing to me," said Marian.

"Oh, my, no," Emma responded, continuing her pedagogical air, "that would be nasty. I don't tease. I build desire and expectation—and eventually satisfaction. It is just that I manage how far along that continuum any particular episode will go. And because I control that important aspect of our lives, I control Harry in a number of other matters as well."

Marian looked at her co-worker in a new perspective. "I'm not going to take you very seriously, Emma."

"I assure you that you should," Emma said. "It doesn't trouble me that you would, you know. I merely honest enough to do consciously what most other women do unconsciously."

Later, Marian had given some thought to what Marian said. With some uneasiness, she began to think about the foot rubs that Lars frequently gave her, either at her request or at his own initiative when she commented on the soreness of her feet. They often led to farther ranging caresses by Lars accompanied by playful and suggestive comments that either led to sex or to her having to tell Lars that there would be no sex despite his apparent interest and arousal. It was possible—even likely—that she was doing without conscious intention something like what Emma was consciously doing that she called 'managing' her husband. Marian conceded to Emma that role-playing should be discussed as a teaching technique in their book.

Marian subsequently gave further thought to her own intimate behavior with Lars. She resolved that she would avoid letting Lars proceed on what was for him a pleasantly intensifying progression of caresses unless she was receptive to its concluding with mutual passion. She henceforth made clear to Lars when a massage would be that and nothing more. Even when forewarned, it was Lars's way to ply her with suggestive and humorous sallies, lightheartedly trying to gain what it had been made clear he was not to expect. Marian got progressively better in turning these bantering advances with responses in kind. Lars was more often amused by the tone of these rejections and hence there was clarity between them about the signals of affection and passion between them.

The other aspect to this clarity in their relationship was that Marian was direct and sometimes even blunt about wanting sex when the desire was strong within her. Then, the dialogue which accompanied the caresses was earnest and unequivocal—loaded with the language of intimacy between longtime lovers. Of course, both partners came to realize clearly that control of their sex life was decidedly in Marian's hands. Marian saw no unfairness in this because Lars's desire was not as deep as it was when he was younger. Lars seemed to recognize the favorable dimensions to this new pattern to their physical relationship. She knew, because they'd discussed it, that Lars did find sex that was performed from duty rather than passion a bland pleasure. Marian was convinced that their lovemaking, though less frequent, had an enthusiasm and mutual satisfaction that was surprising and pleasing. Lars often now said that he could not remember when sex had ever been better. When he said so to Marian, she would laugh and accuse him of being a classic male chauvinist, whose best orgasm was always the last one he had had. Yet her own expressed satisfaction when they lay in the afterglow of their energetic play made clear to Lars that he was not alone in finding an extraordinary sweetness to these less plentiful, late season fruits.

CHAPTER 8

Campus Controversy Eclipses Classroom Concerns

One of the joys that Lars had experienced in leaving administrative work to return to teaching was to relate to students other than student politicians and their inevitable adjunct, the student reporter, who was indistinguishable from the professional variety in their unflagging pursuit of self-interest masquerading as principle. In his classes, Lars found students equally charming somehow, whether they chose to invite or fight learning. Most of them had a hard time maintaining their indifference. Overheard in casual conversation, they would profess boredom with everything they were required to study and a large portion of what they chose to study. But the caliber of their minds would betray them into interest in an idea from time to time. Lars relished those moments. They more than over-balanced the apparent indifference of youth, which, even at its worst, did not equal the unpleasantness of the adversarial attitude of students when they dealt with administrators.

Of course, teaching students did have its own moments of unpleasantness. Lars was brought to recollect one of them when he looked up from the notes he was skimming moments before the start of class to find a familiar young woman presenting him with the form indicating that she would become a late enrollee in his course. She had taken a class from him the previous spring and they had not finished the semester under pleasant circumstances. Hence her intending to enroll in his political theory course, which was not required either for the major or in the liberal education requirements, was puzzling. “Are you sure you want to do this?" Lars asked with genuine concern for the future tranquility of both of them.

The milky-complexioned oval face framed with straight reddish brown hair cut in a severe bang across her forehead and falling straight to her jaw at the sides did not betray the move of a muscle when she uttered the single word "Yes." She released the form into Lars's hand and walked to the last row and dropped her backpack into the empty chair next to her. She sat down, slid into her usual position, propped her boots on the chair in front of her, and began to tap a pencil on one of her knees, which peaked from her fashionably torn jeans.

Lars recalled what had passed between them last spring. She had come to his office after he had returned an essay test to the class and said, quite respectfully, that she felt that her paper had been incorrectly graded. She had received a D, an unsatisfactory though passing grade, for an answer that she felt was an accurate response to the question Lars had asked. Adding to her frustration was the comment Lars had written on her paper. He had stated that the answer was extremely well written, but it simply did not answer the question asked. In fact, Lars had given the paper a passing though unsatisfactory grade rather than the failing grade that he normally would have given an answer that totally missed the mark because he was impressed with the quality and organization of the writing.

During a discussion that was mostly repetition after the first few minutes, Lars tried to explain how the young woman had misinterpreted the question and hence had offered an analysis that was unrelated to the appropriate answer. The young woman, in rather controlled but insistent fashion, argued the logic of having interpreted the question as she had. When Lars gave no indication of yielding to her reasoning, the student fixed him with a grave and stolid expression and said, with perhaps not the least intention of being insulting, that she hoped that if Lars were to use that question again that he would revise it into a clearer and fairer wording. Lars was put off by the shifting of the responsibility to him for her problem and pointed out rather sharply that sixty-two other students had experienced no difficulty with the wording of the question and had answered along the anticipated lines with varying degrees of success.

Neither Lars's tone nor his point seemed to impact the student and she began again to explain the validity of her answer. Lars succumbed at that point to her emerging and sincere distress. He was aware of something that the young woman could not be. She had scored a B on the two major tests already given. Her other short quiz grades other than this latest one were as high as those on the major tests. The overwhelming probability was that her grade on the final exam would be similar to the usual grades she had scored. Hence, whether her score on this one quiz were an A or an F would make absolutely no difference in her final grade. Of course, Lars could not speak in those terms, it being against the fundamental unwritten law of American educational culture that, when final grades were computed, all things were possible in the face of predominant prior evidence to the contrary. Thus, it seemed abrupt when he interrupted the earnest young woman and stated that she was needlessly distressed by the grade. He continued that he disliked seeing her so upset about it. Therefore, he said as he reached over and took the test paper which the student had earlier laid on his desk, he would change the grade rather than see her so upset. He crossed out the D at the top of the paper and replaced it with a B, which reflected the quality of the analysis if it had been about the right subject.

Lars handed back the paper and was surprised to see that the young woman, rather than being pleased that she had won her point, had begun noiselessly to cry. She snatched the paper and bolted from her chair and quickly disappeared, leaving Lars guiltily reflecting that his accession, which it cost him some pain to make, had made the situation worse rather than better.

The incident was no longer on Lars's mind several days later when the class in which the unhappy student was enrolled met again. But it came back to him with a jolt when he walked down the hall toward the lecture room greeting students that he recognized as he passed them. His greeting to the formerly troubled familiar face was automatic, but he focused when the greeting was not returned, as was usually the case with students. The consciousness of the incident in which he had produced such unhappiness made Lars awkward in the opening minutes of his class, but soon he was engrossed in lecturing about mid-nineteenth century political controversy. To illustrate a British Tory point of view on diplomacy, Lars read a poem by Benjamin Disraeli that treated the subject of relations among nations. Lars confessed that there was a passage in it that he had always found unclear and appealed to the class for help with the key phrase. A sole student volunteered an explanation and Lars experienced what was for him one of the little delights of teaching. Occasionally someone offers to the instructor a different and more insightful perspective on what has been for the teacher an impenetrable or unsatisfactorily understood phrase, and suddenly it becomes clear as crystal.

Lars was so pleased at the experience that he did not realize for a moment that his benefactor was last week's tearful student. Lars explained to the class his lack of understanding had been caused by interpreting one word in the troublesome phrase as a noun rather than a verb. He thanked the student for changing his perception and clearing away his confusion and complemented her on her insight. On reflection, he noted that the young woman did not look the least bit snide that the instructor who had recently graded her down for misreading a question had now had the benefit of her reading more accurately than him.

Lars had intended to say something personally to the student about the irony in the events and apologize for having upset her. Perhaps from pride or guilt, he did not do it in the weeks that remained of the spring term. The young woman's presence in his class this fall, in her usual casual posture, suggested to Lars that he had been forgiven. He added the memory of the episode to the set of teaching experiences which reminded him that one was obliged to teach well to be worthy of that percentage of one's students who were exceptional. Such rare but nourishing experiences kept him attacking his lectures with extraordinary passion.

A few days later, Lars returned to his office charged with the satisfaction of a class that had gone well. He enjoyed the mood for a few minutes before his telephone rang him back to the mundane moment. The caller identified himself and destroyed Lars's ebullient mood by saying that he was a reporter for the student newspaper. Since leaving administration, Lars no longer was called by the student paper to answer questions about the latest real and imagined crises that were occurring on campus. The very presence of a student reporter on the other end of a telephone brought back an avalanche of unpleasant memories. He had never had an interface—they escaped being what might legitimately could be called interviews—with a student reporter that had not been unnerving. Invariably they phrased their questions with the assumption that they were dealing with a corrupt person who had something to hide. A second basis of their point of view was that whatever sources they had talked to among the faculty and students were truthful and that any contrary views or facts coming from an administrative source were suspect. Of course, attempting verification of conflicting views was a luxury they never indulged in because publishing the unverified was more satisfying than delaying publication until the next issue and in the meantime confirming assertions or facts that were in dispute. The basic operating premise was: if there isn't any proof, the administration is hiding the truth. This basic operating premise conformed to the typical student journalist's self-image as a crusading and courageous investigator dedicated to revealing the unquestionable covert wrongdoing of those who wielded the illusionary power in the university. For Lars, the combination of conditions made every interlude with a student reporter an exercise in trying to avoid a slide down an icy mountain when barefoot and blindfolded. He had been spared the feeling for several years until this instant call.

As usual, Lars found that conversing with a student journalist was an exercise in dealing with the unexpected. The first shock came in listening to the great deference with which he was greeted. "Good afternoon, Dr. Paulsen," the ingratiating voice began, "my name is Mindy Carson and I am a reporter for the Weekly Viking, the student paper. I wonder if you could spare a few minutes to answer some questions for me?" Lars was accustomed during his years in administration to a tone that implied a threat should the reporter suspect anything less than humble compliance; therefore, he almost laughed before he responded that he would be glad to take the time, but he was uncertain that he could or should supply information on an as yet unidentified subject. The reporter acknowledged the reasonability of Lars's response, thus confronting Lars with a first in two decades at three different universities where it had been his lot to be obliged to be interviewed by student reporters.

"The story I'm working on," Ms. Carson began, "is about the faculty union's filing a grievance over the firing of the theatre instructor Eric Gonzales."

"I wasn't aware that that had happened," Lars said, hoping that the call might be blessedly brief.

"The union has issued a statement saying that Mr. Gonzales has given an appropriate accounting of the thirteen thousand dollars that was supposedly missing and that they are requesting his immediate reinstatement," the reporter said. Lars made no response. "Do you have a comment on that?" he was then asked.

"I really don't know anything about this," Lars said. "I can't comment."

"In your role as a trustee of the university," the reporter began, "do you intend to investigate the union's grievance?"

"That would be inappropriate," Lars pointed out. "There is very explicit language in the union's contract with the university about how grievances are handled. It would be wrong for me to inject myself into the process at this point in any way."

"But don't the trustees tell the administration how they must handle things like this. I mean, isn't it your job?"

Lars could not suppress a chuckle. "You're talking about the general way in which the trustees oversee the actions of the administration, I guess. That happens within clearly defined limits. This sort of thing only becomes a matter of trustee scrutiny if some contractual or other legal issue requires our involvement after the administrative processes are complete."

"Don't you think that point has been reached yet? I mean, if it has now been proved that Mr. Gonzales didn't steal any money."

"Whether the trustees will be involved is something that I would be notified about through proper channels, and I have not," Lars explained. "I want to emphasize one thing especially. A trustee would never act individually in this or any other matter. Properly, we must act as a group. We don't have individual fishing licenses, if you know what I mean."

"I see," said the voice that came through the phone, "that makes sense."

This last statement was the most substantial shock Lars felt in the conversation. He'd never had a reporter accuse him of making sense before. Hoping to end the interview on this unfamiliar and most pleasant plane, Lars offered, "Why don't you give me a call at some other time if this matter does reach a stage of development where it would be appropriate for me to answer your questions." The student journalist not only agreed but also thanked Lars for doing what he had not actually done, which was to help her with her story.

After the phone call ended in amiable fashion, Lars sat pondering how the student's perception of his status as a trustee had ameliorated the tone of the interface. He doubted that President Haskell and others in the current NSSU administration who were interviewed on this developing public controversy would be handled with such kindness and generosity.

CHAPTER 9

Social Event Aimed at University Good will Encounters Chilly Evening

In October, Lars approached his second monthly trustee meeting with high hopes for a pleasant interlude. He had succeeded in convincing Marian that she should join him for part of the social activities which always accompanied the two days of business meetings. Chancellor Brown had scheduled a dinner on Thursday evening at the university system chancellor's residence, as he frequently did in conjunction with the usual Thursday-Friday business schedule of the trustee meetings.

While the purpose was avowedly to provide the trustees with a relaxed respite from the Thursday afternoon meetings and to restore their energies for the next morning's sessions, they actually had a functional purpose as well. The dinners gave the opportunity for the trustees to meet informally with various constituencies both internal and external to the university for the purpose of taking input or promoting policy initiatives. Sometimes the goal was to gently persuade groups and individuals whose supportive reaction to trustee actions would be facilitative or whose opposition would be a major obstacle. Of course, no business purpose was ever specified for the event and the presence of the trustees' spouses underscored the apparently social purpose of the gathering.

However, spousal veterans of these events looked on them with a modicum of impatience because they anticipated sitting through a considerable amount of shoptalk. Lars hoped that Marian's professional interest in the university would make her more tolerant of the shoptalk than other trustee spouses would be. In addition, he was pleased to have her in Pauliapolis for the overnight stay, although they had to travel in separate cars because Marian would have to leave immediately after breakfast on Friday morning to meet her classes back in St. Claude by late morning.

Chancellor Brown, his wife and Dr. Appleby, as usual unaccompanied by his surgeon wife, had already welcomed most of the evening's company to the chancellor's residence when Lars and Marian arrived. They were greeted with guest-like deference, though formally Lars and the other trustees were co-hosts with Chancellor Brown to the evening's actual guests. The evening's guests were the university's elite compliment of prominent scholars and researchers. These members of the faculty were, in recognition of their published and noted efforts in scholarship and research, awarded the rank of distinguished professor, a title that was accorded to a maximum of twenty-five of the university's total on three campuses of slightly more than three thousand faculty. The title conferred more than status, since it was accompanied with a substantial pay augmentation beyond that normally given to full professors, which was itself a rank and pay level to which no more than one-fourth of the university's faculty attained.

On the basis of accomplishment in their fields, each one of these select few was unquestionably worthy of the compensation and honor accorded. What was less certain was that they should acquire another benefit that accrued to their status as distinguished professors. The university administration and trustees traditionally viewed them as sages, concluding by some strange reasoning that expertise in a specific science or art conferred on one the wisdom to judge what is judicious in all the goals and operations of a complex contemporary public university. The distinguished professors felt that this privileged position to weigh any and all matters abroad in the university was not only rational but a right that accrued with their academic distinction.

What was ignored both by those who took their views so seriously and by the seeming sages who gave their views so confidently was that they were usually motivated by self-interest rather than objective analysis. Typically, all faculty were convinced that what furthered their interests furthered the university as a whole. That was even more emphatically the case with these most able among them.

In fact, the distinguished professors often initiated a position statement when they felt some administrative action was improper or unwise, letting their views be known even though they had not been requested. They had on more than one instance brought an abrupt end to the career of a chancellor of the university who had displeased some segment of the faculty, for whom the small group of twenty-five were confident that they spoke, though they never took the pains to ascertain what might be the consensus among that group consisting of more than one hundred times their number. If they collectively lacked humility, it was not a unique circumstance for any such recognized group in an American university. Their instructional colleagues concurred in according them the highest level in the academic caste system that prevailed throughout the land despite a constant rhetorical devotion within the profession to an egalitarian concept of what American university social structure was like.

The seating plan at trustee dinners at the chancellor's residence mingled at tables with six places each the guests, trustees, their spouses and the few attending senior administrators—these being Chancellor Brown's three system level vice chancellors and their spouses. Hence Marian and Lars did not have the comfort of being seated together. Marian found herself seated between Trustee Harlan Cartwright, the Pauliapolis business executive, and Dr. Harold Stratemeier, a distinguished professor of geology at the Pauliapolis campus. Trustee Henderson's wife, the student trustee Henry Amberson, and the wife of Marshal Carter, the operations vice chancellor, were her other table companions.

Attempts at conversation topics which engaged Marian's entire table soon diminished. Mrs. Carter was interested in ingratiating herself with Mrs. Anderson, who was focused in being maternal with the youthful trustee Amberson. Amberson's satisfaction in being the focus of the attention by the two matrons left the three others at the table searching for a subject of their own. Stratemeier, Marian soon discovered, was intent of talking across her to Trustee Cartwright, so she was satisfied to devote herself to a rather good fruit salad with an unexpectedly different dressing while the geologist re-established for Cartwright what an ornament to the university he was, and Cartwright reminded the professor what a weighty figure in the business community the trustee was.

Alas, shortly after the entree was served, Marian's quiet devotion to her meal was not to endure. "I understand, Mrs. Paulsen, that you are on the faculty at North Shore," said Dr. Stratemeier.

"Yes," answered Marian, holding to brevity to avoid revealing her irritation on two counts. Stratemeier had either assumed that she did not have an earned doctorate or meant to deny her a form of address that was normally accorded to him. Secondly, though Marian's professional reputation was not as eminent as Stratemeier's, she was of substantial reputation among professors of education nationally. While it was reasonable that the prominent geologist would not know of her professional reputation, a more courteous man would have begun from the assumption that they were professional equals, Marian thought.

"And what do you teach?" continued Stratemeier.

"I'm an education professor—social science is my field," said Marian.

"Social science," Stratemeier repeated with a stress on the second word that expressed his doubts that the word "science" could correctly be applied to Marian's area of expertise. Marian thought her silence at this point might lead Stratemeier to drop the topic; however, the distinguished professor asked, mindful that he was addressing the spouse of a university trustee but exploring from a viewpoint rigidly formed long ago, "And just what scientific facts are they that you teach youngsters aspiring to be teachers?"

Marian reflected at that moment that Lars often joked that she had no capacity to convey abrasiveness. On the other hand, she felt that she always successfully suppressed it while he, in her view, too often gave in to it. Her mastery of combativeness was equal to the moment, however, and she stated, "The fundamentals of several disciplines actually—history, sociology, a bit of anthropology and political science."

Stratemeier responded with a playfulness that struck Marian as being more for Cartwright's ears than for hers, "You're not worried that you might produce that situation where a little knowledge is a dangerous thing, are you?"

"No," Marian answered, smiling as she began an answer she could give with complete comfort. "It's a matter of grounding the student in basic concepts from which they can build a more extensive knowledge and learn independently. Much the same as you do with you beginning geology students, I expect. I'm sure that you give them a good foundations and within a few years the best of them are working with you as research assistants."

Marian had, as she hoped, struck a rich vein, not for conversation but certainly for monologue. Stratemeier began a long account, which he permitted Cartwright to interrupt with an occasional brief question, of how he started students in the science of geology and developed them into high caliber researchers. By the time he was finished, he had long since forgotten the exploration he had begun of Marian's being a lesser light in the academic firmament. It was, in fact, a lengthy enough monologue that Marian's dessert was being set before her by the time it was ended.

As he turned to his dessert, Stratemeier seemed to have exhausted his account of how he produced superior geologists, and Marian feared she might not get to enjoy her chocolate mousse without another ego battering. She resorted to the universal topic most likely to re-start a conversation. "Of course, Trustee Cartwright," Marian began, the faculty member in her not permitting her to use the trustee's first name, though she'd been invited to do so, "Dr. Stratemeier's modesty no doubt prohibits him from mentioning how much external funding he and his research assistants produce for the university budget."

Cartwright, whose interest had been flagging increasingly during the geology professor's lengthy account of the nurturing of fine scholars, perked up immediately at the mention of money. Marian knew it always stimulated the interest of a businessman that a professor generated money rather than being the agent for absorbing it. He earnestly queried Stratemeier on the particulars of his revenue-producing research activities. Stratemeier was delighted to specify not only the amounts and sources of funding but also his role in the research which had been given such substantial financial support. For a competent academic like Marian, Stratemeier's was a routine story, hence, boring, but preferable to being the focus of Stratemeier's unfounded but nonetheless annoying contempt for academics who trained teachers for the public schools. As Marian savored her chocolate mousse, she resolved to tell Lars that she would not relish accompanying him to these trustee social functions in the future.

Lars himself had not had a relaxing dinner, though he did not suffer the personal irritation that Marian was to report to him vividly when they left the dinner for their hotel room. His dining experience had proven to be a business session of such intensity that he barely noticed what the food was that he had eaten. He was seated between his fellow trustee Martha Collins and the wife of trustee Ugstad. Mrs. Ugstad, Lars soon realized, was a shy woman who endured these events for two reason, she had always accompanied her husband on business trips, and each monthly meeting provided the opportunity to shop in Pauliapolis for things that were not available in as wide a selection or quality in the small town where they lived. Hence she was quite happy to enjoy her meal and limit her participation in dialogue to brief pleasantry and small talk. Her presence would have made for a relaxing meal for Lars if Martha Collins had not been in a genuinely conflicted state over a matter that she wanted to explore with Lars.

Collins had been approached by trustee Pete Henderson to support a resolution that he was going to propose the next day obliging the administration to institute a one percent across-the-board cut in all its programs to fund immediately the clean up of the pollution of Little Moose Lake. Collins was among the first of the trustees from whom Henderson had solicited support and was surprised that Lars had not been approached yet. She could not decide how she would vote on the resolution. Collins shared the legitimate environmental concern over the damage to the lake, and she took seriously the possible reprisals against the university by the sportsmen over any delay in their returning to one of their pleasant and convenient hunting and fishing sites. Of course, Martha was also conscious of the hardship it would be on the university's programs to lose money that they had planned on for the two-year state budget period. Her distress was increased by Lars's pointing out that since the first of the two budget years was well underway, the assessment of a one percent cut would probably have to be applied in the second year, which would actually make it a two percent reduction for that second half of the budget period. Martha looked genuinely grave as she asked Lars whether he would support Henderson's resolution or oppose it.

Lars told Martha quite honestly that he didn't know on the spur of the moment how he would vote. He had not expected to have the matter of cleaning up the lake come up again so soon. He had expected that the administration would not find the funding in the current budget to clean up the pollution without removing promised funding from existing programs. Thus, he anticipated that the administration would include a clean-up funding request in the next biennial budget request that they would prepare for the board to submit to the state government a year hence. No doubt the board would support that item unanimously, and the sportsmen could shift their pressure for action to the state government. The state's sportsmen undoubtedly would not be happy to wait a total of three years to return to the lake, but that seemed a preferable course of action to diverting money from other university programs to secure immediate action.

To delay the clean up until the next budget cycle had ramifications sure to annoy two powerful groups, the legislators who would have to find the money to augment the university's budget and the sportsmen who would surely be incensed at what they would consider an unconscionable delay at addressing environmental damage of the university's own making.

Lars was a captive audience to Martha's exploration of the problem from all angles, repeating facets tirelessly when every nuance of the possibilities had been identified and no painless course of action seemed possible. Lars respected his colleague's intense desire to do the right thing, but he was both fatigued and frustrated by her inability to let the topic go and allow the evening to be a respite from the challenge that Henderson's proposal would no doubt bring in the morning. It was more from desperation than conviction that he heard himself say, "I wonder if the administration has thought of applying to the federal superfund for the money to do the clean up. You know—that federal money that's been identified specifically to handle pollution problems." Lars had no idea whether the possibility had been considered or whether the project would qualify for the fund, which was primarily intended to remedy the worst cases of environmental damage. However, he did not express these reservations to his dinner companion, since she seized on the possibility as a solution which would satisfy all concerned parties close at hand—and more importantly would relieve the trustees of either pressure or criticism.

Lars felt a bit guilty about remaining silent about the unlikelihood of his idea working out, but his guilt did not prevent him for having one more glass of wine in a more relaxed state before the remarks after dinner by Chancellor Brown and Trustee Chair Appleby. The theme of both speeches was similar. Appleby affirmed for the trustee professors what a valuable and much appreciated resource they were to the university. Chancellor Brown cited the most recent research accomplishments and externally funded projects by certain members of the group, perhaps causing those distinguished professors not mentioned to reflect that academic giants shrink to normal professorial size inexorably unless they pump themselves up by repeated accomplishment. Finally, Brown applied salve to any inadvertent wounds by affirming that the national prominence and respect accorded the university resulted from presence on its faculty of the entire cadre of distinguished professors.

Lars knew all too well that a fundamental reality of the American higher education scene was being recognized. The achievements of a small group of successful researchers are the basis of the reputation for excellence of an American university. Given the presence of a few academic stars, the public and the media assume the high quality of the instructional activity at a university, whether that excellence is a reality or not. As did any experienced professional in higher education, particularly one who had served as a senior administrator, Lars knew that there was no necessary connection between the two conditions. His experience told him that his fellow trustees did not know that. His fellow trustees' belief would have depressed Lars, except that he knew that they did not share a parallel assumption believed by an astonishing percentage of the

American populace. The majority of Americans believed that there is a correlation between the success of a university's athletic teams and the quality of the education it offers. Clinging to the single, sanity-supporting fact that his colleagues on the board did not believe that success in athletics and educational quality are inseparable, Lars endured in moderately amiable spirits until the dinner adjourned for the evening.

As they buckled into their car seats to begin the short drive back to the hotel, Lars ventured, "That wasn't so bad."

Marian did not receive his opinion in tranquility. She recounted with painstaking detail the condescension she had suffered at the hands of Dr. Stratemeier without mitigation by way of trustee Cartwright's having introduced a different topic of conversation. Re-living the episode did not calm Marian. In fact, Lars's offer of an explanation for Stratemeier's abrasiveness only made things worse. Marian had not known that Stratemeier had been the nominee of the Pauliapolis faculty for the faculty trustee position. Had the faculty of all three campuses unified behind him, he most likely would have been the appointee. Because the North Shore State faculty union had for the first time proposed their own candidate, who also attracted some support at the Beau Prairie and Pauliapolis campuses, Stratemeier was the first ever Pauliapolis nominee to be disappointed. The lobbying by the two factions was what had made the governor turn elsewhere to fill the faculty trustee seat, thus resulting in Lars's selection. Hence, Lars pointed out, Marian was the victim of a bit of anger at Lars that Stratemeier still nurtured. She would not experience such a situation again when she accompanied him to trustee social functions, Lars assured her. His speculation that her experience had not been typical did not sway Marian, who asserted with finality that he was unlikely to have her along at any more trustee social events.

Lars barely saved himself from adding to Marian's irritation when he suppressed saying what was often the opening of a playful episode when they traveled. Hotels were a mild aphrodisiac to Marian. A nightcap in the bar often concluded with his asking her up to what he termed "his" room, as a predatory male might a woman casually encountered. Marian would assume the role of a stranger and ask Lars what he had in mind. The subsequent dialogue and activity was always mutually satisfying. Now, Lars almost said, "I suppose asking you up to my room is out of the question." He knew that the developments he hoped for were impossible, so he did not increase Marian's annoyance by posing the question.

CHAPTER 10

U Trustees Torn by High Kicks and Sportsmen's Nix

Pete Henderson sought recognition immediately after Chair Appleby's call for any new business. Though the normal planning and mode of operation of the trustees meetings made any so-called new business a rarity, Henderson's proposal came as a surprise to no one because of his energetic efforts to line up sufficient votes in advance for its introduction. Not having been approached, Lars wondered if Henderson had been successful. After Henderson moved his resolution proposing the one percent across-the-board cut to fund the pollution cleanup, a lengthy silence followed Appleby's call for a second. The board was motionless as well as silent, like rabbits hoping that the dogs would not pick up their scent. Henderson fixed his gaze on trustee Bensweiger, who reluctantly mumbled a second that he appeared to have promised Henderson that he would deliver. Henderson then made a passionate argument emphasizing not only everyone's duty to protect the environment but also the university's moral obligation to the state's sportsmen, who pursued an interest that the state was traditionally noted for. It was an effective declaration of two verities in a region that prided itself on its natural beauty and the avid pursuit of the recreational interests that the largely unspoiled environment of the state provided.

Another silence followed Henderson's endorsement of his recommended solution to the Little Moose Lake problem. Lars studied the faces of his fellow trustees to see who would be first in coming to the support of Henderson's idea, which obviously would be unpopular with the faculty, and possibly the students as well. Lars saw Chancellor Ivor Brown studying the board members' faces as intently as he was. When it became clear that Brown could proceed without intruding on any trustees' desire to speak, he sought the floor and began his remarks in the deliberate fashion that was intended to imply that everything that he said had been carefully thought out and that he was incapable of being either hasty or emotionally reactive.

"Chair Appleby and members of the board," said Brown, "be assured that every member of the administration shares your commendable concern for a speedy solution to the pollution problem on university property. After yesterday's meeting, I directed the staff to explore the cost of cleaning up the problem and the possibilities for funding an immediate clean up within the university's current budget. The cost would be substantial, because it includes not only digging up the leaking barrels in which the hazardous waste was buried, but paying for a new means of dealing with the waste in a way that both meets current, more stringent regulations and, hopefully, will be permanent. The staff estimates the cost at between twenty-five and thirty million dollars. It will be expensive to do it right—we should not forget that. When this waste was buried thirty years ago, the method was thought to be a permanent disposal of the problem. We now know that more safeguards—hence greater expense—are a necessity to avoid a repetition of the problem."

"The staff has nearly completed a plan to divert the funding from other programs if you wish to proceed with the clean up project immediately," Brown continued. "I must tell you that the staff has, with my concurrence, taken a different approach to identifying funds than what has been proposed in Trustee Henderson's plan. To do as proposed in the motion now before you would diminish the funding next year for every program in the university, both instructional and non-instructional. "The solution that the staff is working on recognizes that the university as a whole has been underfunded for a number of years. Hence it would be unwise to divert funds from highest priority of the university—instruction. Instead, the staff is identifying certain non-instructional programs for total elimination so that the core activity of the university will remain undamaged. I hope that you will agree with that principle. If we decide to proceed with attacking the pollution problem immediately—we should proceed in a manner that will not adversely affect our most important activities."

His own administrative experience having made him painfully aware of the truth of Brown's statement about years of underfunding, Lars believed that the trustees should avoid re-allocation from the current university budget at all; however, if his fellow trustees did commit to funding the clean up immediately, he was relieved by the soundness of the method that Brown was proposing. He was on the verge of asking for recognition to say so when Trustee Marsha Brandwyn sought recognition and was given the floor by Appleby.

"I am not yet convinced that we should begin with the elimination of the Little Moose Lake problem immediately, but how we vote on that matter is obviously related to where the money would come from and how much damage would be done by diverting those funds."

Brandwyn paused for emphasis, then began again with heightened earnestness. "Word has reached me from supporters of one of the programs that would be eliminated under the plan that Chancellor Brown has his staff working on. Some of those supporters are present here today and I would like the board to hear their concerns."

Lars was still mulling over the astonishing speed at which information was abroad about staff activity that the chancellor had initiated just the previous evening when Chancellor Brown whispered quickly to Appleby, and Appleby announced Brown's name as the next speaker.

"Chair Appleby and members of the board, with all due respect, I ask you to consider whether it is wise to air this concern at this time. As I stated earlier, the plan for program eliminations is not yet complete. It may change considerably before it is finalized. At this point, it is not definite what programs will be on the list. If you desire to review the plan at the next meeting as a basis for funding the clean up, is that not the appropriate time to consider all the programs that would be eliminated?"

Brandwyn was quick to request the floor for rebuttal. "I don't think it would be fair to make these people, who are concerned parents of university students, to wait to be heard. Perhaps hearing one case of the implications of a program elimination approach will help us decide whether or not we want to direct the administration to stop consideration of so drastic a course of action. Why create panic in certain programs that they are on a hit list if we would not consider implementing such a course of action?"

That Brandwyn would want the board to hear a special plea for one program at a premature time was no surprise to Lars, or more veteran members of the board as well. Her reputation as the board's bleeding heart was well established. She was the member that opponents to any developing administration action—and it was the norm that there were always opponents, no matter how cautious and well-reasoned the contemplated action was—approached to get themselves a conduit to speak directly to the board. This trait created great ambivalence about her because she was indiscriminate in her advocacy. She urged the board's hearing everyone, whether they be blatantly self-interested or thoughtful and unselfish.

Appleby, whose parliamentary role it was to keep the board on task, asked his colleagues, "I do not think that Trustee Brandwyn's suggestion is, in the strictest sense, in order with regard to the motion before us; however, if the board wants to hear the spokespersons that trustee Brandwyn wishes us to hear, I will not rule the presentation out of order. How many favor hearing the presentation?" Lars kept his arms on his lap. Appleby looked less than pleased when enough hands when up to clearly constitute a majority. "Fine. We will hear the presenters if they will come forward now."

Two men and a woman stood up within the audience seating area and began to make their way toward the speaker's chair at Appleby's left. By the time they reached the front of the room, two additional chairs had been placed in the speaker's position so that all three could sit. One of the men took the chair in front of the microphone and his companions sat in the flanking chairs.

The spokesperson was a man in his late forties or early fifties. His round, florid face displayed a tendency to fleshiness that made his expensive, conservative suit fit snuggly. He shuffled some sheets of paper until he was satisfied with their order and leaned down closer to the microphone than necessary to be heard.

"Chair Appleby and members of the board, thank you for the opportunity to express to you our concern about the plan to eliminate a university program for which the members of our group have a very high regard. Our children are currently participants in this program and derive great benefit from that participation. In fact, many of these students only chose this university to attend for their education because they could participate in this program. No only would we regret the loss of this program for our children, we deplore its unavailability to future potential students who will chose to attend other institutions because the program is no longer unavailable here."

Lars speculated which among the university's non-instructional programs the speaker was discussing. An initial round of program elimination invariable focuses on programs which are sparse in participants and not closely related to instruction while also entailing some significant cost to offer. He was not familiar enough with the Pauliapolis campus's non-instructional activity to infer likely candidates, but the speaker's passionately delivered remarks did make the program sound like one of some significance.

"Our group consists of the parents of the students who participate in the dance line," the speaker said, finally achieving some long needed specificity. Only Lars's considerable experience as an administrator kept him from an audible reaction to the information. His experience had been that, even in the midst of considering the weightiest matters, a relatively minor matter would claim equal or even preeminent consideration. Be it physics or football, every existing activity within a university would be defended with equal and near religious vigor by its advocates when conditions suggested that some activity had to go to reduce or re-allocate expenditures. Hence Lars was not surprised that the parents of the students who performed dance routines between portions of the football and hockey contests had risen in alarm at the possibility that the program might be eliminated to fund some other activity.

The speaker spoke passionately of the long existence of the dance line, of the important crowd appeal it added to athletic contests, of the skill required of the dancers, who developed it in long hours of rehearsing dance routines of their own creation, and of the benefits to the young dancers of what was learned about dedication and discipline through this participation.

Lars decided, as the impassioned parent reached his final emotional appeal, that silence would be the better part of discretion in the discussion now to begin. Having a dance line was a refinement that his own campus in St. Claude shared with the Pauliapolis campus, though their athletic programs participated at very different levels. He had not seen the Pauliapolis dance line, but he imagined that the routines were similar, consisting of high kicks in chorus line formation combined with occasional acrobatics and a great many synchronized movements not unlike calisthenics. It was all harmless and pleasing to the eye when well executed, but hardly something that anyone except a doting parent would place on a list of minimally meaningful university level activity. Such a sentiment, Lars recognized, would be well to leave unexpressed.

Trustee James Middlebrook, a humanities professor at St. Stephens college, a prestigious private college in Pauliapolis, was unable to restrain himself when the dance line advocates had finished their heartfelt appeal for the continuation of the program so dear to the hearts of themselves and their student offspring. St. Stephens was a small, expensive, socially elitist college, and it would sooner have nude, mixed doubles tennis than a dance line. Hence Middlebrook's doubts about the necessity of an educational institution's having such a program might safely be inferred. While Lars was normally irritated with Dr. Middlebrook's arrogant condescending perspective on issues arising at a large public university system, he expected that he was about to enjoy himself.

"I'll confess to being unfamiliar with the activity being discussed," said Middlebrook with discernible pride. "As you know, St. Stephens does not have the high emphasis athletic program that there is here in the university; hence we have not acquired trappings such as a dance line and the like. Therefore, I perhaps have the advantage of a more objective perspective on this activity.

"The pollution problem we must deal with is a very serious matter. If we wait until the next budget cycle and include a request for funds for the clean up, we have no guarantee that such a request would be funded. Then we would be facing, two years hence, exactly the same situation that we face now. We will be searching internally for the funds to accomplish the clean up. Surely we would be derelict in our responsibilities to delay any longer than the next budget cycle to deal with this matter. Thus, if we are forced to implement a solution funded by the internal transfer of funds, I would favor the program elimination approach rather than an across-the-board cut. In that case, I believe the peripheral nature of the program we are discussing is incontestable. Notwithstanding the hard work and commitment that some students—and I feel compelled to point out it is not a large number—put into the program, I would have no hesitancy in voting for its elimination."

One of the other parents who had accompanied the initial spokesperson injected without waiting to be recognized to speak that it made no sense that the dance line should be eliminated to correct a problem that it had absolutely no part in creating. Let those, he asserted, who had created the pollution problem bear the burden of eliminating it. He began a passionate declaration of how hard his daughter, who had participated in her high school dance line before entering the university, worked in creating routines when Dr. Appleby cut him short as being out of order.

The woman who had not yet spoken sought recognition. She wisely sensed that some conciliation was in order. She stated that the pollution problem was the shared concern of everyone in the university, and that it seemed to her that the fairest course of action would be that all the university's programs, without exception, should share the cost of the clean up.

Appleby thanked the woman for her statement and noted that it had, in its content returned the discussion to the subject of the motion on the floor. He told the three visitors that unless they had more to add, they could be excused, and the board would return to further discussion of the motion of the floor.

No one seemed eager to speak to the motion. Finally, Martha Collins asked for recognition and said, "I am not comfortable to vote on this motion that finalizes the course of action we will take when we have not had a chance to explore alternatives. We have not seen the plan that the administration is preparing. Also, I've been made aware that some federal agency—or perhaps the state environmental protection agency—might be a source of funds for this task. It seems premature to decide this now."

Henry Amberson hastened to contribute. "I agree with Trustee Collins that a decision would be premature. I would like to have the chance to gather the opinion of the students on the possibility of budget cuts and other possible solutions."

Pete Henderson showed some impatience in responding. "The board should know that I have brought forward this proposal after I was approached by several large and important citizens groups—the farm organizations and the sportsmen's organizations. And I can assure you that they are very impatient and getting angry. They don't understand how the university can in good conscience delay in correcting this problem. We might as well stop hoping for money to drop from the sky and take care of this matter with our current funds. We're all aware that the university's support has been eroding in recent years. If we don't do something about this right now, it is bound to erode even further."

Following Henderson's testy assertion, which had more than matched the passion of the dance line parents, all the trustees except Lars who had not yet spoken to the motion acted out the board's most cherished ritual—rallying to the side of the angels. Each spoke earnestly to their total opposition to pollution and their commitment to its elimination on university property. However, in keeping with this ritual, each was careful to avoid stating his position on the proposed solution or any of its alternatives. So customary was this ritual that Walter Appleby looked toward Lars to see if he wished to make his bold statement against pollution. Lars sought recognition with a slight flexing of his hand and, being recognized, said, "I move to table the motion until the next meeting." Though Pete Henderson reacted with an expression of disgust, ten other faces unsuccessfully tried to hide an expression of relief. The motion passed on a vote of eleven to one.

The crisis of the month having been concluded, the board disposed of the rest of the agenda rapidly so that they could proceed toward home through the sunlit and colorful autumn countryside. Lars enjoyed the effort that ten of his eleven colleagues took to wish him a pleasant trip home.

CHAPTER 11

Intent of Profs Collusion Questioned

Lars sat in his office daydreaming about nothing in particular. It was a pleasure he had returned to since resuming his teaching duties. On a day when his classes had gone well—when the coherence of what he had planned to say was actually manifest in the delivery; when the students had responded insightfully and extensively—then one felt a satisfaction in which one could simply sit and saturate oneself. There was a gentle knock at the open door followed by a liquidly uttered statement. "I hope I'm not interrupting the formulation of a major statement of theoretical political science."

Lars smiled broadly at the woman who entered the small office and now stood before his desk with a smile that combined impishness and allure. "Alas, we'll never know," Lars said with mock gravity. "If there was a great thought emerging its completely gone now."

"I don't seem to have that disruptive effect on any other man except you," said his visitor as she sat and made herself visibly comfortable. Lars had not seen Connie Mercutio in over a year, and in that instance for only a few minutes of conversation devoted to reporting the state of their lives at the moment. In fact, their only prior extensive contact had been four years earlier, Lars's last year of administrative work. Connie had been a candidate for tenure that year. Because she was an exceptional teacher and scholar, to award her permanent employment status would have been a routine matter except for Connie's involvement in some feminist activity that led to vocal community opposition to her further employment at NSSU. As the editor of the woman's resource center newsletter, she had written a number of columns deploring the actions of local groups opposed to abortion. It was only the support of Lars, who, as vice president for academic affairs, was the principal recommender to the president on her tenure award that had made common sense prevail. Lars was also convinced that he had saved the university a lawsuit that Connie would surely have won over the matter.

Actually, Lars's efforts had been motivated by more than duty. He admired the woman. She was bold and forthright in her support of the right as she saw it, which, Lars had to admit, corresponded with his own views. This demeanor, coupled with her gifts as a teacher and her accomplishments as a scholar, made her the model of what Lars hoped for in the younger generation of academics. Lars, though reluctant to admit it to himself, was conscious of Connie's charms beyond the intellectual. At five foot nine, she matched his own height. Her body had the willowy athleticism that it retained since her days as a collegiate tennis player. As Lars had learned to his dismay several years ago, she was more than his equal as a golfer, a fact that Connie had been careful to make only limited use of as a topic for humor in their rare meetings during the last several years.

"How have you been?" Lars asked.

"Fine. Just fine," Connie answered.

"I thought as much," Lars grinned. "I haven't heard of any lynch mobs pursuing you across campus."

"That's true," Connie smiled, her expression developing into a look that crossed amusement and anticipation. "Of course, I'm not sure how long that situation will last."

"Oh, God," Lars began with a tone of exaggerated concern. "What are you into now?"

"I've just taken on a new, shall we say, professionally related assignment."

"I can hardly wait to hear what it is," Lars said, continuing his pretended apprehension.

Connie's eyes joined in the sly mirth conveyed by her smile and announced, "I am the new faculty union grievance officer."

"I don't believe it," Lars retorted. "Ev Lawlor would never give up the greatest joy of his life. He has been the grievance officer since before I got here, and that's twelve years. I think he likes rattling the administration's cage more than he does sex."

"Well, he's probably giving that up too," Connie said and registered a serious expression. "He's had a mild heart attack and his doctor has recommended that he give up all avoidable stressful activity."

"I know I'll sound unkind," Lars sighed, "but Ev gave a helluva lot more stress than he got through his actions as union grievance officer." Lars paused a moment before adding, "I *am* being unkind. I wish him well. But," Lars continued, "what possessed you to take on such a thankless and time consuming burden?"

"I didn't agree to at first. I'm up to my ears this semester. I have two big classes, a couple of committees assignments, and a research project I must wind up before the end of the school year," Connie sighed. "But then they worked on my conscience."

"Ah, that." nodded Lars feigning exasperation. "Yours is drastically overactive, you know. But then you must be aware of that, with the frequency that it gets you into trouble."

"I don't know that I get more than my share of trouble—from acting on principle, that is." Connie's expression became serious. "The truth is, they made me feel like some kind of freeloader. I'd never been active in the union—even to attend meetings—let alone handle any kind of assignment."

"That could be said of more than ninety percent of your fellow union members, many of whom have been here a lot longer than you."

"Yes," Connie said and shrugged her shoulders. "They have to deal with their consciences and I with mine."

Lars was struck with a discomforting thought. "With regard to consciences, don't tell me that they've sent you here to stir mine because I've never joined the union since I came on to the faculty?"

Connie laughed in the unaffected manner that Lars heard in few people. "Your not having joined is a matter of constant comment, as a matter of fact. But that's not why I'm here. In a way, I'm here to do the administration a favor."

"My God, they've transplanted Ev Lawlor's brain into you," Lars groaned. "Or is it that you've already developed that weird line of reasoning that happens to anyone who becomes a grievance officer?"

"Oh, for pity's sake, stop acting like an administrator—or worse yet—a trustee, and hear me out."

Sensing her seriousness, Lars dropped his playful mood and listened.

"You no doubt know about the administration's summarily firing Eric Gonzales," Connie began. "The stated reason is that there appears to be thirteen thousand dollars unaccounted for in the records of last summer's repertory theatre, which he managed. The union has recently entered a grievance on Eric's behalf because he wasn't given adequate due process before the decision was made."

"That's a standard position on the union's part. They fight every dismissal, and, if there isn't any substantive basis for the grievance, they always say the process was faulty. I've known Pres Selkirk for years and I've seen how he administers. Not only is he a fair-minded man, he's one of the most thorough administrators I ever worked with. I'm sure Gonzales had ample opportunity to tell his story. As for Weaver, who took my place as recommender to the president, the truth is that he is, if anything, overly cautious in cases like this."

"It now seems," Connie sighed, "that there's more to the story than Eric has previously admitted. The professional technical director that Gonzales brought in for the season has stated in writing that he was paid the thirteen thousand dollars in addition to his contract salary because Eric insisted that he do last minute set modifications after the tech director had completed the agreed to designs."

"And Gonzales hadn't thought to mention this before?" said Lars disbelievingly.

"He says that he was afraid that putting it in the records would make him look like a bad manager."

"So he'd rather look like a crook?" Lars injected sarcastically.

"It was the summer theatre's first season in the black in five years," Connie reported. "He didn't think that there'd be such a thorough audit."

Lars had great faith in Connie's integrity. However, a lengthy career in administration had taught him that no alleged wrongdoer in a university ever lacked an explanation that absolved him or her of responsibility for his or her actions. "Do you believe this late breaking explanation?" Lars asked, trying to limit his skepticism so Connie would not feel insulted.

"Gonzales says that he realized at the last minute that the set for the musical was all wrong. When he asked the man—Driscoll's his name—for a whole new set after he'd finished constructing the design Gonzales gave him before, Driscoll cited his contract and refused unless he was paid additional salary. We have his written statement now."

Lars shook his head. "If it's true I can't believe Gonzales wouldn't have said anything before now."

"He says that he was worried that he wouldn't get to manage summer theatre in future years, which, of course, would be income that he normally counts on. The main thing from the union's point of view,' Connie said earnestly, "is that there's no evidence to say that his explanation isn't so."

Lars sighed, "if it's true, he may be an inept manager, but he's not a thief. Certainly his actions are no grounds for dismissal—discipline maybe, but not dismissal."

"We're hoping that the administration would see it that way," Connie offered.

"Have you talked to them yet?" Lars noticed he had used the collective reference for the campus's leadership rather than specifying an individual. Apparently, he was completing his transition to a professorial mentality.

"No," said Connie, accompanying the word with an instructor's gesture that Lars might have used himself to signal that a crucial point was coming. "That's why I've come to you. I'm trying to get the union out of the automatic adversarial posture that they adopt in every case of employment status controversy. It's the main reason that I took the assignment of grievance officer. I'm not alone within the faculty of the opinion that a lot of situations can be resolved without resort to the formal processes called for in the contract."

"That's commendable, Connie, though I'm not optimistic that you can change some long engrained behavior—on both sides. But why have you come to me? I don't see what I can do."

Connie looked at him with the earnestness that accompanies a sincere person's making the clinching argument. "President Haskell hasn't responded to the grievance yet. He's more likely to listen to you than to anyone else—certainly not the union grievance officer—that he doesn't have all the facts. The Gonzales termination seems certain to be overturned by an arbitrator. If he accepts that from you, a lot of time, money and public embarrassment can be avoided."

Lars would have been amused by Connie's perception if it also did not bring to mind some painful personal history. "You want me to go to the man who removed me from the position that is officially responsible for giving him advice on these very matters and convince him to back off from a very significant decision that he is publicly on record for."

"Oh, please," Connie said, rejecting Lars's statement yet managing a sympathetic tone, "everyone on this campus knows what respect for your judgment Haskell had. It's well known that his dumping you was about pure self-interest, not about how you did your job."

Lars snorted ruefully, "If that's the case, there isn't one damn soul on this campus who's ever said that to me."

"Except me," Connie said, her eyes meeting his to emphasize her sincerity.

"That's true," Lars admitted. His mind continued to dwell on the painful subject of his lost administrative career. It was a foolishness, since he realized his life was more pleasant and productive now; yet he had never overcome the feeling of failure that clung to the circumstances of the end of his term as academic vice president.

"Besides, I hate to bring this up," Connie began, though it seemed to Lars that she sounded anything but reticent, "your recent appointment to the board—about which I've been neglectful in not offering congratulations, I confess—does significantly increase the intensity of the attention that President Haskell will give to anything that you say."

The transparently false innocence with which Connie expressed the circumstance broke Lars's dark reverie and made him smile. "You know, professor, understatement is an infrequent rhetorical style with you," Lars said, good humored in spite of himself, "so I suggest that you should be careful not to tinge it with cynicism when you do use it."

"Me? Cynical?" Connie gasped with an exaggerated, wide-eyed expression. "How could one be a woman faculty member in an American university and be cynical?"

Lars's reluctance to fulfill Connie's request vanished as much before the woman's charm as the sheer common sense of it. "O.K., O.K., I'll go do your whispering for you."

Connie smiled broadly, her sharp brown eyes at their attractive best. "Great. Then I won't take any more of your time," she said as she rose from her chair. "Thank you. And good luck. It's really better for all concerned."

"We'll see," Lars said hopefully.

Connie turned and got into the doorway before she turned to face Lars again. "Oh, by the way," she said looking the model of an innocent who had a sudden thought, "you wouldn't want me to send you a union membership card, would you?"

"You're pushing your luck," Lars responded with mock irritation.

His colleague was still smiling as she disappeared.

CHAPTER 12

Mystery Shrouds Confidential Dialogue

Knowing that President Haskell would face a deadline in responding to the grievance filed by the faculty union on behalf of Eric Gonzales, Lars immediately requested an appointment with Haskell after Connie left. The president's schedule was juggled to make time available that very afternoon. Reflecting that he had had greater difficulty getting on the president's calendar when he had been his chief subordinate, Lars could not help but be amused at the magic evoked by the title trustee.

Late that afternoon, as he settled into the couch in Haskell's office that had been his usual position when Haskell was being collegial and did not sit behind his desk, Lars thought that Haskell wore an ambivalent expression. The unexpected visit by or a phone call from a university trustee was not often good news for a university administrator, Lars knew. Lars's beginning with a request that his visit be off the record did nothing to remove Haskell's apprehension.

"I have come across some information that could simplify your life considerably," said Lars and watched Haskell's expression warm immediately.

"You have, I understand," Lars continued, "a formal grievance before you filed in the matter of Professor Gonzales." Haskell nodded and reverted to a dubious facial expression.

"There appears to be some new information which makes your decision rather obvious. And it would be a popular course of action with both students and faculty as well." Lars smiled with conviction, inviting Haskell to share a lighthearted mood.

"Sounds irresistible," Haskell brightened.

Lars leaned toward his now captured listener and provided a context for his information. "Since the grievance was filed with you, the union has received an accounting of the thirteen thousand dollar expenditure which seems to clear Gonzales of any illegality, though the story wouldn't make one an admirer of his administrative abilities or good sense."

His preamble complete, Lars provided the specifics of the information he had received from Connie. "The thirteen thousand was an additional salary payment to the professional technical director, who demanded that payment because Gonzales wanted a new set for the musical production after the tech director had completed the one that Gonzales originally requested."

"I've already read the grievance, nothing like this is asserted, leave alone documented," Haskell reported with the skepticism of a veteran at reading grievances.

"Apparently, the union itself didn't know until it received a letter from the technical man stating it was so after they filed the grievance."

"And Gonzales himself never mentioned it, even after we'd summarily terminated him?" Haskell queried, skepticism reverberating in every syllable.

Lars shrugged. "He claims he was afraid to look like such a wasteful manager. He says he was afraid he'd never get to manage summer theater again."

"He's right about that," Haskell snorted. "But that would have been better than dismissal. You think that he'd have owned up if it were true."

Lars paused to let the information settle itself into Haskell's thoughts. "I'll admit that I've heard more convincing stories, Jim, but the fact is that the union now has a written affirmation of what happened to the money that clears Gonzales of thievery. It would likely prove compelling if they took the case to arbitration."

Haskell meditated briefly before he answered. He began reluctantly. "That's true, provided—please don't take offense, Lars—that this information is so."

"My source is very reliable, Jim, but you'll have to forgive me if I don't name it."

"Oh, of course," Haskell hastened to assure trustee Paulsen. Haskell bowed his head in thought a while longer before he said, "My problem, as I see it, is that I don't actually have this information in hand, even if I did want to use it as the basis for my grievance response. I'd be deciding the grievance on information that I technically don't even have. The central administration might think that I've lost my mind, to have argued for termination and then several weeks later, with apparently no additional information in hand, reversed myself and re-instated the person."

"If you've got a few days left before the deadline, you could ask the union if they have any additional information or argument to add to their position," Lars suggested. "That way you'd get the information and not appear to have had prior knowledge of its existence.

"I wouldn't have time to check it out before the deadline, of course. Besides, a request like that so rarely occurs," Haskell reasoned. "How many times did we do it during your seven years as vice president?"

"Twice, at most," recollected Lars.

"The request, so soon after they got the information, might set them wondering if I have a source within their organization." Haskell rose from his chair and paced briefly. "That could complicate life for your source, mightn't it?"

"That's a good point," Lars agreed emphatically. "I don't expect that I'll be approached with such information again, but I wouldn't want to cause anyone a problem for trying to help out in this one instance."

"Perhaps the best thing to do is to pretend that I don't even know what I've just been told," Haskell reasoned. "If I reject the grievance, the union will no doubt take it to the next level. If they include this latest information in the grievance argument, Chancellor Brown will no doubt decide to reinstate. He can be the hero, but there'll be no onus to me since I technically didn't have the information that was the basis of his decision."

Lars was relieved at the thought of Haskell's taking the course of action that he had just outlined. It protected Connie and would get Gonzales his job back without the local administration looking neither draconian nor weak. Lars rose from his chair. "As usual, Jim, you are the soul of subtle judiciousness."

"Kind of you to say it, Lars," Haskell smiled, showing the good spirits that came from getting past a problem that had been vexing him since the union's grievance on behalf of Gonzales had arrived. "Of course," the president added, savoring a successful episode of some intimacy with the new faculty trustee, "it helps to have friends who warn you of the pitfalls before you step into them." Haskell offered his hand and enclosed Lars's hand in a hearty grasp. "I really appreciate your help, Lars, and more so, your guidance." The last phrase was a little too much for Lars. He had almost never been thanked for his advice when it had been his job to give it. Now it came tinged with the flattery he fell heir to with his new title. Lars nodded and sent Haskell a wan smile as he took his leave.

Lars realized that his participation in the afternoon's events had been quite unorthodox, but he felt that he had been useful and that the result would be all to the good. He arrived home in good spirits. However, his happy mood was no match for Marian's, who greeted him with food and drink and an exuberantly celebratory air. He barely entered the kitchen where she was putting the finishing touches on a tray of appetizers and had yet to shed his coat when she announced that the book which she had been writing with Emma Hardesty had been accepted for publication.

Lars understood and shared Marian's exuberance. She had published more than a score of articles in the most prestigious professional journals devoted to research in the subject matter and the pedagogy of the social sciences that had established her as a nationally known and respected scholar, but this was her first book length publication. It not only was the most significant publication of her career, the innovative research that was the basis of the pedagogical aspects of the book would, if favorably received, make Marian and her co-author figures of note. While a favorable reception might not mean great financial compensation, the recognition would lead to numerous speaking invitations and reviews that would enhance the careers of Marian and Emma both. Lars asked the details of publication while he opened a bottle of wine. Soon, they sat at the kitchen table demolishing the tray of appetizers and replenishing their glasses while they speculated on the exciting possibilities that might unfold for Marian. By the time they decided to go out for a lavish dinner that neither of them really wanted but felt necessary to do justice to the importance of the day events, Lars had completely forgotten his maneuvers performed for the good of several people and their supporters that had arrayed for battle barring some outbreak of truth and sanity.

CHAPTER 13

Questions Surround University Personnel Activity

Lars had not been surprised at Chancellor Ivor Brown's request that he arrive in Pauliapolis early for the November trustees meeting so that they could confer about the NSSU faculty union's grievance on behalf of Eric Gonzales. Undoubtedly, Brown and Haskell had discussed the matter, and Brown wanted to meet to emphasize for the faculty trustee that he, as much as President Haskell, was attentive to the advice of a member of the board who had provided specific information to enlighten an administrative decision.

Since Lars could not tell Brown any more than he had already told Haskell and since that same information was no doubt contained in the grievance statement filed with Brown by the union, Lars entered the building which housed the offices of the central administration of the university system with an amused air. He expected a ritualistic meeting in which Brown would, with the smoothness and indirectness for which he was well known, convey to the faculty trustee how valuable his input was. Lars was aware that he shared the weakness of most of humanity for feeling important. He considered it a failing he could control if he kept the foolishness of it in mind.

He had to laugh at himself for looking forward to his meeting with Brown because he thought of how provocative his experiences in the building in which he now walked had been to him during his administrative days. His most frequent visits to the building had been to negotiate funding or program approvals with the academic vice chancellor, an arrogant, physically small former chemistry professor who considered the two campuses outside the city of Pauliapolis both an inconvenience and an inexcusable financial drain on the prestigious Pauliapolis campus. Lars had always found the little man impervious to logical argument and never without a set of figures that differed substantially from the ones Lars had presented. It was as though the academic vice chancellor had some staff whose assignment it was to produce data that undermined any numerical presentation that established a need for more support in St. Claude or Beau Prairie. In frustration, Lars had labeled the man, Michael Caswell, Myopic Mike because his administrative vision seemed incapable of conceptualizing any educational enterprise beyond the city limits of Pauliapolis. Since becoming a trustee, Lars's contempt for Caswell had increased because the man was attentive to Lars's words in a way that he had not been when such listening would actually have had some greater functional effect.

When he entered Chancellor Brown's suite of offices, He found Brown standing before the receptionist's desk arranging some detail of scheduling his activities. Lars was quickly and deferentially invited into Brown's office and directed to the most comfortable chair. Lars made himself comfortable and looked placidly at Brown as the chancellor settled himself in a chair across the large, low table between the two men. Brown was a lean six-footer with a pleasant face and receding but silvery hair. In all, he looked the part of a university leader. His temperament confirmed the impression made by his physical appearance. There was not an overtly combative bone in his body. He was not without strength, but it was manifested in a steadfastness that parried direct blows and seemed to offer none. Brown's opponents were always so surprised at their defeat that they were never quite sure who had done it to them. If he was ever unsure of himself, it never showed. It gave all his statements an air of wisdom, even when they were predictable, bland and unimaginative, which seemed to Lars often the case. Of course, Lars had to admit, Brown had survived for several decades in various progressively senior administrative posts at several different universities, something that Lars himself had not managed to do. Lars rationalized that he had never mastered inoffensiveness; yet he knew what a tightrope university administration was, and he respected Brown for managing to navigate it successfully.

"You probably suspect why I asked to see you, Lars," Brown said amiably. "Jim Haskell suggested that you might have some guidance to give me about this Gonzales grievance."

"I'd be happy to help if I could, Chancellor Brown, but I doubt that I can. I assume that the information that I took to President Haskell on the matter has been included in the version of the grievance statement that has been filed with you."

"I wish you'd call me Ivor, Lars; we shouldn't be so formal." Lars had actually received this invitation years before, when he was a newly appointed administrator at North Shore. He could never explain to people that it was not standoffishness that made him use titles but a sense of decorum that had nothing to do with feeling subservient. He nodded in conceding to Brown's request rather that get sidetracked into an explanation. Brown focused on Lars earnestly. "It's true that the information that you brought to Jim Haskell is now formally part of the grievance argument, but it introduces questions about that facet of the case that I wanted to ask you."

"I'm afraid that I don't know any more than what I told Jim," Lars said with equal seriousness.

"I didn't expect you'd have any additional information. It's your judgment I'm interested in," Brown told Lars in a tone that did not seem intended as mere flattery. "I wondered if you believe the story that the money was paid to the technical director as additional salary."

"Well," Lars said, drawing out the word slowly as he struggled with his reluctance to express an opinion. It would be difficult to keep the dialogue brief and objective once the speculation began, and Lars thought that he should avoid involvement in Brown's decision. "I don't know anything that would contradict the man's affirmation that he got the money, and I'm hard put to imagine why anyone would say that he got money if he hadn't."

A mild, meditative expression was fixed on Brown's face as he ruminated. "That's logical, but you and I have both been around academic personnel matters long enough to know that logic often has absolutely no place in them."

Lars observed that even when Brown said something cynical he still wore the expression of a well-behaved choirboy. "You're right about that," he agreed.

"I've had the summer theater records checked, Lars," Brown reported. "There's no canceled check or any sort of record to establish that Gonzales paid his technical director this extra money. We're apparently supposed to believe that he was paid it in cash."

"Are there records for the salary payments that the tech man was contracted for?" Lars asked.

"Oh, yes," Brown affirmed. "The thirteen thousand is only amount that doesn't show anywhere."

"Has Gonzales been asked how the money was paid?"

"Cash, he says," Brown stated, his mouth turning up at the corners a millimeter, which was apparently as much display of a dubious feeling that he cared to reveal. "What's the likelihood that there'd even be that much cash on hand?" asked Brown, seeming to expect that Lars could answer so specific a question out of his familiarity with the North Shore campus operations.

"It's not impossible. A lot of ticket sales are done in cash on the night of a performance," Lars recollected. "Of course, I'd expect that money to be deposited quickly and regularly. One would have to hang on to the cash from daily ticket sales for quite some time to have thirteen thousand dollars cash on hand."

"You see why I'm reluctant to reinstate the man on the basis of this accounting of the money, then," emphasized Brown. "Maybe this technical director is just saying he got the money to help a friend out of a predicament that Gonzales got himself into by pocketing the cash. If I award this grievance, I could be putting a thief back on the North Shore State faculty—and I'll be seeing his name on a tenure award list a few years from now."

"And," Lars added, "there's no way you could deny tenure to someone who was seemingly wrongly accused of theft and then re-instated."

"Exactly," Brown stated with an open palm gesture of his hands which indicated his dilemma. "I don't know what to do."

"Have you considered this?" Lars began, the idea only forming in his mind as he spoke. "If you could get the union to agree to a time extension for your decision on the grievance, you might be able to have your staff dig up something to confirm or refute the technical director's story."

He had Brown's interest. "What possible line of investigation would there be, Lars?" asked the chancellor.

"Actually, I wasn't thinking of uncovering any information now existing. I thought it might be worthwhile to offer Gonzales and his friend a chance to stumble. What I have in mind is a little manipulative, but, If it doesn't reveal they're lying, Gonzales ought to be given the benefit of the doubt and have his grievance awarded."

Brown again registered his dubious look. "You're not suggesting something illegal?"

Lars was offended that Brown would think him capable of what the chancellor had so quickly inferred. Certainly there was nothing in Lars's administrative history that would lead Brown to his rapidly expressed apprehension. He was of the verge of telling Brown to forget the idea, but he thought that such a reaction would appear to confirm Brown's inference. "No," Lars responded tersely, then after a pause to calm himself added, "I just thought it might be relevant to know if Gonzales's friend is going to report the thirteen thousand as income on his tax return a few months from now."

Brown's face brightened. "If he doesn't report it, maybe he never got it," the chancellor recognized.

"Maybe," smiled Lars.

"Of course, maybe he's just a tax cheat," Brown observed. "You know how imprecise some people are about reporting every dime of income that they received in cash."

"But in this case, he has an employer who will be reporting his income to the government," Lars pointed out.

"You mean we should include the thirteen thousand in the earnings statement that we send him at the end of the year."

"I admit, I had something more devious in mind," Lars said. He read the puzzlement on Brown's face and continued. "Send him a statement initially that states only his contracted salary. Give him time to start to prepare his return on that basis, then, around the end of March, send him a corrected earnings statement that adds on the thirteen thousand. If he didn't get that money, he's suddenly got a tax problem that he has to deal with in short order, whether he has already filed his return or is one of us normal, last minute filers."

"I see," Brown smiled. "He's either got to pay taxes on some money he never got, so that he keeps his story straight, or he's got to want to get out from under the extra taxes by changing his story."

"That's what I was thinking," Lars confirmed. "Perhaps it's too devious a course of action for your taste." Lars prepared for another blow to his feelings if Brown should decline the tactics as a violation of his scruples.

He need not have steeled himself. "How do I get all the extra time to play this scenario out?" Brown asked. "You know that there's a deadline for responding to this grievance that comes up just before Thanksgiving, just a couple of weeks from now, months before the income tax filing deadline."

"Of course, the union would have to agree to a ninety day extension for your decision. Don't forget, the grievance response deadlines are based on working days and not calendar days—with the Christmas break and the semester break, ninety days must come very close to April fifteenth—may even pass it, for all I know. If it doesn't, it will come very close."

Brown went to his desk and leafed through the desk calendar. He spent a minute counting, leafing, and counting again. "The semester break isn't on here yet, but just approximating it, the ninety working days comes very close to mid-April." Brown's smile was momentary. It faded quickly, and he asked, "How do I get the union to agree to this generous extension of time? That length of extension would be unprecedented, if memory serves me."

Lars recognized that Brown had identified a major snag. He could imagine Connie's reaction, as the union's grievance officer—let alone that of Gonzales and the union leadership—to a request to keep a faculty member—and his family—without income for months while the administration mulled over its decision on a grievance in which the available evidence strongly argued for restoring the person to his job.

"You could say you need time for another audit of the theatre's records for last summer—and any previous years that Gonzales managed it—which wouldn't be a bad idea, by the way. But even that wouldn't make for an easy sell, unless you were willing to change Gonzales's status to a suspension with pay, including salary payment back to the point of termination."

Brown frowned and shook his head adamantly. "I hate that. I hate paying people for not working." He strode back from behind his desk and returned to the chair opposite Lars. He stared at the table, his face wearing a rare truculent expression.

Lars could share Brown's distaste for the course of action; however, he felt compelled to point out, "I don't think that there's any chance of an extension without the suspension with pay." Brown said nothing as he continued to look for some enlightenment from the tabletop. "Of course, you could award the grievance. Maybe their story is the truth. You know, Gonzales is supposed to be a fine teacher. It's not like you'd be putting an incompetent back on the payroll. I can tell you that the students and his colleagues would be delighted if you awarded the grievance."

"No, no," Brown sighed resignedly, "I don't want to award the grievance. I truly have doubts about the explanation for the thirteen thousand." Brown paused again. "Besides, even if it's true, the man's a little short of common sense. I'm not sure he should be around, even if he is a great theater man." Brown looked up and met Lars's own look. His determination was plain to see. "I'm going to ask for the extension. I like the way you put it before you explained your idea. We should give them a chance to stumble." Brown stood and reached for Lars's hand. Lars stood and extended his own hand for Brown to grip. "Thanks, Lars, you've been a big help."

"I hope they go for the extension," Lars said encouragingly and proceeded toward the door.

As Brown walked beside he said, "So do I." Opening the door for Lars, Brown smiled affably, "Well, at least this stickler got us together. We should do it more often."

Lars accepted another handshake as he recognized the re-emergence of the official chancellor in Brown's demeanor. "Under better circumstances," Lars offered, showing that he could play an official guise himself.

CHAPTER 14

Trustee Finds Monthly Meetings not All Business

During the walk back to his hotel, Lars considered whether or not he should alert Connie Mercutio about the request that would be coming to the NSSU faculty union for an extension of time for the chancellor's office to respond to the grievance on behalf of Eric Gonzales. As the union's grievance coordinator, she would have a significant role in the decision to agree to or deny the extension. It might be in her interests to give her time to consider the possibility before she had to discuss it with Gonzales and the union leadership. In addition to telling her what was coming, Lars could point out the reasons it would be in everyone's best interests to delay the chancellor's decision. If later developments revealed that Gonzales was unworthy of the union's support, much time, effort, and expense would be saved for the union to cease fighting the dismissal at the time damning information emerged. Notwithstanding that eventual possibility, the union could claim a partial victory in restoring Gonzales to paid status in the interim. If nothing occurred to undercut the defensible explanation of the use of the money, both adversaries in the matter would look good. The administration would look fair-minded in not implementing a termination that became to a lost cause in arbitration because of information it did not have when it made its original decision, and the union would no doubt take the opportunity to bask in the glory of its successful effort on behalf of one of its members.

However, none of these rational reasons for delay would necessarily protect Connie from criticism if she were to counsel the union to accept the delay. The role of the grievance officer was to press for outcomes favorable to the employee-grievant, be the case strong or weak. In the light of the union's having presented what appeared to be a compelling argument, Connie would look timid to the adversarial members of the leadership if she recommended an action that apparently had no advantage for the union and the person it represented. At best Connie would be criticized as deficient as a grievance coordinator, less kindly, she might be labeled a tool of the administration.

Of course, there was the remote possibility that the audit of records of prior years' summer theatre seasons—conducted hurriedly during the two weeks before Brown had to respond if there were no extension—might show some irregularities that could not be explained away. In that case, the dismissal would stand and Gonzales might wish he had taken the suspension with pay which would at least garnered himself several months additional salary. Anyone who had counseled for the extension would look wise under those circumstances.

The complexities and hazards inherent in all of the outcomes, Lars concluded, suggested that Connie could choose the most defensible position if she had the greatest amount of time to weigh the possibilities. Therefore, he resolved to alert her immediately if he could. He thought it unwise to phone her at her office. Anyone who identified the caller might raise inquiry about why the faculty trustee was talking directly to the union grievance officer. He needed her home phone number or her address to talk to Connie confidentially. Being in Pauliapolis, he was puzzled for a moment about how to get the information to reach her. He realized it would be foolish to call his department office at NSSU and ask the secretary to provide Connie's home number phone number. Then, he remembered that the office of the trustees' staff had the phone directories of all of the campuses, which contained every employee's home as well as campus phone number. He could look up the number himself. It only would take a short detour from his direct path to the hotel.

Lars spent the remainder of the afternoon trying Connie's home phone number unsuccessfully. Between efforts, he spent his time familiarizing himself with the current trustees' agenda. That document, because of the extensive explanatory and contextual material, was, as usual, an inch-thick loose-leaf notebook. Most of the topics were routine matters not requiring more than brief examination, but it was wise to identify any potentially complex or controversial item so that one could approach it cautiously during the meeting itself.

The single item in the agenda Lars was perusing which required close reading was the long awaited report of the study committee on intercollegiate athletics at the Pauliapolis campus. Lars recalled that a study of the athletic programs at the Pauliapolis campus had been commissioned over a year ago before Lars had joined the board. It was so long overdue that Lars had forgotten that such a study was underway. Lars began reading the report avidly. As an enthusiastic fan of intercollegiate athletics, he had always had considerable interest in the high emphasis athletic programs at the Pauliapolis campus. In fact, the success of many of the PSU teams made intercollegiate athletics a good public relations tool and support builder for that university. The single exception to the teams that were a source of pride to alumni and the public in general was the football team. The football team competed in one of the most prominent and competitive leagues in the nation and had, at one time in the past, been a power to be reckoned with; however, for over two decades the Pauliapolis Prairie Dogs had been a perennial door mat. Irritation among the state's population, which was impatient to see the return of what the local press had then termed the Dynamic Dogs, was near universal, since the Pauliapolis State athletic teams were the only ones in the state that played at a level where success drew national recognition. The usual solution of changing coaches had not yet managed to bring the passionately desired miracle of uninterrupted victories about. That had been the impetous for the study which was now concluded. Of course, since it would have seemed too blatant to charge the committee with the assignment of developing a plan to have a winning football team, the charge to the committee had been to study the entire intercollegiate program of the Pauliapolis State University. It was understood that the committee would not belabor its comments about the teams in sports other than football, other than to applaud their success. The major feature of the report was to be a set of recommendations to achieve the return of a winning football team.

Lars was engrossed in that particular part of the report when there was a gentle knock at the door. He opened the door and found Marian, with a small overnight bag in hand, smiling broadly. She crossed the threshold, set down her bag and stamped her lips enthusiastically on his.

Before Lars could react, Marian had taken up her bag again, set it on the bureau top and began to empty its contents. "Aren't you glad to see me?" she grinned, obviously enjoying Lars's dazed look and speechlessness.

"Of course I am," blurted Lars as he recovered himself. "But you know I wasn't expecting you."

"You don't mind my dropping by," Marian said with an air of pretended casualness that betrayed her excitement.

"I'm delighted to have your company. You know that," said Lars. He went to her and, interrupting her unpacking by encircling her in his arms, returned Marian's kiss with a bit more intensity than she had conveyed on entering.

"Well," Marian sighed as she patted a stray lock of Lars's hair against his temple, "I'm afraid that I'll be a bit too busy to be much company." She looked eager to convey some news. "I'm giving a seminar for the graduate faculty of the Pauliapolis school of education tomorrow morning."

Marian was glowing with pride, and Lars understood why. In every college and university in the state, from the church-related little huddles where what passed for the liberal arts was a narrowly focused prescription for living according to a particular religious dogma to large scale public emporiums where liberal education was an ill-defined collage lost in an obscure corner apart from a multitude of professional programs, there was a program for training teachers for the public schools. However, the school of education at Pauliapolis State, with what would have been justifiable pride were it not so extreme, rarely recognized the existence of any other program than their own, let alone credited any other program with any merit. Even the program at North Shore State, at what was a sister institution that provided a considerable percentage of PSU's better graduate students, hence providing at least one meaningful confirmation of the quality of the NSSU teacher education program, rarely was admitted to be respectable by the graduate faculty of the school of education at Pauliapolis State. Never that Lars could remember did that group feel that some education professor at NSSU had anything to say that might enlighten them so that they invited that person to give a seminar. Marian was being accorded a significant professional recognition by a group of colleagues whose attainments were only exceeded by the extent of their own pride in them.

"You mean that these Brahmins down here have finally admitted that you have something to teach them?" Lars chuckled.

"I don't know if they're going to listen, but I'm pretty sure that I've got something to tell them," Marian laughed.

"Of course you do," Lars said and pressed a kiss to Marian's forehead. "I'm happy that they could swallow their pride sufficiently to admit it. You must be feeling pretty good." Lars glanced at his watch and saw that it was past the time when he and Marian normally had dinner. "We should go out for a special dinner to celebrate your crashing through the impregnable pride surrounding the campus down here. No one else from the NSSU school of education has ever done it."

Marian touched her hand gently to Lars's cheeks. "We can celebrate with food later," she said as she looked invitingly into her husband's eyes. "I was thinking of another kind of celebration first."

Lars smiled in anticipation. "One that we won't have to leave the room for?"

Marian began to unbutton Lars's shirt. "One that we definitely won't have to leave the room for," she smiled.

Lars was both amused and aroused. He had long held the belief that success was an aphrodisiac, at least so for men. In their younger days, Marian responded to his periods of sexual insatiability with amused participation. She disparaged light-heartedly Lars's conjugal exuberance as generated by some career accomplishment rather than passion for her. Eventually, Lars realized that there was some truth to the explanation. Success elevated his self-worth, and self-worth elevated his libido. As he and Marian helped each other off with their clothing while they interrupted the disrobing with increasingly eager kisses and caresses, he wondered if Marian now shared the notion that success was an aphrodisiac for women as well as men. Certainly Marian's desire, which had been dormant for several weeks, strongly suggested the possibility. Recalling how Marian's analysis of that motive for sex had diminished his own ardor at that time, he did not dare spoil the moment by wondering aloud at the timing of this long awaited interlude of passion.

Of course his amusement at this unexpected delight was secondary to his arousal. Marian had long since stopped tolerating sex when she was not interested. So their lovemaking was less frequent than Lars would have liked, though the infrequency was not a great frustration to the lower burning fire of middle-aged desire. In addition, Lars had never found sex with a compliant but unenthusiastic partner the epitome of joy. Hence Marian's occasional and unpredictable moments of genuine passion were like a gift. He relished them. He could not imagine when the pleasure might have been greater. He would never understand people who became bored with a familiar lover. He was not one who had ever become bored with a familiar and well-loved symphony. How could he ever be bored with caressing one who had excited him for decades and who knew what to do to heighten that excitement? Perhaps it was only sex that was ever fresh despite being familiar, and to Lars that was what made shared passion with Marian all the more precious.

Later that evening, when they had finished a sumptuous meal and shared a broad smile as they emptied their often refilled wine glasses, Lars could tell that their mutually satisfied mood had more to do with the intense passion that they had earlier brought to a boisterous climax than to the taste of the meal whose considerable savor was incapable of matching their earlier pleasure.

CHAPTER 15

U Trustees Tossed for Loss Over Pigskin Proposal

When Lars arrived for the trustees meeting the next morning, he was surprised at the size of the crowd of people in the hall outside the meeting room. When he had worked his way down the hallway through the noisy group that was chatting while they sipped courtesy coffee from plastic cups, he found the meeting room itself fully occupied in both the audience and media sections. Several television cameras on tripods had been set up at the end of the media gallery, and technicians bustled about while their on-camera colleagues stood with microphones in hand searching among the arrivals for likely possibilities from whom to secure a sound bite that might be further abbreviated to become a part of their next news broadcast.

Lars was puzzled for a moment at what might be the cause of the excitement. His examination of the agenda the previous day hadn't struck him as containing anything likely to arouse intense public excitement. Then he recalled that Marian's arrival had stopped his reading of the athletics study group report, to which he had never returned. There must be some aspect of that report, Lars concluded, that had enough people aroused that the media smelled the possibility of a story with controversial potential.

Lars hurried to his usual seat at the meeting table and quickly found the section of his agenda notebook which contained the athletics report. He was still flipping hurriedly back and forth among the pages of the report looking for a "hot button" when Dr. Appleby, the board chair, rapping the table with a forcefulness that was not normally required to quiet the room. The room stilled to a restless quiet and the meeting began. Both the audience and the media squirmed through several routine matters of business, somewhat like playgoers awaiting the opening curtain of a popular play. When Appleby called on the chair of the athletics study committee to present that item of business, a bespectacled man with a fleshy face and matching body was not as quick to rise from the audience and come forward as were the television camera crews to rush to their equipment.

To Lars, the man who settled into the presenter's chair did not look like he had devoted himself to the study of athletics because of either a present or past participant's interest in some athletic endeavor. When Appleby introduced him as a professor of accounting, Lars concluded that the man had been requested to undertake the committee leadership to supply the expertise for the financial aspects of the committee's explorations. When the presenter himself began his remarks by calling attention to the list of committee membership, it became apparent that people from a variety of instructional disciplines had served on the committee. Lars recognized the membership as the customary attempt to assure that the full range of constituencies and special interests within the university were represented. This minimized the possibility of the outcome's being challenged as biased. Of course, it also minimized the likelihood that the report would recommend any course of action that outraged any special interest group, be its size minuscule or multitudinous. What then, Lars wondered, could be in the report that had drawn so much interest that word of mouth had brought so many people and the media here before the contents of the report had been made public?

The presenter began his review of the report by paying tribute to the recent success in competition of the men's basketball and hockey teams and the women's volleyball team, three groups that had capped league championship seasons with enough playoff success to near national championships. Lars recognized in the accounting professor's statements the customary inordinate pride that educational institutions, be they tiny liberal arts colleges or major research universities, take in the success of their athletic teams. Success, in the context of American collegiate athletics was, of course, winning. This was the real standard despite any rhetoric about the intangible value of athletics for the student participants and the practical value to the university of the good feeling created among students, alumni and general public by a nationally known winning athletic program.

The study committee chair proceeded to applaud the progress that the university had made toward achieving equality in athletic opportunity for women through the creation of new teams in soccer and field hockey. While recognizing that the goals of equal expenditure on men's and women's sports and equal numbers of male and female participants were yet far from achievement, the report concluded that further progress toward such equality was prevented by the financial situation of the athletics program as a whole. The attainment of equality by creating additional teams for women rather than decreasing the number of men's teams required increased expenditures for athletic programming. The only sources of additional money for athletics were revenue produced by the teams themselves or the transfer of money from the general fund budget committed to teaching and research. Since the instructional and research budgets were already deemed to be Spartan in support level, said the presenter, the additional funding needed must be generated by the athletic programs themselves.

Lars was not surprised that a committee consisting of instructional faculty had reached that conclusion. What came next was no surprise. The presenter continued that it was unfortunate that the majority of athletic teams, both male and female, were not producers of sufficient revenue to be self-supporting, let alone profitable enough to contribute funding to other sports. In fact, only football, men's basketball and men's hockey could produce revenue in any substantial amount. And these only did so in those years when the winning record of the team not only generated sold out contests but substantial income from appearances on television and in post-season competition.

Coming to the financial dilemma that was familiar before the study had recounted it, the accounting professor and committee chair was brought to the most significant one among the committee's recommendations. He began by stating that the football program was a revenue deficit rather than being profitable. Thus, the committee had concluded, it was imperative that the football program be restored to a success level which would made it once again the revenue producer that it had formerly been.

Lars's mind raced to a conclusion about what had brought so many people to today's meeting. He was surprised that he had not spotted what he inferred the report contained, a recommendation to fire the football coach. He leafed through the report and found the recommendation regarding the football program—noting peripherally that the teams in high emphasis collegiate athletics were never "teams" but "programs." He read the text and found the recommendation different than what he expected. The committee was recommending that the contract of the football coach, who would be serving the final year of a four-year contract in the next year, be extended for one more year.

Here, frowned Lars, was a puzzle. Coach Walter Meeker, the latest in a long line of football coaches who had served the university since the end of its era of football glory, had been no more successful than his predecessors, if won and lost record were the criterion of success. There had been the usual high expectations when he was hired, but the football team was in its third mediocre season of performance since he had arrived. Despite Meeker's upbeat and effusive style, which was keyed to motivating the players through moralistic sloganeering and pietistic exhortations, opposing teams had regularly been unkind enough to score with considerable ease against the Pauliapolis State Prairie Dogs football team. "The Purple Peril," as it continued to be called in the local press, had for years been perilous to nothing other than the patience of its long suffering admirers. Because the team could score rather frequently itself, Coach Meeker repeatedly delivered optimistic predictions that the team would soon begin to outscore its opponents and begin to win consistently. In fact, since each season began with non-conference opponents whose competitive skills were well below the level of the Great Lakes Conference opponents that The Purple would face in the latter three quarters of its season, each of the last three seasons had begun with several promising victories. However, when the conference competition was faced, even though The Purple managed to score thirty or forty points, the opposition could be counted on to score one to three touchdowns more. Lars, whose enthusiasm for college football was tempered by its increasingly blatant commercialism, was not surprised that those who had come to call the team "The Puny Purple" were calling for the immediate firing of Walt Meeker. Neither would he have been surprised if a bit of kindness within the committee had led to a recommendation that Coach Meeker's contract, which accorded him a higher salary than either the president of Pauliapolis State or system chancellor Ivor Brown, not be renewed after it was completed the next season. However, he found it unimaginable that there was a recommendation to extend it, which would leave Meeker in place for two more seasons beyond the one in progress during which the football team continued in its lusterless ways.

The presenter of the athletics report, perhaps vainly hoping that the boulder suspended by a thread would pass unnoticed, concluded by mentioning that the report contained some very carefully considered recommendations, and offered to answer any questions. The usual pause which preceded the start of the discussion did not occur, as Trustee Harlan Cartwright began motioning for recognition as the final syllable of the presenter's statement was uttered.

"I'm sure the committee was very thorough and deliberate in its explorations," Cartwright began, preserving the custom of politeness even in those instances where one was going to challenge the good sense and sanity of some group's work, "but I find the recommendation for an extension of the football coach's contract puzzling. Before the last change in coaches, we recognized that maximizing the income from football was crucial to the soundness of the total program in intercollegiate athletics. To achieve that, it was recognized that there must be a sellout of every home football game. It was hoped that the current coach could produce the kind of team that would draw the spectators to achieve those sellouts—to that end, a bonus clause for producing a certain level of attendance was placed in his contract, as I recall. I note in the report that we are averaging a little over 28,000 in paid attendance at home games—just slightly more than half of what the stadium holds. In the light of that situation, how can the committee recommend the extension of the coach's contract?"

The accounting professor collected himself before answering. He looked to Lars to be attempting to hide a lack of conviction. "The committee felt that Coach Meeker has not yet had time for his efforts to improve the football program to produce results. Since Coach Meeker was hired late in the spring and was not able to recruit for his first season here, he has only been able to recruit through two cycles of high school graduations. The players he's chosen are only freshmen and sophomores. It was felt that the full impact of his efforts can only be judged when the team consists entirely of players that he recruited and trained." Lars recognized an undeniable logic in the reasoning just given, but also recognized that it was identical to the defense one might give of the coach of a professional football team whose early seasons had not met with success.

The presenter's expression changed to one that looked a bit more convinced of the defensibility of what he would say next. "In addition, it was felt that Coach Meeker brings certain qualities of leadership to the football program which are highly desirable and perhaps rare in division I intercollegiate programs today. The committee felt that caution was warranted before the university should sacrifice those qualities solely to trying to improve the won and lost record of the team."

Lars silently groaned. It was one of the quixotic and contradictory characteristics of this state that people could retain lip service to the philosophy that there were more important aspects to athletics than winning while they desired to compete successfully at a level where the reality was that winning was the only thing that counted. Regionally there was a tacit acceptance of two irreconcilable beliefs—that you could pursue intercollegiate athletics in a mode that required huge amounts of money as the only means to success and survival and that you could retain the belief that intercollegiate athletics was most importantly devoted to the development of the characters of the participants. Lars, as a devoted fan of intercollegiate football, wished that the game were a part of college life because of its intangible benefits to the players, but he did not delude himself that the game as it existed in an era of full scholarships, multimillion dollar stadia, and similar sized annual budgets had anything to do with developing the characters of participants, many of whom were only looking for the notoriety to make them candidates for lucrative professional careers.

Trustee Pete Henderson was quick to seek recognition when it was apparent that the chair of the athletic study committee had completed his response. "I think it's important that we not let ourselves get sidetracked into any fanciful ideas as we deal with what is basically a financial problem. I respect Coach Meeker for the moral principles that he makes the basis of his coaching approach. I believe that the players are better off for working with a coach of his character. But the reality is that we cannot fill the stadium without a winning football team, and those gate receipts are vital to maintaining the entire athletic program. The report is clear on that point, and that just confirms what we already knew. I don't think that we can afford more time to see if Coach Meeker can produce the results that we need. I can tell you that the alumni that I talk to have serious doubts."

Anderson's bluntness resulted in an extended silence at the table and an interruption in the buzz and restless shifting about within the audience. Lars had lived in the region long enough to recognize that Anderson had strayed from the behavioral norm of the dominant regional pattern. In fact, residents who prided themselves on their ancestral roots in the region admiringly called non-confrontational behavior "Nordic Nice." Its tenants were simple. One could take issue any time, but all confrontation was to be veiled. Criticism was always indirect or asserted to be for the subject's own good. Opposition was always denied to have a personal element to it. Aggressiveness and downright hostility—behaviors no less frequently occurring here than elsewhere—were cloaked in a rhetoric of principle, though the target ended up just as damaged as if the attack had been frontal.

The tense silence was broken by Trustee Marcia Brandwyn's addressing the chair. "Mr. Chairman," she began in a voice that added an element of breathlessness to its usual ministerial unctuousness, "I am surprised by the tenor of Trustee Anderson's remarks. Have we come to the point of being willing to sacrifice anything to winning? It was Coach Meeker's values that were an important reason that several of us supported his appointment. Even those of us who are not enthusiastic followers of athletics have noticed that he has functioned entirely as expected in promoting the values that we found so commendable in choosing him. His personal appearances around the state and in the media always produce favorable comments about what he has said and stands for. I am appalled that anyone would so quickly give up on someone who brings such important and desirable values to an area of university activity that vitally needs them."

Lars recognized that Brandwyn was totally sincere in her endorsement of Meeker's moralistic approach to coaching and athletics in general. He personally found Meeker's pietistic and didactic pronouncements to his players, the public and the media indigestible. To Lars, sport was activity that was worthwhile for its own sake, utilizing skill and determination in approximately equal parts. The appeal of it was in the moment. That was proper for both participant and spectator. To moralistically glorify it in anticipation or recollection perverted it, a fact that spectator-mad America had yet to understand, to the detriment of themselves and sport as an activity. Any effort to see sport as more than an engaging moment was not only misplaced but also potentially injurious to the good health of the enterprise. He knew that Marsha Brandwyn meant well, but she was hoping for a happy marriage of idealism and commercialism that was unattainable within the current circumstances of collegiate sport. He would never say so publicly for fear of being thought cynical for stating the reality. He wondered if anyone would. At the end of the table, the three BUT trustees, Bensweiger, Ugstad and Talbot, had their heads together and were quietly engaged in discussion.

After a moment the two of the triumvirate who'd leaned in to produce the conversational huddle straightened and the center one, Trustee Ugstad, motioned for recognition. "I think we can all be sympathetic to the point that Trustee Brandwyn is trying to make," he began, "but (Lars wondered if the three knew that they were known by that trademark word) don't we have to look at this situation in the reality of the provisions of Coach Meeker's contract? His employment status is clearly tied to attendance. Obviously, the desired goal in attendance has not been reached. His contract specifies a time period during which a goal should be reached. I am sure that none of us would want to give him less time than the contract calls for. And just as surely, I hope that we would not want to extend that time." Ugstad looked to each side of him to confirm if he had caught the spirit of what his cohorts intended. Each gave him an affirmative nod.

Another pause ensued. Chair Appleby patiently awaited further discussion. Beside him Chancellor Brown looked inscrutable. The presenter looked hopeful that his ordeal might be at an end. "Are we ready for a motion?" asked Walter Appleby.

"I move that we accept the committee's report and implement its recommendations," said Marsha Brandwyn with firmness and clarity in her voice. After a brief pause, young Henry Amberson seconded the motion.

When Appleby invited discussion of the motion, his look fell on those trustees who had yet to be heard from. He seemed to be signaling that this was a matter on which no trustee could remain silent. Stanley Konjeski, the trustee who represented the region in which St. Claude and the state's northern extremity called "The Ridge" were included, was the first to respond to Appleby's silent urging. "I can tell you, Mr. Chairman and members of the board, that the Purple Peril football team is a part of the university that people in my part of the state take great pride in; no other part of the state has larger or more devoted Purple Pride fan clubs. But there hasn't been much to be proud of for a long time, has there? No question that support for the university in general is diminishing in my area because of this."

Trustee Middlebrook, who taught at a college where the faculty gave athletics slightly less tolerance than it did the crabgrass in their lawns, was stimulated to react to Konjeski's statement. "I am sure Trustee Konjeski did not mean to imply that support for the university rests solely on the success of its football team. Undoubtedly it is true that part of the public—and certainly some alumni—are stimulated to support the university because of the success of its sports teams. I don't think we should encourage such an attitude. We certainly would be unwise to let it control our decisions. We should want the university to be worthy of support for the caliber of its instructional programs and the skills and character of its graduates rather than something so peripheral as its football team. I have no quarrel with a university's having all the athletics that it can afford. If the case at Pauliapolis State is that the current expenditures for athletics are unaffordable, then that must be dealt with. Perhaps less programming rather than more expenditure is the answer." Lars had to admit that there was more to Middlebrook's position than intellectual snobbery.

Besides appealing to the instructional nurturers of young minds whose salaries were a fourth to a third that of the football coach, it would appeal to that segment of the public who worried that the emphasis and expenditures on intercollegiate athletics indicated a drastic confusion within education about what a university's function ought to be. During Lars's career as an administrator, he had occasionally fretted that one of the sideshows—even in universities where the athletic programs was described as "low emphasis"—was overshadowing the main event.

When Appleby's gaze fell on Martha Collins, she looked bewildered. The topic was apparently one she found unfathomable. Unlike Middlebrook, Lars knew from past experience, she did not have contempt for things that didn't interest her. "It would help me, Mr. Chairman," she said, looking earnestly for some form of relief, "to hear what Chancellor Brown has to say on the subject."

Lars's interest was now genuinely aroused. He smiled and fantasized while Brown collected his thoughts that the chancellor would say something other than the predictable exercise in fence straddling that Brown would recite. He imagined the chancellor saying, *"If I'd been half as ineffective as Meeker, whom it irritates me to note that you of the board pay almost twice what you pay me to manage the entire operation, you'd have sent me packing long ago."* However, Lars knew that this totally justified assertion would never be uttered. In fact, what Brown did say was exactly what an intelligent administrator with normal survival skills would say. "I believe that the university should strive for the highest level of excellence in everything that it commits itself to do. That should be no less true in athletics as in all other areas of instruction—and I hope we would not forget that athletics are an instructional situation. I can assure the board that the administration will explore every possibility to solve the current financial dilemma in the intercollegiate athletics program. I am confident that a solution will be found."

Lars smiled. Whether one thought Meeker should be decapitated or canonized, one would find nothing to irritate him in Brown's statement. Collins looked comforted, but no more enlightened than before Brown spoke.

Now Appleby looked to Lars. Rather than search his mind for a statement of appropriate ambivalence, Lars said, "Mr. Chairman, I move to divide the question, separating the recommendation on the extension of the appointment of the football coach from the rest of the report."

Appleby's expression indicated that he saw some value in Lars's proposal. "The effect of Trustee Paulsen's motion, if adopted, is that the board would vote separately on the motion to accept the committee report and the specific recommendation to extend the contract of the football coach. Is there a second to the motion?" Cartwright provided a second and a voice vote on the non-debatable motion to divide was quickly taken and unanimously passed. Appleby called for further discussion on the report exclusive of the now separate recommendation on Meeker's contract. There being no further discussion, the motion to accept the report passed by another unanimous voice vote.

Appleby then invited further discussion of the recommendation of Meeker's appointment extension. His eyes went from face to face around the table, silently urging discussion. His desire to have as many members as possible state a position before a vote adhered to a faithfully pursued board custom. Having the all of the committed members go on record permitted undecided members to smell out the likely majority and register their vote in accord with it. No one was moved to speak, despite Appleby's making his stare as insistence has he could. "We seem to be ready for a vote," Appleby concluded. He called for a voice vote, which sounded too close for him to announce a decision. When he requested a vote by a show of hands, only four of the group, Brandwyn, Amberson, Middlebrook and Collins, voted to extend the football coach's contract. Lars felt no guilt that Meeker was now in the position of having to deliver at last a year hence on his three years of optimistic predictions of a winning football season. The reality that governed the sideshow aspects of university life was that they are governed by the dynamics of the marketplace. Fame and fortune were assured those who succeeded in these irrelevant but treasured spectacles that had been added to the purpose for which universities existed. Just as certainly, those who failed could count on being forced into a major career change.

The rest of the morning's trustee business was routine. Lars sat impatiently through it. He and Marian had arranged to meet at their hotel for lunch so that he could get a full report on how her seminar to the Pauliapolis State education faculty had gone. As he hurried down the stairs out of the building, he found Marian waiting for him in the entry.

Lars greeted her and asked, "Did I get it wrong? I thought we were meeting at the hotel."

"We planned to, but I hope that you won't mind if I change our plans," Marian said as she put her hand on his arm.

"Is everything all right?" Lars asked, though Marian showed no sign of distress.

"Everything's fine, but I hope you'll let me cancel out of lunch."

"Sure," Lars assured Marian, though he was puzzled by the change. "Did the seminar go O.K.?"

"Better than that," Marian said and burst into a broad grin as she squeezed his arm. "They really listened. They asked lots of great questions. We ran over a whole hour. They were so enthusiastic that they invited me to lunch to talk about my presentation further."

"That's great," Lars said and smiled as broadly as Marian. He had feared that Marian might meet with condescension, no matter how meaningful her presentation. Pauliapolis faculty were known for their unwillingness to recognize the value of scholarship by NSSU faculty, no matter how valuable the work might be. Lars could understand Marian's joy.

"You don't mind if I desert you?" Marian asked.

"Of course not," said the proud spouse. "You must really have been super to impress that gang. Go give them more of that good stuff."

Marian squeezed his arm with both of hers and kissed Lars on the cheek. "Thanks, darling. I'm going to have to drive home right after lunch. I see you at home tomorrow, O.K.?"

Lars nodded his agreement as Marian sailed out the door. He was still in time to go to the usual lunch that Chancellor Brown provided for trustees. Lars would eat well, he knew, at no greater price than listening to mundane information from Chancellor Brown's staff. He would much rather have been a listener at Marian's lunch with the education faculty, where his pride would no doubt be more filling that the meal.

Lars walked rapidly across campus to the most modern of the several dining and student activity buildings that served the massive Pauliapolis State campus. The mid November chill that had stripped the central campus grove of oaks and the flower gardens around the buildings that surrounded that inspiring stand of century old trees had left no reason to tarry outdoors. Lars was crossing the first floor student lounge toward the elevators that would take him to the trustees' private dining room on the top floor when he spotted Connie Mercutio standing at the elevator doors. She turned and saw him as he approached. With exaggerated gravity and a taunting grin, she greeted him, "Good day, Trustee Paulsen. I hope that you did not find the morning's deliberations too taxing."

"I thank you for your concern, Dr. Mercutio," Lars responded in kind. "I am surprised to find you here rather than back in St. Claude molding young minds."

"Oh, I'm here on business," Connie responded, and continuing the fake formality, added, "so you need not have me investigated for deserting my university responsibilities."

"Business?" Lars asked, dropping the fencing match and making honest inquiry.

"Yes, the union leadership decided that their new grievance coordinator should acquire some first hand experience with trustee meetings and got someone to cover my classes so that I could observe the whole of a monthly meeting of your august group."

"Oh," Lars nodded, "you were there this morning? Perhaps I should be glad. It won't take much more of sitting through dreary dramas like that to wean you away from union activity. I'll confess that I'm hoping you'll realize that it's not worth your time and energy to be a union leader," Lars said candidly.

"But I'd have missed your adroit handling of the football coaching crisis at P State," Connie countered, showing no desire to take Lars's genuine concern seriously.

"No doubt you were impressed to find what significant matters related to providing the next generation with a sound education absorb the time of the trustees," Lars stated with calculated cynicism.

"Sounds like it's you rather than me that ought to be thinking whether your activities are a worthwhile expenditure of your time."

"There are redeeming compensations," Lars said.

"Such as?"

"I am sometimes in a position to be helpful to union grievance coordinators. As a matter of fact, I've been trying to reach you, but you apparently don't spend much time at home. Could you spare me some time now?"

"I was on my way to sampling the delicacies in the food court of the student deli downstairs," Connie said. "You are welcome to join me."

Lars accepted the invitation and soon they were seated in the noisy student eating area beyond the cafeteria where they had chosen two of the less wilted salads that struggled to provide what fresh vegetables could be had as the approaching northland winter removed the possibility of local crops.

Adding more dressing than he should to his salad, Lars began. "Please forgive me if I seem abrupt in getting to business, but I've something to tell you and something to sell and not much time." As briefly as he could, Lars summarized for Connie that the university administration would be requesting a time extension for responding to the Gonzales dismissal grievance and why the grievant and his union ought to consider granting it.

"I'm not quite grasping why the union and Gonzales should agree to an extension of time before Brown is required to respond to the grievance," Connie mused. "Frankly, I think that we've got a winner. Without the extension, Brown's going to have to reinstate Gonzales in a few days with back pay. What's the advantage to Gonzales to be suspended with pay while the university takes more time to investigate?"

Lars put down his fork and mustered all the candor that he could. "Have you considered that Gonzales's explanation isn't as convincing to other parties as it is to his advocates? You have only the technical director's word that the money went to him. Even without disproving that explanation, Brown could let the matter go to arbitration—which, incidentally, could keep Gonzales unsalaried for several more months until that hearing takes place—to test whether people are willing to testify to the explanation under oath. Bluffs tend to collapse in hearings, you know."

"But if it's not a bluff—or, to be blunt, even if it's a successful bluff—Gonzales gets his pay eventually," Connie underscored.

"If he goes along with the extension, he can start getting his money now, even if the case goes against him later. He has nothing to lose through the delay and possibly something to gain."

Connie maintained eye contact with Lars an unusual length of time.

"Do you think that the explanation of where the money went isn't going to hold up?"

"I have no idea, one way or the other," Lars said as he returned Connie's look. "But I believe one thing. It's no better than even money right now whether Brown will grant the grievance or let it go to arbitration. With those odds, I'd agree to the extension if I were in Gonzales's shoes."

"Well," Connie sighed as she returned to the remaining portion of her salad, "I'm sure that it will get some heavy discussion between Gonzales and the union leadership." After several distracted mouthfuls, she pushed the plate aside and said, "I should think through what I'm going to say when my opinion is asked."

Lars stood and gathered his things to depart. "That's why I wanted to get to you—to give you some thinking time."

"Not to mention the strongest argument for doing what the administration wants," Connie said with a mixture of humor and skepticism.

Lars knew that the reasons he had sought Connie out were so convoluted a mixture of professional and personal reasons that it was best not to respond substantively. "You know that we trustees only want what's best for the university, professor," he said hopeful that banter would obviate the need for meaningful response.

Connie arched her eyebrows, silently showing that she gave the statement no more credence than it deserved.

CHAPTER 16

U Trustee Prefers Academic Joys to Bored Work

During the next few weeks after the November board meeting, everything but teaching and other scholarly concerns blotted the politics and other peripheral sideshow of university life from Lars's mind. He was totally absorbed in his work. He had been asked to write a review of a new book on the post World War I disarmament conferences for Foreign Policy Quarterly, a prestigious political science periodical. He enjoyed the highly specialized reading and the task of appraising fairly and thoroughly the writer's reporting of the facts and his interpretation them. He enjoyed rather than was troubled to re-write his review four times to remove awkward pedantry and unwarranted cleverness at the expense of the competent and careful author. Reviewers who sacrificed fairness to cleverness had always been a particular irritation to Lars, so avoiding the fault was a particular goal with him. The last revision was devoted to removing abstractness which impresses but fails to communicate—a sin he had never overcome permanently—from complexity required for his analysis.

The review was a labor of love that infused additional enthusiasm into his lectures to his students, though the topics were different. A kindled intellect was not selective or narrow about where it threw its light. It was one of those happy periods where he and Marian, she similarly engrossed by her own scholarly concerns, were happy though apart or ignoring each other even when they were both at home. In fact, they both confessed to relief that their children had been unable to come home for Thanksgiving, letting them restrict celebration of the holiday to a restaurant meal on Thanksgiving itself so that they both could devote the bulk of the five-day hiatus in their teaching schedules to scholarly pursuits.

Even Lars's contacts with students when the university was in session were pleasantly academic. The approach of the end of a semester always brought a heightened interest in their studies among students who had delayed their reading until now and found that they actually were interested in the material in spite of themselves. Lars was surprised that even his erstwhile friend, the agile student politician Butch Kirk, approached him on an academic matter. A management major, Butch was doing a research paper for a class in finance on per capita funding of instruction in public and private universities. He had several technical questions that Lars, out of his administrative experience in a public university, could answer.

Lars remained so completely oblivious to the sideshows of his profession for more than two weeks so that it was a shock when Connie Mercutio called him the day he returned to his office after the Thanksgiving break. She asked him a question which assumed that he knew that Eric Gonzales and the NSSU faculty union representing him had agreed to the time extension for Chancellor Brown to respond to the dismissal grievance. Connie asked that, if he could do so without violating confidentiality, would he tell her how the administration's investigation into the case was going? Lars surprised himself to have to say that he knew nothing at all of the matter. Connie was reluctant to believe him until he assured her that, if he did learn anything about the matter that he could pass on without being improper, he would tell her. He meant to honor the promise; however, he resolved that he would not seek out any information, though he would honor the commitment if any information that he could share came his way.

CHAPTER 17

U Administration Balancing Act is no Hit with Anyone

The arrival of the agenda document for the December trustees meeting was preceded by several days by a letter from Chancellor Brown to the board. Its subject, the proposed university budget for the coming year, was unusual. The budget proposal itself would be in the agenda document in its entirety. Normally, if the chancellor felt it necessary to provide a position brief on any agenda item, that communication was placed in the agenda document as a preliminary to that subject for action itself. Brown's letter of explanation and advocacy was intended to give the trustees additional time to think about the implications of the constructive but potentially divisive budget plan he and his staff had developed. Brown also pleaded that any trustee who had questions on the budget plan discuss it with him in advance of the meeting. Lars was aware that Brown liked to arrange for board support of his positions in advance of the meeting itself to minimize the possibility of contrary dialogue in the meetings—and most importantly from Brown's point of view—to avoid any challenge to courses of action that he had decided on.

The letter summarized that the budget plan was designed to accomplish two important goals. The first was to fund the clean up of Little Moose Lake. The second was to increase support for the academic programs specifically by making access to computing more available at reasonable cost to all of the university's students. The necessity of achieving the first aim, the chancellor wrote, was sufficiently obvious and the subject of such extensive prior discussion that it needed not be dwelt on. The clean up would be funded partially by cuts in or elimination of non-instructional university programs and services.

The improvement of student access to computing was intended to correct a deficiency in the university's support of its students that had now reached an embarrassing state. Students in the natural sciences and engineering were paying increasingly larger computing fees for access to computers in courses that were crucial to their majors. Students in other areas of study had more and more need to have computers available to them for word processing and the developing qualitative aspects of their majors. Not enough equipment was available for non-science majors. To supply it by introducing the burdensome fees like those already existing for science students did not seem an appropriate solution. Instead, Chancellor Brown's staff proposed a one percent increase in tuition. The amount would actually lower the cost to science students and make computers readily available to all other students at a very modest cost. The tuition increase would yield enough funding to create, equip and staff a large number of additional computer labs that would be available to all students around the clock daily. The course-by-course computing fees would be eliminated. Admittedly, though the plan now created an indirect computing fee for all students, the cost per student would be low by spreading the burden among everyone. On the beneficial side, the application of computing to a number of disciplines where cost now restrained developments would be eliminated. Brown's discussion included a candid admission that the improvements in student computing could be done with two thirds of a percent rather than the full one percent. Those funds would be used to fund the balance of the lake clean up that the cost cutting in non-instructional areas did not cover. This action was defended as a preferable course of action to cutting even more services to students and faculty.

Brown closed with the assertion that, while the plan would draw some anger for increasing the cost for some students while decreasing it for others and for diminishing or eliminating some administrative services, the combination of actions seemed the most rational way to correct two expensive and embarrassing problems that urgently required action. Lars probably spent less time mulling over the implications and benefits of the Chancellor's budget plan than would his eleven trustee colleagues. His experience in university administration told him that the balance of costs and benefits in the plan weighed heavily on the benefit side. No doubt his trustee colleagues would agonize in anticipation of the screams of anguish that the plan would cause among both students and university employees, but Lars saw Brown's plan as courageous and appropriate and resolved that he would support it. He said precisely this to board chair Appleby, who called him two days later to try to sample how divisive a situation he would have to cope with in the following week's meeting on the matter.

In fact, the discussion of the matter was less than twenty minutes old in the midst of the first morning session of the December board meeting when it was apparent to the entire board that consensus on the budget would be hard to reach. Of course there were some views that were unanimously held. No one liked tuition increases, which in recent years had exceeded the rate of inflation and had become a heavy burden on students and their families. No one liked pollution. No one liked to decrease services to students and faculty. No one liked waste, rising costs, college graduates who were ignorant of modern technology, and—just for the record—high taxes or diminishing support for public higher education. All these sacred cows having been milked, Lars noted, the matter of endorsing the budget proposed by the administration or substituting an alternative remained untouched.

With Appleby coaxing his colleagues to address specific parts of the budget proposal, certain positions eventually did become known. Trustees Brandwyn, Konkeski, Amberson and Collins favored more computing access for students but didn't think tuition ought to be raised to provide it. Trustees Cartwright, Anderson, Bensweiger, Ugstad and Talbot favored additional computing access and thought it proper that more tuition pay for it but would hold the amount of the increase to just what was needed for computing. Middlebrook, who recognized the necessity of computing access for science students and deferred to the unfortunate introduction of quantitative approaches into business curricula, questioned the value of computing approaches in the liberal arts and social sciences. Hence, he concluded that the present handling of computing costs for students was appropriate and opposed to raising tuition of all students to pay for a tool that was not similarly used by all. Appleby did not press Lars for a position, Lars presumed, because the chair did not think the timing favorable to support all the provisions of the budget plan as proposed.

As to funding the clean up, Cartwright, Anderson and the three BUT trustees would fund it entirely with even deeper cuts in non-instructional services than those proposed; but the other five who spoke would only support cuts that did not require layoffs, which the administration plan admitted would happen if the anticipated attrition did not occur, permitting savings by leaving vacancies unfilled.

Lars's trustee colleagues joined him in an inert silence when they had finished making it clear that they unanimously liked the aims of the administration budget proposal but could not achieve a majority on the implementation actions proposed in the plan. Walter Appleby let the silence reign until the stalemate settled heavily on the shoulders of his colleagues. He then opened a folder and began the distribution of some sheets of paper to his fellow board members. "We seem to be stalemated on accepting the administrative budget plan or proposing any consensus alternative to achieve a pair of goals that we all seem to believe are worthy," said the chair as his trustee colleagues each took a sheet of paper and passed the remainder on down the table, "I anticipated that this situation might happen. I have developed an alternative for your consideration. The sheet that I have just handed out contains the actions that I propose and the figures that would result, achieving fully or in part the goals proposed in the administration plan."

Each board member studied the sheet with the appearance of intense concentration as Appleby continued. "The proposal on the sheet before you calls for a one-half of one percent increase in tuition. That will cover most, but not all, of the cost of implementing the computing improvements—and eliminating the present selective fees. The rest of the cost of computing improvement will be covered by the cuts—in the amounts specified in the administration plan—in non-instructional services. As you will note from the figures, only a fraction of the cut savings will be needed for computing; the remainder of the savings would be used to fund the initial phase of the pollution clean up. You'll note from the figures that the savings not devoted to computing will cover slightly less that one-half of the estimated cost of the lake clean up. I am hoping that this effort on the university's part will encourage the legislature to provide us the balance of the clean up money when we make our biennial request a year hence."

The bowed heads around the table continued to stare at the sheet of paper in silence. Finally, Trustee Middlebrook gestured for the floor. "Mr. Chairman, I don't know if it was your goal in arriving at this plan to try to design one that would make everyone unhappy, but that is what you have obviously done. Though some of us have opposed a tuition increase, you have included one; though some of us think the students ought to pay for computing, you would only make them pay for part of the improvement; though we all want the clean up to occur, you would start it but not finish it; and, though some of us oppose cuts in service, that remains one of the ingredients. This seems to be a plan designed to make everyone unhappy."

Middlebrook's assessment floated in a stillness at the table which was counterpointed by prominent murmuring and restlessness in the audience. Lars gestured for recognition, feeling an obligation to be the one who pointed to the reality the board was avoiding. "Chair Appleby and members of the board," Lars began, with no relish for the role of urging his colleagues to do what they must all find distasteful. "I will confess to looking at the alternate budget plan not so much as a board member but more from the point of view of an instructor and a former administrator. We are unanimous in feeling an obligation not to delay too long in cleaning up the pollution, though the university should feel no guilt about it. After all, the problem has not resulted from reckless or improper action."

Lars looked a moment into the eyes of each of his colleagues around the table before turning to his next and most dearly held position. "We will continue to do our students a serious disservice if we send them into the world of work without familiarity with the technology that is rapidly becoming a universal feature of both work and other aspects of daily life. The only question before us is not *if* we should correct these deficiencies but *how*. I am sure that Trustee Middlebrook is correct. The alternative plan will make everyone unhappy to some extent. But sometimes creating universal unhappiness to a similar degree in all constituencies is one of the virtues of a plan—particularly if a painless course of action is not possible. I believe that is the situation we face. This plan, which spreads the unhappiness universally but evenly while meeting two pressing obligations, is our most judicious course of action. I move that we adopt it."

The board settled into another silence. The audience joined in the board's paralysis. In the palpable tension, Lars's motion was like a leaky boat gradually filling up with water and soon to sink. Appleby let the funereal silence endure a while before he asked, "Is there a second to the motion?"

The silence was not immediately broken, but finally Trustee Martha Collins addressed the chair and, being recognized, supplied the second to the motion. No one responded to the chair's invitation to discuss the motion. In the voice vote that Appleby called, the motion passed unanimously.

The apparent lack of enthusiasm for the course of action on the budget that the trustees had taken did not create a sullen mood for the rest of the trustee meeting. The trustees seemed relieved to have a course of action that placated everyone partially though it distressed them as well. They could all make half-a-loaf statements to the media and various constituencies when asked. There were ample grounds to appear responsible, prudent and financially cautious.

Hence the atmosphere at Chancellor Brown's annual Christmas dinner for the trustees Thursday evening had an even more festive air than could be attributed to the approaching holidays. University business was almost never a subject of conversation, except for an occasional brief tribute to the wisdom of what they had done. Lars wished that Marian had been there to experience the jovial and self-congratulatory mood; however, he was sure that she, just as he, would have been less than enthralled with the lengthy program of seventeenth century English Christmas carols. He was certain that the PSU music professor had given them the entirety of her repertoire. Lars was convinced that there was no song from the period that the singer had overlooked.

CHAPTER 18

St. Claude Couple Finds New Year Full of Surprises

December is a frenzied but joyful month for university professors. There is the unavoidable rush to wind up their teaching responsibilities because the semester ends before Christmas. At least for the conscientious ones—which are that majority that includes the Paulsens—there are the students' research papers to read; examinations to prepare, administer and grade; and recordkeeping to complete. With these professional tasks completed, the happy hysteria of preparing for the holidays can finally be engaged.

With Christmas only nine days away, everything that the Paulsens had held in abeyance until their teaching responsibilities were complete was attacked energetically, if not methodically: a tree was bought and decorated (the children, though adults, would be deflated if they did not find it to examine and appraise on their arrival); lights were strung on the spruce in the front yard; food was bought for the special meals that both the children and their parents would delight in (Marian took special pleasure feeding her offspring deliciously and abundantly when they made their infrequent visits); and presents were bought (notwithstanding that Marian accumulated presents all year long for the three members of her family.) In sum, four people of independent spirit whose lives consciously centered on their work more than their family ties reunited and effortlessly re-awakened their affectionate feelings for each other, which, though usually submerged, were no less strong and binding for that.

The reality of what transpired in the four days that the Paulsens' son and daughter were home surpassed even the expectations that were constantly a part of the parents' preparations. With pride, the children reported the latest news regarding their careers. The pleased parents' enjoyment in hearing of these accomplishments was heightened by seeing these competent professionals resort to the peculiarities and juvenile enjoyment of their developing years. Even when the pair disappeared to be with childhood friends, there was a special enjoyment for the parents in reviewing the fresh awareness at what the children did and had become. The twinge of pain the elder Paulsens felt in seeing their children leave—each in a car that was more luxurious than the ones their academic parents drove, though Lars and Marian could now afford luxuries that were beyond them during the early days of their marriage—was tempered with a feeling of happiness at the lives that the children had made for themselves.

Lars and Marian each felt a lesser but equally satisfying pleasure as early January brought them new teaching assignments and new students. A change of lecture material was always an energizing experience. A new cohort of students meant dozens of new personalities to discovery and unique abilities and minds to see displayed. Even the frustrations and disappointments were either new or a change from the recent past. For couples like the Paulsens, who shared the same profession and a joy for it, a new term always meant fresh dinner table conversation. Education, they had long since agreed, was perhaps the foremost profession for providing such endless novelty to enliven a lengthy marriage.

Life finally returned to a mundane level for Lars when Marian left to attend a Wednesday through Saturday conference in Chicago during the same week when he was scheduled for the monthly Thursday and Friday trustees meeting. The evening before his trip to Pauliapolis, Lars could not stay awake reading the humdrum agenda comprised of a multitude of minuscule matters destined for decisions which were foregone conclusions.

In fact, the topics were so uninspiring the Lars hit on a pleasanter thing to do that to attend the Friday session. The sunny and cold but dry weather was predicted to hold through the weekend. With an early start, Lars could make the eight hour drive from Pauliapolis to Chicago and be at Marian's hotel by late afternoon. There would be time for dinner and—if fate favored them—the symphony before spending the night together at the hotel. He was sure that Marian would not mind the long drive home rather than coming by plane if they made frequent stops along the way. In fact, the return trip would take them by not only several decent restaurants but also a shop that sold some unique baskets of birch made by local people of Norwegian extraction who practiced a traditional craft. Marian admired the artfully shaped and constructed containers for their practicality as well as their beauty. She had several in the house as well as one in her office. She had also given several as presents and would no doubt be happy to examine the current stock of handcrafted work as possible gifts.

Lars made the uneventful drive to Chicago as planned and at 4:30 stood at the registration desk of the hotel facing Grant Park only a few blocks from the symphony hall. He explained to the clerk that he wanted to register to stay in his wife's room. The clerk recorded the information and cheerfully informed Lars that there would be no charge because his stay was covered by the conference rate that Marian was paying.

Lars asked for a key to the room. It was likely that Marian would be in one of the meetings taking place on the conference level of the hotel. He planned to leave his bag in the room and roam the conference in search of her. It would not be difficult. The conference group, consisting of a particular set of educational specialists, was not large. He paused for a bit at the house telephones near the elevators and thought about calling Marian's room in case she were taking a break from the day long series of meetings that were in their third day. Deciding that it would be fun to surprise her, he went to the elevators without phoning.

A packed car full of people wearing conference lapel badges emptied before him, and he entered alone to rise to what was now his tenth floor room. The car stopped on the fourth floor and a man got on carrying a small bouquet wrapped in tissue paper. Lars got a brief sight of violets nestled inside the tissue before the man turned his back to Lars and made the usual intense study of the changing display of numbers above the elevator door, as people do when they wanted to avoid eye contact or conversation with their fellow occupants of the small cubicle. Lars smiled as he wondered if the stranger was a husband who did not normally make romantic gestures to his wife and was a bit sheepish at carrying a bouquet.

When the elevator door opened on the tenth floor, the other man exited ahead of Lars and started down the hall to the right. Lars glanced at the key envelope showing his room number and at the room numbers and directions on the wall and started left down the hall. In a few steps he realized that the room numbers were heading in the wrong direction and looked as his room number again. He had misread 1016 as 1061, so he re-traced his steps back to the room number indicators, which sent him down the hall in the opposite direction from his original course. Shortly, he turned a corner and heard the sound of several taps on a door. He looked a few feet down the hall where his violet-carrying companion from the elevator stood before a door that was now opening to him. He heard the sound of the voice that was unmistakable to him beyond all others express her delight at the gift of flowers. A few steps closer gave him a sight of the embrace and the kiss in which the two bodies were locked. Lars stood in stunned silence for a few moments before he turned back toward the elevators. Before he turned the corner into the elevator area, he heard the sound of a door closing. He thought that it probably would not have sounded as loud to anyone else as it did to him.

CHAPTER 19

Professional Skills no Solution to Personal Conflict

Lars began the drive from Chicago to St. Claude with no thought if it made sense to start a ten-hour drive in the dark of night in mid winter after already having spent eight hours on the road. Anger had provided more than enough energy to stride like a charging bull through the hotel lobby and back to the garage where he re-claimed the car he had parked less than an hour before. When he found himself on the open and rapidly flowing interstate ninety minutes later, he realized he had driven through the rush hour traffic without a moment's consciousness of what he was doing. Still seething with an anger that kept his foot heavily on the accelerator, Lars spun fantasies of punishment and revenge as he rushed northward through the dark. Uncounted miles later, a moment's attention to his driving led him to notice that the fuel gage showed empty. He wondered how long it had read thus. If the warning bell that accompanied the visual display had rung, he had not heard it. He took the first opportunity to fill the tank. When the tank took more fuel than he could ever remember having put in at one time, he decided to drive for two more hours and find a room for the night. The primary criterion for the motel would be whether or not the bar was open. He wondered how much brandy it would take to give him any chance at all of sleeping that night.

In fact, despite considerable brandy, Lars did not fall asleep before the middle of a movie that started at 2:00 A.M. Nonetheless, he was up before 6:00 A.M. and decided not to wait until the motel restaurant opened for breakfast before he got back on the road. As he drove, anger still assaulted him. However, in moments of diminished anger, other themes than punishment and revenge mingled in the welter of his thoughts. He saw the necessity of planning his immediate future. He would be home shortly after noon. Marian's plane arrived at 6:00 P.M. She, as arranged, expected him to pick her up at the airport. After a perfunctory greeting and the brief drive home, what would he say and do? If he confronted her with what he had seen, would she say her hotel tryst had not gone beyond a kiss or two? He wouldn't for a moment believe such an explanation. Yet, only an admission on her part would confirm the adultery of which he had seen the passionate prelude.

Could he remain silent and pretend that he had never gone to Chicago and seen what he had? It was unlikely that he could manage to do that. During his thirty-year marriage to Marian, Lars had given her total fidelity and had never doubted that Marian had lived by a similar commitment. The betrayal he felt made it doubtful that he could consider Marian's infidelity a one-time lapse from decades of loyalty and harmony and go on as though no violation of their bond had occurred. Now thinking of Marian from a new perspective, he felt no certainty that yesterday had been a first occurrence or would be a last one.

Whether Lars would be torn by suspicions after their initial dialogue or struggling to deal with Marian's admission of adultery, what did he intend to do after that first face-to-face meeting? The tangle of anger and rumination was engrossing enough that Lars gave no thought to either breakfast of lunch before he arrived in St. Claude. He paced the house indecisively for a couple of hours. Unable to decide how he would behave, he decided to avoid meaningful conversation or contact with Marian entirely that evening in the hope that the next morning would find him calm and resolute about what to say and do. The North Shore State hockey team was playing at Northfield College, which was seventy miles away from St. Claude, that evening. If he went to the game, Marian would be asleep by the time he returned, and the difficulty to be endured would be postponed until tomorrow morning.

He phoned the airport and asked to have a message given to Marian when she arrived telling her what his plans were. He considered for a moment that, as furious as he was with Marian, he did not want to put her to the annoyance of waiting pointlessly for him when she could immediately take a taxi home. Then he realized that his motive was not unselfish. Not knowing what Lars knew, Marian had no reason for restlessness that might prevent an early bedtime and slumber. His message was intended to avoid distressing Marian so that she was certain to be asleep when he returned. That Marian would still be feeling the tranquility that was completely lost to him re-fueled his anger.

When he returned to the house shortly after midnight, Lars was no more settled about what to do than he had been when he left. He was relieved to find the house was completely dark. He knew that the sound of the garage door opening and closing did not usually disturb Marian's sleep. He took off his shoes in the garage. By keeping the noise of his preparation for bed to a minimum, he would be able to slip into bed without awakening Marian. He was cautiously feeling his way across the dark but familiar living room when light from the lamp beside the couch burst into his eyes. When his sight adjusted to the glare, he saw Marian sitting on the couch fully clothed.

"I thought you would long since have been asleep," Lars said. "Was your plane late?"

"No, it was on time," Marian answered, with a tone and facial expression that Lars could not quite interpret. He hoped that she was not about to express annoyance at not having been met at the airport. He was certain he would not be able to react civilly to that. "I've been sitting here waiting for you since I got back."

"In the dark?"

"Yes. I seemed to think better that way," Marian said.

"You must be as tired as I am," Lars said, hoping to avoid a discussion of anything when he was tired, hurt and angry.

"It's important that we talk now," Marian pressed. She shifted about restlessly for a moment before she settled and fixed a confident gaze on Lars. "Emma Hardesty says that she saw you in our hotel in Chicago yesterday."

Lars stared at his wife of thirty years. It was perhaps inevitable that she looked different to him. The face and figure that made her the handsomest woman of her age that he knew were the same. However, the facial blush and grave expression that she always brought to any critical situation were missing. Customarily, Lars showed and spoke his nervousness more than Marian did, so her calm demeanor was no surprise. But her facial expression at this moment went beyond calmness almost to placidity.

"Were you there? Between four and five in the afternoon?" Marian asked. Lars nodded affirmatively.

"Have you been checking on me?" Marian asked coldly.

Lars restrained the impulse to explode. "If you're trying to made out that I'm the one of us who's done something wrong, I advise against it. I was just planning to offer my wife dinner and the symphony for the evening. Obviously there was other entertainment that you had in mind."

Marian moved to a more guarded posture; yet still showed confidence. "All right," Marian said as though closing a matter. She sighed and said, "You were never supposed to find out. I'd never do anything at home to embarrass you."

"You mean it's O.K. if no one knows? What a novel idea," Lars offered sarcastically.

"It isn't novel, is it? A rather common masculine explanation, I believe," Marian retorted.

"We're not going to discuss this in terms of what men have done to women since the beginning of time, are we? There's a difference between being discrete and being loyal—and loyalty's what I've given you for thirty years." Lars had spoken like a card player laying down trump.

"I can match you with as many years of faithfulness."

"Who is this irresistible man that brought that to an end?"

Marian responded with one slight shake of her head. "That's not important."

"How long has it been going on?"

"It hasn't been 'going on' at all," Marian said with a trace of impatience. "It was something I just decided to do."

"It was that easy to decide?"

"It was within a specific frame of reference. I was away from home. My paper had gone well. The attention felt good. It was just one more part of the success. And I meant to enjoy it—I apologize for the wording, it sounds cruel—in total privacy. Emma was the only one there who knew me, and I took care that she wouldn't know."

"Someone knows. He's probably already looking forward to the next conference he goes to."

Marian again showed some irritation at Lars's consistent sarcasm. "Don't make me sound like a slut. Some occasional un-involved sex is not all that rare, even in good relationships."

Lars, still on his feet since entering, took several steps toward the hallway. He considered leaving before he exploded. His next thought brought him back to face Marian squarely. "I'm wondering if you'd be justifying yourself with that rationalization if I hadn't years ago let you have control of our sex life."

"Me? Control? That's ridiculous. When have I ever controlled anything? What I've wanted has always come second in our marriage and you know it. Where we lived; when we moved; if I worked and where I worked—all your decisions or consequences of your decisions. God, even when we had our second kid was determined by your career, not mine."

"If you had even a shred of awareness about the frequency of my unmet needs, you'd see how firmly you are in control of our sex lives."

"How am I supposed to know what you want? Can't you just tell me?"

Lars felt exasperation replacing his anger. "There's a limit to how blunt requests can be without a situation becoming like a business transaction. Besides, we do make arrangements sometimes and you more often than not forget or don't care to indulge. That's when you treat my desperate little hints and touches with an unresponsiveness that leaves me struggling with my grouchiness for several days.

"Maybe you should try a little adventure of your own," Marian offered with a blandness that Lars found astonishing.

Lars smiled wryly as he renewed his pacing. "Somehow, I thought I owed you a loyalty that stood in the way of a solution like that."

"Consider it getting even, if that's what you need to do to get past this situation."

Lars let more sharpness break into his voice and retorted, "Keeping the score even hasn't been my idea of our relationship."

"Have you considered that maybe you've just got wounded pride? There's been no harm done by what I did. Maybe you should try it." Marian's endorsement of extra-marital activity brought Lars as close to striking her as he had ever been in thirty years of marriage. "If you could do it secretly, would you do it again?" he asked.

Marian thought some moments before she answered, "I can't say now."

"Well," Lars began with all the ice in his voice that he could muster, "I'm going to leave tomorrow morning to find a place to stay. When you can say, why don't you let me know?" He turned and proceeded down the hallway to his son's room, where he intended to spend the night.

CHAPTER 20

Young and Old Share Unusual Valentines

Four weeks passed without Lars and Marian speaking a word to each other. He found a winterized lake cottage not far from town to rent. Lars assumed that Marian took precautions similar to his own to prevent their meeting. He made several trips to the house for clothes and other personal belongings he needed when he knew Marian was teaching. He knew where she preferred to buy groceries and avoided the place. Even when they had lived together, their paths rarely crossed on campus. It only took a little extra wariness to prevent chance meetings. However, it was with greater than normal enthusiasm that Lars traveled to Pauliapolis for the February trustees meeting because it meant that being constantly on guard would be unnecessary for a few days.

He checked into the hotel on the edge of the Pauliapolis campus and was in the midst of a couple of hours of reading before dinner to familiarize himself with the agenda of the meetings that would begin the next morning when the phone rang. The voice that returned Lars's greeting was recognizable as that of Chancellor Ivor Brown. After identifying himself, Brown apologized for doing some business over the phone that would have been more proper to do face-to-face. However, the chancellor explained that he meant to prevent the press from getting a sensitive story before he had a chance to announce the matter to the board. Therefore, Brown explained, he was phoning each board member that afternoon rather that waiting until the morning to try to break the news to them privately before the public session began.

Lars heard the chancellor draw a deep breath before he continued in a tone of voice that seemed to convey satisfaction rather than crisis. Brown told Lars that he would be resigning the chancellorship of the system of the three state universities to assume the directorship of a large foundation in Houston which funded experiments in educational innovation. Lars could tell that Brown was enormously pleased at the change of careers that he was undertaking. He asked a few questions that gave the chancellor the opportunity to make enthusiastic statements about the opportunity he would have to serve education in a different, wider capacity. Brown hinted discretely that he would be doing so at a considerably higher salary that he now received from the state university system.

Lars expressed congratulations and genuine pleasure to Brown at his news. It was Lars's experience that, although people occasionally managed to survive in the same university position for a lengthy term of service and retire from it, the more frequent pattern—even for able university administrators—was to move periodically before they inevitably wore out their welcome, no matter how effectively they had served. Lars respected the fact that Brown was making a practical decision, no matter what his new circumstances would be. Brown thanked Lars for his good wishes and excused himself from further conversation, stating that he had a number of other calls to make if he were going to reach certain people who might be offended if they saw the news in print before they heard it from him.

When Thursday morning came, Brown's circumspection of the previous day proved unnecessary, since the morning paper was silent on an impending change in university leadership. However, there was a prominently featured story that doubtless would be the focus of the university board's labors that morning rather than the routine set of topics in its printed agenda.

The morning paper gave front-page space to a controversial situation which had developed at Beau Prairie State within the last twenty-four hours. The annual Valentine's Day issue of the student weekly newspaper had appeared two days before, that being its last regular publication date before the holiday which would occur the coming Saturday. It had long been the custom at Beau Prairie State to treat the Valentine's Day theme in satiric or outrageous fashion, usually succeeding in amusing the campus at large, though not always the community of Beau Prairie itself. This year, however, any displeasure that was felt in the community paled in comparison with the anger and dismay created on the campus itself. In fact, if it had been the intention of the young journalists to outrage student adherents to the entire spectrum of social values, they had succeeded spectacularly, despite their subsequent insistence that their intention had been to amuse rather than offend.

Each copy of *The Beau Prairie Spokesman*, which for the Valentine issue was entitled *The Beau Prairie Playmate*, had come with a condom attached. While the editorial stated that the device was being provided to encourage safe sex in these times when precaution was common sense, the wording in which the editorial crudely encouraged the sex act and broadly hinted in which dorms eager males would find the most willing and indiscriminate women was appalling rather than amusing. Both the religious fundamentalists and feminists among the students had found the editorial insulting. Students less enamored of chastity and accepting of healthful practices in sexual activity had found the piece tasteless rather than clever.

The gay, lesbian and bisexual student group had found its basis for anger in the section of the paper devoted to personals purportedly for seeking dates, a feature now quite common in daily papers across the country. However, the self-descriptions of people soliciting partners were so grossly insulting and the activities for which partners were being solicited were described so perversely that the students of less traditional sexual orientations felt demeaned and demonized. They were not mollified when the newspaper staff pointed out that the ads in the concocted straight section of the dating pages were just as bizarre as those in the distorted alternative life style section. In this section as with the editorial, those who were not personally offended simply found the unsuccessful attempt at humor distasteful.

The consequence of the outrage over the content of *The Beau Prairie Playmate* issue was that the campus's Gay, Lesbian, and Bisexual Alliance had taken it upon itself to confiscate all the copies of the student paper from the racks around campus where it normally was placed so that students might avail themselves of the free weekly distribution. The staff of the paper had called the removal a blatant and illegal act of censorship and contacted the Pauliapolis daily paper to bring attention to the violation of their first amendment rights. The professional journalists in Pauliapolis were, of course, delighted to give significant attention to the situation for two reasons. Tempests within the academy always had a juiciness because the combatants always took themselves so seriously. Secondly, the selfish interests of the press led them to see every event remotely related to freedom of speech as a matter of major implication. It was an opportunity to promote their goal of being completely unfettered to write whatever they wished without fear of being called to account for untruthfulness, inaccuracy, sloppiness, unfairness or outright bias. Thus had appeared the prominent and lengthy story that Lars had read with dismay. It would no doubt divert the day's meeting of the university system trustees from whatever else they were scheduled to do.

The meeting of the trustees no sooner was convened than Chair Appleby announced that he would entertain a motion to modify the published agenda to hear a report from the president of Beau Prairie State, Stuart Richardson, on the controversy at that campus over the current edition of the student paper. The motion passed without discussion and President Richardson quickly made his way to the presenter's chair. He was a slight and bespectacled man of medium height whose apparent meekness was, Lars knew from experience, a contradiction to the firm, principled character of the man. In his typically understated fashion, Richardson recounted the facts in the situation regarding the current issue of the student paper at his campus. Lars noted that the campus president's version was not significantly different from the newspaper story. Richardson went on to say that he had last evening met with the membership of the Gay, Lesbian, Bisexual Alliance and the staff of the student paper.

The student journalists were adamant that their first amendment rights had been violated and that it was the responsibility of the administration to see that the Valentine's Day issue of the paper was distributed immediately. The student group refused to return the papers, which they admitted that they had not destroyed. Their intention was to make them available at a public forum where they would publicly address what they considered the malicious and prejudicial content of the writing. They demanded not only that the administration support the forum but cancel classes at that time so that all students could attend. In fact, the more extreme among their number asserted that attendance at the forum should be required of all students as a first step in sensitizing the entire campus community to alternative lifestyle issues.

Richardson closed by saying that he had promised both groups that he would announce a course of action at 4:00 o'clock this afternoon. So that the board might read the controversial material for themselves, Richardson added, he had brought along copies of the editorial and the date match sections for the board to examine. He explained that they were sheets of paper rather the newspapers themselves because neither group, the paper staff who had just a few file copies, and the student protestors who held the entire press run, would provide him with copies of *The Beau Prairie Playmate* edition.

Lars was not surprised at what he read. The writing was heavy-handed and crude, the result when a writer attempts humor motivated by his own intolerance rather than his subject's vulnerability to caricature. The women who had been asserted to be promiscuous merely because they lived in certain dorms were no less abused than those whose lifestyles had been made grotesque. It was an exercise in free speech that would amuse only those who shared the writers' intolerance. Lars recognized a dilemma he had encountered himself as an administrator. Should one permit the suppression of speech or writing that was nothing more that intolerant vilification or must all expressions be permitted on principle? The answer was easy for those who believed free speech an absolute right. It was less easy for those who saw a distinction between ridicule and demonization or were reluctant to have fellow humans with variant lifestyles portrayed as unfit to share the society.

Walter Appleby asked the group if they had any questions of President Richardson. After a few factual inquiries, a series of statements tumbled out of members of the board that revealed how the speaker thought Richardson ought to decide the matter. The tenor of the remarks was predictable. Though all the speakers asserted the writing to have exceeded the bounds of good taste, some believed that the paper had to be distributed out of regard for the principle of free speech. A few saw the confiscation justified by the egregiousness of the presentation. Whether the student journalists should apologize or not was variously supported or opposed, though no speaker linked his position to his tolerance or distaste for the life styles of those who had been pilloried. Everyone thought that the angered students should conduct a forum if they chose, but special university sanction of it or dismissal of classes was unanimously deemed inappropriate. Finally, Chair Appleby reminded the group that the subject was on the agenda for discussion and not action. President Richardson, Appleby pointed out, would be making his decision later in the day after consultation with the university attorney's office. With that, the discussion, which had been energetic but not divisive, was ended. The group was surprised to find that it had expended the entire morning on the matter and adjourned for lunch determined to dispose the entire day's scheduled concerns during the afternoon session.

In fact, not only did the board dispose of the entire Thursday agenda that afternoon but also began handling the Friday morning session with similar dispatch. It was mid-morning, therefore, when Chancellor Ivor Brown concluded his monthly Chancellor's report with the announcement of his resignation effective two months hence to accept the prestigious foundation directorship which he briefly described. Other than the board and a few senior colleagues of the chancellor who had been informed in advance of Brown's announcement, the audience reacted predictably at the unexpected development. A stunned silence was followed by a buzz of excitement and much stirring among the media personnel who were present. Walter Appleby brought the room to order with a sharp rap of his gavel. After a brief statement of commendation and thanks to the chancellor for his service, Appleby stated that that Chancellor Brown would be available in a few minutes for a press conference in the auditorium one floor below. The board, the chair announced, would adjourn for fifteen minutes and convene in executive session to discuss the process for selecting Brown's successor as chancellor.

Lars made his way out of the room for a respite from the noise as a group of well-wishers milled around Brown. He stood in the stairwell enjoying the relative quiet. Outside the board room, the noise prompted by Brown's announcement persisted. He turned away from the window at the approach of footsteps to find Ivor Brown approaching to descend the stairs. Lars smiled and said, "Amazing that the word didn't get out."

"It was a minor miracle," said Brown as he stopped to shake Lars's hand. "You've been an asset to me on the board. I appreciate it."

"I was glad to help."

Brown patted Lars on the shoulder. "I've got to run."

Brown got half way down the steps and stopped. "Lars," he said, "I thought you'd like to know. You recall the dismissal case at North Shore—Gonzales? His explanation of the missing money was that the technical director was given additional pay, you'll recall. The technical director appears to have accepted the earnings statement that didn't include the supposed additional salary. It starts to look like the union's grievance will fall apart." Brown waved and disappeared down the stairs.

Lars felt a moment of satisfaction that the strategy he'd recommended to Brown had proven to be a wise one. His pride dissolved quickly when he considered what trouble the turn of events might make for Connie Mercutio.

CHAPTER 21

Sources Say Friends in Conflict Over Ethics

Lars pondered all weekend whether he should warn Connie Mercutio that the grievance position that she was advocating in good faith for Eric Gonzales was about to be rebutted convincingly. She seemed destined for some amount of embarrassment. Either she would appear naive to have accepted a false explanation for the missing money, or she would be seen as a willing party to a misrepresentation. He knew that Connie had an idealistic view of her work as the union grievance representative. She had confidence in the union's process for screening out insubstantial complaints and representing only those grievants who appeared to have been unfairly treated. She would be disappointed to have been deceived. Lars considered that he should cushion Connie's disillusionment. Yet he had faith in her tough-mindedness. She was realistic enough to know that complainants occasionally lied or neglected part of the truth. Perhaps he should let the situation play itself out. Lars didn't think it a bad thing that Connie would be disillusioned with union involvement. She was an exceptional scholar and teacher. Her productivity was no doubt diminished by time she spent rescuing people who often did not, in Lars's mind, deserve her efforts.

By Monday, he decided that he should pass on to Connie what he knew, not because he thought she needed protecting, but because he wanted to start her thinking that union involvement may not be worth her time. He reached Connie by phone and briefly reported that the set designer had accepted an earnings statement for tax purposes that excluded the thirteen thousand dollars that Gonzales claimed to have paid him as additional salary. Faced with the contradiction, Lars went on, the man must now either pay taxes on money he never received or retract his statement that he had received it. Lars candidly predicted that the designer would withdraw his earlier statement; hence again leaving Gonzales without an explanation for the missing money. He recommended to Connie that she and the union leadership confront Gonzales so that they could consider whether to withdraw the grievance challenging his dismissal.

Connie had been silent throughout Lars's report and recommendation. She was slow to respond after Lars had finished. "Maybe he just hasn't noticed the discrepancy yet. There's still some time before the tax-filing deadline. Maybe he hasn't even looked at his tax records yet. When he does, he may ask for a revised earnings statement from the university."

"Or maybe he'll ask Gonzales for some money to pay the taxes on income he never got," Lars offered.

"You can't believe that the union would be a party to anything like that," Connie stated forcefully. "Besides, Gonzales couldn't come up with money for that even if the union were unethical enough to go along."

"Maybe the union won't even know if it happens," Lars pointed out

"Maybe you're just too cynical and mistrusting," Connie shot back.

"And maybe you are too—" Lars began before he checked himself. "Listen to us. About to get into an argument over conflicting speculations about matters beyond our control."

"Something's not beyond my control, if you have no problem with my doing it," Connie said tentatively. "I could raise the matter of the earnings statement discrepancy with Gonzales and the set designer and ask for an explanation."

"No doubt they'll want to know how you know about the discrepancy," Lars pointed out.

"I'll tell them I heard a rumor. They don't need to know more than that."

"I don't know," Lars countered. He could see a maze of complication looming.

"You're not afraid that there's a reasonable explanation, are you?"

"Come on," Lars chided. "I've got no investment in this."

"Then why'd you call?" Connie asked.

"I thought I might confidentially save a friend a little embarrassment. I guess I made a mistake." Lars felt some bitterness.

Connie responded quickly. "You didn't deserve what I said. I apologize."

"Accepted," Lars said as he settled down quickly. "On reflection, I should have expected that you'd want to pursue the matter. I have no doubt that you'll be able to keep me out of it. Do what you think you have to."

"You're not angry?" Connie asked, her concern clearly coming through.

"Of course not," Lars could say unreservedly. "I'll be interested to see what develops." On that note, he ended their conversation.

Three days later, Connie called Lars to tell him the outcome of her inquiry regarding the earning statement discrepancy. The cheerful tone of her voice in her greeting and explanation for her call let Lars infer that she was suffering no anguish over what she had been told. Connie admitted that she had had to prod Gonzales for some time. Finally, he had asked for time to talk to the set designer, who was on the road with a show at the moment. When he had talked to the designer, Gonzales called Connie with an elaboration of his earlier explanation of the use of the money that still appeared to absolve him of wrongdoing. Connie told Lars, "The set designer has now told Gonzales that he paid the money as salary to a member of the stage crew who actually had done the re-design of the musical show rather than his doing it himself."

"And why didn't the designer say this before?" Lars asked skeptically.

"Two reasons, he now says to Gonzales," Connie answered. "First of all, as a union scale professional, he was ashamed to admit that he had relied on an amateur's work. Secondly, she was a student working in the summer theatre for graduation credit, and she was not really eligible to accept salary."

"Sounds to me that this information just exchanges one cause for dismissal with another, if Gonzales just passed salary on to a student through the professional," pointed out.

"Apparently," Connie began with what seemed to Lars like an ambiguous tone, "that is not exactly what happened."

Lars failed to suppress a chuckle even though it risked irritating Connie. "Let me guess. Gonzales asserts that he knew nothing about these arrangements between the designer and the student."

"That's what he and the designer both say."

Lars continued to pursue his doubts. "Of course there is still the impropriety of awarding both credits—which no doubt are listed with Gonzales as instructor—and a salary."

"That difficulty apparently can be remedied," Connie explained, sounding to Lars unenthusiastic. "The young lady is going to forego taking the credits that she earned and report the income on her tax return."

"How ingenious," Lars commented sarcastically.

"Perhaps," Connie agreed, "but certainly helpful to Gonzales and a relief to my colleagues in the union leadership."

Lars found the entire tale unconvincing. "Do you believe this story?"

"I have no reason to disbelieve it. I'm the union grievance coordinator. If there is no evidence to the contrary, we owe the man representation."

Lars breathed a sigh of resignation. "You're right. It's the position you got to take in the job you've got." Lars felt that there was a growing unseemliness to the affair; yet he would merely annoy Connie by expressing it. O.K., professor," Lars said trying for a joviality that he did not feel, "you've got to do what you think is right, but just remember, if you hear the sound of the ice cracking, head for shore."

"But, Trustee Paulsen," Connie said with a tone that tried to match his own effort at lightness, "I don't even go ice fishing."

"See, you're sensible in so many ways," Lars countered, "grievance representation must be the one thing you do as an exception." Satisfied with this parting shot, Lars hung up before Connie had a chance to retort.

CHAPTER 22

Locals Seek Thaw in Marital Weather

Shuffling through the day's mail that had come to his office, Lars found a surprise. There was a letter from his son Mark. Lars tried to recall if Mark had ever written him before. He could not remember another time. Mark had faithfully kept in touch with his parents from the time he went away to college, but the telephone was his medium. The calls were invariably about achievements and enjoyments. Not only did Mark mesh well with people but also the boy's high ability for science, his sound training as an electrical engineer and his willingness to work had made his adulthood an uninterrupted procession of happy experiences. As Lars tore open the envelope, he hoped Mark was not reporting that the parade of pleasantry had not been interrupted.

The subject of the letter was as surprising as its having been written. Lars read it twice without pausing.

Dear Dad,

I've called home over a half dozen times in the last two months and asked to talk to you. Each time, Mom said that you were out. When I finally pressed her about this string of coincidences, she told me that you had moved out. I'd have written sooner, but it has taken some time—and considerable thought—for the fact to sink in. Mom won't say why you've left. At first she said that she didn't know. Then she said it's personal between you and her. I accept that I don't have a right to know. I also accept that you think that you have your reasons. What I don't want to accept is that the problem—what ever it is—can't be worked out. Dad, when I think about getting married myself, I hope that I will be as happy as you and mom were—or seemed to be—when I was growing up. I can't believe that it wasn't so. I can't believe that you'd want to give up that happiness without trying to save it. Won't you please try? Mom says she's willing to talk. She feels the first move is up to you. Maybe she's asking a lot. I don't know. Even if she is, I wish you'd try. Amy and I have talked about this. She's really upset. Mom won't discuss it with her. She's going to write to you too and ask you to talk to Mom. Please, please do, Dad.

Love,

Mark

Lars's thoughts and feelings tumbled and tangled in his head. Focused on his own anger and hurt over the break up, he had not thought about how his grown and departed children would react when they knew. His initial resentment at Mark's attempt at intervention gave way to the recognition that his son had a right to be concerned. He felt some embarrassment at somehow having failed the boy. His anger blossomed at Marian's having told their son that Lars should initiate the attempt at reconciliation. He was the injured party. It was Marian who should approach him, he felt. After staring motionlessly at nothing for a quarter of an hour, Lars tucked Mark's letter into his jacket pocket and left the office undecided what he would do—if anything, even to acknowledging to Mark that he had received his letter.

Mark's letter had an unfortunate effect on what had been Lars's improving mental state. His fractured personal life returned to dominating every moment of his waking hours that were not spent before his classes. Even his preparations to lecture, which frequently absorbed him even more that delivering the lecture, were distracted by anger and frustration. He was often annoyed with himself when he realized that he had sat for ten or fifteen minutes before an open book with pen in hand pointlessly re-opening his wounds. He was in the midst of such a rumination when someone knocked softly on his office door. He invited the person in without rising from his chair. A smiling Lisa Hytonnen, one of the campus's two student representatives to the board of trustees, greeted him and stood before his desk. Lars returned her smile and invited her to sit. He was genuinely pleased to see Lisa, not just because her coming had stopped his hostile contemplation, but also because his experiences with the young woman had always been pleasant.

"I've had some trouble deciding whether or not I should come and talk to you," Lisa began.

Lars expected that Lisa was faced with some difficulty in her academic work and was reluctant to discuss it with anyone in authority. Lars had always admired Lisa's avoiding using her position of influence for personal advantage. "We can be off the record, Lisa, if that will make it any easier," Lars offered.

She nodded affirmatively. "That would help. It's a little awkward to talk about." Lars grew suddenly apprehensive that the young woman was about to discuss some personal rather than academic matter. He had never been wise at helping students with their personal lives. In fact, the few times he had been pressed into giving advice on personal matters such as relationships with parents or lovers, his advice had been invariably disastrous. He chose silence rather than urging Lisa to continue.

"I was recently appointed as the student representative on the committee which will be choosing the acting chancellor who will serve from April 1 until a permanent appointment is made."

Lars felt relieved. "Congratulations, Lisa. I'm pleased. You will do a good job, I'm sure," Lars said with strong conviction. "But—is this something you and I can talk about? The committee's deliberations are, after all, confidential and I'm not a member."

"Oh," Lisa began with a vigorous shake of her head, "I wouldn't want to break procedure. But committee members are supposed to pursue relevant sources of information, and there is something that only you can tell me about."

"In that case," Lars smiled, "I'll be glad to help if I can."

"I've been talking to Butch Kirk," Lisa said, pausing as though she was uncertain that she had chosen the right opening.

Knowing that he and Lisa shared a fondness for her well-intentioned but sometimes overly facile colleague, Lars interjected, "Now there is someone who'll not be shy about giving you his views."

"Actually," Lisa sighed, "it's his having done that which has brought me to see you. I have a personal question to ask," Lisa said and paused. "I'm afraid that it will make you angry."

"If it's relevant to your committee work, go ahead," Lars offered. He smiled to enforce his assurance to the student. "I promise not to bite your head off."

Lisa struggled with her reluctance and then spoke rapidly, as though the words had to be forced out before they were suppressed. "Did you resign from being academic vice president of this campus or were you fired?"

The question did not outrage Lars, though he was surprised. His quietly forced resignation from his administrative post was a subject he had never discussed with anyone except his wife. He knew that people on campus had speculated about the matter at the time, but he thought the subject had long since been forgotten. He felt a little embarrassed at the prospect of answering Lisa's question. He would have felt awkward talking about his firing to someone older, let alone a young student.

"Why do you want to know?" Lars asked, still considering whether he ought to evade the question by telling Lisa that the matter was too personal to discuss.

"It is related to the work of the acting chancellor selection committee," Lisa explained. "We'll be voting on a short list very soon." Lisa paused again. She looked like she wanted some encouragement to continue. Lars remained silent and avoided staring at the young woman. Lisa's expression became resolute. "It's been public that our campus president, Dr. Haskell, is one of the people who was nominated for acting chancellor and has applied." There was another pause before she asserted, "Butch says that I should vote for anyone except him."

Lars was uncertain whether it was proper to let Lisa continue, yet curiosity now mingled with discretion in his mind. "Did Butch say why he thinks that?"

"Butch has great respect for you, Dr. Paulsen. He thinks that you were a really good administrator, so he thinks that anyone who fired you shouldn't get to be chancellor."

Lars could not refrain from smiling. The forced end of his administrative career at North Shore State was far enough removed that the memory held no pain. In addition, the pleasure that he had found in his return to teaching and research left no room for bitterness. "Lisa," Lars began, resolved to be as deliberate and disinterested as he could, "though I'm flattered by Butch's good opinion of me, I hope that you will not follow his advice for several reasons. First of all, the appointment will almost certainly not last more than a year and, by agreement already announced, not be a stepping stone to the permanent appointment, which means that the person you choose will not have a long term impact on the university one way or the other. Secondly, the conditions of the appointment—a short length of service and ineligibility to apply for the permanent appointment—make an internal appointment inevitable. I infer that all the other candidates are from the Pauliapolis campus. I shutter at what that might mean in the short run, which inevitably includes one budget cycle."

"Butch also expressed some very strong thoughts on Vice President Caswell of the Pauliapolis campus."

Lars shook his head. "It's best if I don't comment on candidates, Lisa." The statement took some forbearance. Lars agreed with those who called Caswell "Myopic Mike" because of his indifference to either of the universities outside of Pauliapolis. "What I can tell you is that, while it is true that President Haskell gave me a leave-or-be-fired ultimatum, I bear him no ill will. He is an able administrator. Obviously I think that he could have handled my case differently, but it was his prerogative to deal with a situation and I respect that."

Lisa was studying his face intently. Lars hoped that she would not ask any more questions. He thought he had said everything that she needed to know to fairly consider Haskell's candidacy for acting chancellor. He preferred not to talk about the end of his administrative career any further. He wryly thought that he had greater pain closer at hand to cope with.

Lisa nodded and stood up. "I shouldn't take any more of your time. I really appreciate what you have told me. You would have been totally justified to tell me that what I asked was none of my business. But it has been a help to me and I thank you for that." Lars nodded and smiled, relieved that the session was ended. Lisa returned his smile and left, closing the door gently behind her.

Lars felt certain that the most trying part of his day was past, but that turned out not to be the case. Just as he was closing his briefcase to leave for the day, his phone rang. The caller was his daughter Amy, who began by apologizing for calling his office, but pointed out that she knew no other number to reach him by phone. Lars told her that Mark had led him to expect that he would be getting a letter from her. Amy explained that she had decided that she could not adequately put all she wanted to say in a letter, hence her call.

"Amy, Mark wrote me that you were upset," Lars began sympathetically, "but you shouldn't be. You've got your own life to live now. Besides, nothing that happens between me and your mother changes how either of us feels about you."

"Dad," Amy responded quickly, "a child doesn't stop caring about its parents just because she's grown up."

"I didn't mean to suggest that, Amy," Lars responded. He tried to sound as conciliatory as possible. "I'm simply saying that your mother's and my problems don't affect our love for you. Just accept that your mother and I have got to live our own lives and don't let what ever happens between us upset you."

"Dad," Amy returned impatiently, the volume of her voice rising, "stop saying that I'm upset. If that's what Mark said, he's wrong. Have you forgotten what I do every day? I'm an urban social worker. I spend the majority of my working hours on family crisis problems. I understand the dynamics of what's happening between you and mom better than you do. I'm just surprised that you'd be the kind of man who's so unfair as to abandon his wife."

Lars struggled with a sudden surge of anger. "You don't know what you are talking about."

"Don't I?" Amy asked scathingly. "I've seen so many men walk out on their wives that it's like a parade. Just because mom doesn't face the financial problems that the women that I work with do doesn't make leaving any less a betrayal."

"Obviously, your mother hasn't told you my reason for moving out."

"No," Amy responded with a knowing air. "But which one of the two biggies is it in your case, dad, a younger woman, or the middle-aged need to feel free?" Amy asked sarcastically.

"I don't think that I care to say. Your mother can tell you if she wants."

"She's much too fine a person to go into it. She just says that she hopes that you'll re-consider. Isn't it time you did?"

Lars was deeply angry now. For a moment he considered bluntly telling his daughter exactly what had driven him from his home. Then, to tell his daughter that seemed like the widening of a gulf within the family to perhaps unbridgeable proportions. Marian had not admitted her adultery to their children to preserve their good opinion of her. Lars was not so bitter as to want to restore his children's good opinion of him at the expense of damaging their opinion of their mother. Nevertheless, he was angry that Marian had not described the separation in some light that their children would not assume that their father had willfully and unjustly abandoned their mother.

Though he had no desire to speak to Marian about reconciling, he now felt it necessary to meet with her. He would tell her that he was angry that she had let the children infer that he had some selfish reason for the separation. He would demand that she give them a harmless impression of his actions. "All right, Amy," Lars said coolly, "I think that I will get in touch with your mother." Unwilling to hear his daughter's reaction, he hung up.

CHAPTER 23

Public Gathering Fraught with Tension

Lars found it difficult to phone his estranged wife of thirty years. Shortly into the conversation, he had some regret that he had done so. Marian's voice did not convey any pleasure at his having called. Furthermore, she expressed reluctance when he asked that they meet. She asked several times what he wanted to discuss. When Lars repeated that the matter was best discussed face-to-face, Marian asserted that it would not be wise for them to meet alone. Lars was hurt by the implication and almost confirmed Marian's apprehensions by losing his temper. He suggested that they meet at a restaurant for dinner the next night, pointing out that the public setting would protect her from unpleasantness. Marian still was doubtful. Anxious to repair his relationship with the children, Lars persisted.

Finally, Marian agreed to dinner the next night if the restaurant were the one familiar to them both on the shore of one of the lakes about fifteen miles from St. Claude. Lars was puzzled at her condition and was tempted to ask if she were ashamed to be seen with him where they might be recognized. However, he was afraid that any expression of sarcasm might cause Marian to change her mind. He wanted so badly to plead for his request that she give the children a good account of him that he suppressed any expression that might destroy the opportunity for discussion.

Lars arrived for dinner twenty minutes early. He did not want to try Marian's patience by being late. He need not have worried, since Marian arrived fifteen minutes late. He watched her stride determinedly the entire length of the long narrow dining room, which had been configured to provide the maximum amount of seating facing the lake. He had chosen a table at the extreme end of the room because it was most likely to provide a degree of seclusion. Marian apologized for being late and asked him if they might move to a table closer to the center of the room where the view of the moon reflecting off the icy surface of the lake could be seen. Lars noted that it was also closer to other diners, but said nothing, convinced that Marian was more concerned with restraining his behavior than enjoying the view. That appraisal was confirmed when Marian took the chair that put her back to the window but let her see the proximity of everyone in the room.

Marian managed the process of ordering a drink and dinner with dispatch. This would be no leisurely meal. Lars felt like he was on a blind date than had already gone sour. Small talk was haltingly pursued while waiting for dinner to arrive. Lars asked Marian about the progress of her research, a topic with produced the most responsiveness. Marian reported succinctly, as she might have to a promotion committee, that not only had the analysis of her results gone well, but also a publisher had expressed interest in having her do a book based on the findings. Lars offered congratulations. Marian said how satisfied she felt to have brought her scholarly career to the level of success that she had always felt she could reach if she were granted the stability necessary for sustained effort and concentration. Lars got the message Marian intended. His career moves had detrimentally forced her to start repeatedly at the bottom of the professional ladder. He suppressed his usual response, which stressed the benefits of a larger family income and the life style it provided. Instead, he said that there had never been any doubt of her abilities and that her success was well deserved.

Their dinners were served, and they both ate earnestly, as though the act required maximum concentration that made conversation impossible. With such determined effort, the food was quickly consumed. Lars realized that he had better broach the subject for his requesting a meeting. Marian might decide to escape the tension that they were both feeling by saying that she didn't want dessert and leave abruptly.

"I had a letter from Mark—and a phone call from Amy," Lars reported. "Amy's call was especially disturbing. She's convinced that I've left you for another woman, or am going through some ridiculous male midlife crisis—I don't know which makes me look worse."

Marian's gaze, the first she's fixed on him the entire evening, was defensive. "Surely you can't think that I gave her any such notions."

"No, no," Lars hastened to assure her. "Amy's career has not given her a high opinion of how husbands treat their wives. She just inferred that our situation was more of the same that she deals with repeatedly."

"That is hardly my fault."

"Of course not. But I hope that you will help to correct the notion that I've wronged you. I don't like having her think so ill of me."

"You could do that easily enough yourself."

Lars assumed that Marian meant that he could tell Amy about her mother's infidelity. "I'm not going to repair my situation at your expense," Lars said firmly.

"I appreciate that," Marian said more softly than she had spoken all evening, "but I'd have been surprised if you had done that, or would do it." Her eyes matched the softness of her voice. "I actually had something else in mind. I haven't changed the locks at home, you know. You could come back any day that you want."

Lars was surprised. Marian's face revealed no element of a plea, but she did look conciliatory. He studied the frozen lake surface outside for a long time before he answered. "I want to be honest. I haven't given a thought to trying to go back to the way we were."

Marian looked into his eyes unblinkingly. "I want to be honest too. I wasn't suggesting that we go back to the way we were." Her expression returned earnestness. "I can't promise that I wouldn't succumb to the appeal of a discrete adventure."

Had Lars come seeking a reconciliation, he would have been outraged. As it was, he was stunned. "What's happened to you?" he asked, not really knowing what he meant to ask.

"Not so much, really," Marian said, showing the only animation she had revealed the entire evening. "Maybe I've just awakened to where I am in life. I'm enjoying success. It's changed my whole outlook. I don't know how long it will last—at my age it can't be for long. We're the same age. Don't you feel it too—the urge to explore things before it's too late?"

"The bent of your 'explorations' is not something I can live with."

Marian's eyes did a quick circuit of their immediate surrounding before she leaned toward him and spoke quietly. "Lars, I'm not planning to become a public slut. Maybe I'm just responding to middle age the way a lot of men do. Have you considered that you might enjoy a little discrete freedom yourself?"

"I'm not immune to fantasies, Marian. We apparently don't feel the same restraints about acting them out."

"My God, Lars, we've been married for thirty years."

Lars surprised himself that he could feel no anger. "Yes. For you that's a reason to change, and for me it's a reason to keep things the same."

They both recognized that the conversation had nowhere to go. After a brief silence during which they both gave careful attention to their empty dinner plates, Lars said, "I'll get the check, you needn't stay."

Marian stood and put on her coat. "I'll talk to Amy. I'll tell her that we've just grown apart. That it's no one's fault."

Lars watch his wife's exit, thinking that Amy would likely accept Marian's explanation. After all, it had the ring of truth to it.

CHAPTER 24

U Trustees Closet Selves with Chancellor Finalists

Lars hurried toward his office after his early morning class. His not canceling it gave him a tight schedule for reaching Pauliapolis in time for the special afternoon session of the board that had been called for interviewing the finalists to be acting chancellor. He was surprised to see Connie Mercutio waiting outside his office door. As he neared, she smiled at him broadly.

"You look like you're in a rush, but I just had to see if I could catch you for a minute," she said.

Lars invited her in but she refused, saying that she didn't want to delay him. "I owe you thanks once again. I didn't want to delay saying it because you're going to hear the reason in the paper or on TV shortly," Connie smiled.

"As much as I enjoy being thought worthy of thanks," Lars responded, "I can't think of anything I've done to deserve it."

"I assure you, you do deserve it," Connie nodded, "but I'm the only one who knows of this particular good deed."

"Thank God, at least my reputation wouldn't be soiled."

Connie adopted a serious expression. "You remember giving me some information about the Gonzales situation—about the set designer not claiming the extra income Gonzales said he paid him?"

"I remember. You told me what the latest explanation was."

"The union decided to amend the grievance to base the defense on, as you call it, 'the latest explanation.'"

"Damn," Lars fretted, "I hope you aren't being pressured now to reveal you source for the information."

"Believe me," Connie continued with special urgency in her voice, "no one has an inkling of my source or is even interested."

"That's good news."

"I have better," Connie assured. She gestured a little like a magician displaying the results of her slight of hand. "The administration has thrown in the towel. They have reinstated Gonzales with a reprimand and the condition that he cannot manage the summer theatre again."

Lars patted his hands together in a silent mode of applause. "And now the union thinks that you are the greatest grievance coordinator since the beginning of collective bargaining."

"Perhaps not," Connie countered, "but they are impressed."

Lars liked to see Connie happy. He would not say what he really felt. This victory would keep her involved in union activity when he had hoped that something would happen to prompt her to give it up. He was sure that many of Connie's colleagues with less teaching talent and scholarly inclination would gladly replace her. But he could not say any of this to a friend who felt that she was making a valuable contribution to be involved.

"That's fine," Lars nodded. "It's well that it's over. The university doesn't need the hassle any more than Gonzales does. Now he can get back to doing what I understand he does very well—directing plays and teaching acting."

"I'm sorry that he'll never know how you helped, so I guess my thanks will have to do." Connie extended her hand.

Lars took the offered hand. Connie's was a firm and honest handshake, just as one would expect of her. "That's what friends are for," Lars said.

Connie offered another broad smile. "It's a shame that I can't reveal that friends can be found even among the university's trustees. So my thanks alone are your only reward." She was still smiling when she turned and walked away down the hall. Lars wished that he had said that he had gotten the only reward he wanted.

Lars quickly collected several books he wanted to take on his trip and had his coat on when the phone rang. He needed to get started. He considered letting it ring but his conscience got the better of him. In response to his greeting, he was asked to hold for Governor Sanderson.

In a moment, he heard the voice made familiar from the television news address him. "Dr Paulsen, good morning, Barry Sanderson here."

"Good morning, governor," said Lars, feeling no basis for familiarity despite the governor's informality. In fact some formality seemed wise to Lars for a second reason. Since appointing Lars to the board of trustees, Sanderson had made no request of Lars regarding what position or vote he wanted taken. Perhaps now was the first time. Lars felt that an air of formality in the dialogue would help him to resist pressure to do something that he did not want to do.

"I understand, Dr. Paulsen," the governor began deliberately, "that the board will be interviewing three candidates for the position of acting chancellor today."

"That's so, governor," Lars replied, "but you are a bit better informed than I am. I didn't know even the number of interviewees."

"Well, I do have my sources," Governor Sanderson chuckled amiably. "It's not really an impressive feat of information gathering. The names will be in the evening paper, of course."

Lars accepted the governor's knowledge as only a minor discretion, aware that the names would be required to be public after the afternoon's interviews. He was not surprised that the information had leaked slightly in advance of the required public disclosure.

"You've had extensive administrative service in the university," Sanderson stated. "So you probably are acquainted with all three of the candidates, but one particularly well."

"Again, governor," Lars responded, "you know more than I do. The board members who are not on the selection committee—of which I'm one—wouldn't know the names until we get to the interviews."

"Suffice it to say that I do know the names, Dr. Paulsen," the governor stated with certitude. "One of them is your own NSSU president, Jim Haskell. You worked closely with him for a considerable length of time. I'd like you to give me your impression of him."

Lars was pragmatic enough not to be shocked that the governor had inside information. A university administrative selection process that did not leak was actually unheard of. Still, the governor's request gave him pause. He would rather not have been asked about Haskell. However, if he were to be permitted an appraisal of Haskell, he ought to be accorded the privilege of assessing the other two candidates as well.

Lars was a little slow to answer, but he did so without wavering. "I have a lot of respect for President Haskell's abilities as an administrator, governor. The acting chancellorship—which will last a year, give or take a few months—basically requires someone who will mind the store effectively and prevent confusion and loss of purpose. I have no doubt that President Haskell is up to the job."

Governor Sanderson chuckled heartily. "How did you get that reputation of yours for blunt speaking, Dr. Paulsen? That was very carefully done. Perhaps my approaching you is responsible for your caution," Sanderson inferred. "Let me tell you why I'm getting involved at this stage of the process."

Lars refrained from pointing out that technically the governor had no part in any stage of the process. "I'd appreciate that, governor," Lars admitted, "unless it's something that I'd be better off not knowing."

"Nothing sinister, I assure you," said the governor. "I am getting considerable pressure for sportsmen's organizations from all over the state demanding that the clean up of the pollution of Little Moose Lake be accomplished during the next year. They see the decision to do it or to delay as a matter largely in the hands of the acting chancellor. They are urging me to use my influence to see that no one is appointed acting chancellor unless he will commit himself to the cleanup during the next year."

"I'm just guessing wildly, governor," said Lars, making no effort to disguise his amusement, "but I suspect it's been arranged that each candidate will be asked to make such a commitment during his interview."

"Actually, the situation is somewhat more structured than that," responded Sanderson. Then, perhaps gauging from Lars's tone that the confidentiality he required to be candid existed, he revealed, "The two candidates from the Pauliapolis campus have already made such a commitment—off the record, of course."

Lars did not want to ask the names of the two candidates in question, but anyone familiar with the rumors and preliminary reports could infer the most likely possibilities. One was the dean of the college of liberal arts at the Pauliapolis campus. She was capable and well liked by her faculty—just the kind of amiable egalitarian who invariably ran second in the political brokering of a university selection process. The other likely candidate was Vice President Michael Caswell, the "Myopic Mike" about whom Lars was so unenthusiastic.

"The situation seems sufficiently, as you put it earlier, 'structured' that I don't see the reason for your call, governor."

"My sources tell me, Dr. Paulsen, that none of the three candidates presently have enough votes committed to be elected."

Lars was more puzzled than outraged. "If your sources don't have any firmer information about how the other trustees will vote than they do about me, with whom they haven't talked, I doubt that they know what the situation is."

There was a pause before Governor Sanderson explained. "You must remember that your unique situation on the board—in the faculty seat—does leave you out of the loop in some ways."

Now it was Lars's turn to be at a momentary loss for words. He no longer doubted that the governor knew how the other eleven members of the board were disposed to vote on the three acting chancellor candidates. "I'm sorry to be a bit dense, governor, but don't see what you're asking of me—not that I'm committed to do anything."

"I respect our agreement that I would not expect you to deliver on any request I make, Dr. Paulsen—and let me add, that I've never had a moment's regret about making your appointment—so I'll make my request and leave you to decide whether or not to act on it."

"I appreciate your restraint, governor."

"It's not hard to do business with a pragmatist, which is what I take you to be," the governor said. "I hope that you're not insulted."

"My teaching discipline is political science, governor."

"Enough said," Sanderson chuckled before he continued. "I would like you to tell President Haskell the condition he must agree to if he is to get serious consideration for the acting chancellorship."

Lars did not have to deliberate long to respond. "In view of the discussion with the other candidates, I don't have a problem about doing that. I don't know if I can reach him on such short notice. I do have a question though. Why didn't those who engaged in the dialogues with the two Pauliapolis candidates talk to Haskell as well?"

"I don't want to be too specific," Sanderson stressed. "But suffice it to say that Haskell's support on the board is limited, and it is not among those who are active in this matter of the lake clean up."

Lars needed no further explanation of the situation after Sanderson's statement. Lars pointed out to the governor the need for as much time as possible to accomplish his mission. The conversation was quickly ended.

Lars called Jim Haskell's office and found that Haskell had already left for Pauliapolis. He inquired of the secretary in Haskell's office whether the president carried a phone in his car. Being told that he did, Lars asked that he be called and asked to call Lars at his office number.

He did not have long to wait before Haskell called him. Without identifying his source, Lars briefly told Haskell of the condition required to be considered for the acting chancellorship. Haskell was slow to respond. He asked Lars if he felt that his information were reliable. When assured that it was, Haskell began to think aloud on the generally known information about the pollution problem—its cost, the probability of external funding, the impact on existing university programs if external funding did not materialize. Haskell, Lars sensed, was prolonging the conversation yet leaving something unsaid. Lars concluded that Haskell was wondering why Lars was providing this essential, off-the-record information. Probably he could not believe that Lars harbored no ill will over having been removed as NSSU's number two official.

Lars felt that it would not help the situation to assure Haskell that, while the episode was an unpleasant memory, he sought no revenge. He simply underscored the reality of the situation by restating the condition and broke off the call by suggesting to Haskell that the NSSU president prepare himself to respond to the question about the clean up when it came up in his interview.

Lars was not surprised that afternoon when Jim Haskell responded about Little Moose Lake as did the other two candidates for acting chancellor. Trustee Pete Henderson bluntly asked each one what he would do about the pollution problem if he were chancellor. Each said that he would seek additional funding from the state government to handle the problem, but would proceed without delay by re-allocating existing funds if additional resources were denied.

The trustees began their deliberations to choose one of the three candidates without the Little Moose Lake issue to influence support for any particular one. The discussion began routinely. Trustee Chair Walter Appleby invited each of his eleven colleagues in succession to give an appraisal of each of the three. As to be expected, most of the trustees spoke of all the candidates favorably. However, one could infer the candidate that the speaker favored by his asserting that that particular one brought slightly more knowledge and leadership ability to the job. Lars was familiar with the reason for the strategy of stating only favorable assessments. No one believed that the confidentiality about the discussion which was the required policy actually would be adhered to. Hence, cautious souls expected that their statements would eventually be known by the successful candidate. Circumspect participants wanted to avoid losing their influence if a candidate of whom they had spoken negatively were the eventual selectee.

Lars felt no need for restraint. His goal was to prevent the selection of Vice President Mike Caswell, whom Lars's past experience had shown would be unmindful of the needs of North Shore State, or Beau Prairie State as well, for that matter. Lars began his remarks by saying that the acting chancellor must be someone who could be counted on to tend the needs and programs of all three campuses with equal care. He then asserted his confidence that both Dean Harriet Marshall and President James Haskell had the vision and experience to assure that all the campuses would be well served. His omission of Caswell in his remarks was sufficient to make his point.

When all had given their assessments of the three candidates, Appleby called for a secret ballot, reminding that he would be voting rather than serving in the usual tie-breaking role. The simple majority needed to elect would be seven votes. After what seemed like an unusually long time to tally the twelve slips of paper, Appleby announced the results as five votes each for Caswell and Marshall and two for Haskell. What ensued then was a lengthy discussion. Those who had voted for one of the two deadlocked vote getters spoke unrestrainedly on the favorable qualities of their candidate and with increasing bluntness on the limitations of the candidate with whom their choice was deadlocked. Evening had long since fallen, and everyone was tired when Appleby called for another secret ballot.

It was only a mild surprise to Lars when Jim Haskell was chosen with a bare majority of seven votes. The outcome was one that Lars had seen occur in many selection processes. When some of the people deadlocked over two choices finally did change their votes, they did so to a candidate other than the one who was the closest challenger to their preferred candidate. Lars smiled to find that a North Shore State president had for the first time in the century and a half history of the state university system become its chancellor.

CHAPTER 25

Surprising Developments Make Local Trustee Ponder

For two weeks after the announcement of President Haskell's selection as acting chancellor, the North Shore State campus buzzed with several themes inherent in that development. There was much hopeful anticipation that Haskell's year as the head of the university system would benefit NSSU financially by a more equitable distribution of funds among the campuses. There was intense and conflicting discussion about who would be Haskell's replacement as campus president for the year during which Haskell was headquartered in Pauliapolis. In the arena of pure gossip, there was an oft-repeated rumor, usually delivered with lowered voice and a knowing look, that Haskell had been selected over the strenuous opposition of faculty trustee Paulsen, who was still bitter over his demise as an administrator on Haskell's staff.

For Lars, the crescendo of largely irrelevant dialogue was amusing. In fact, along with the joy of teaching and his hitting upon the first promising research idea he had had since returning to the classroom, the absurd rumor brought his good humor almost beyond containment. He therefore felt a dampening of his spirits when an obviously distressed Connie Mercutio called his office and asked if she could visit with him immediately. Assured that he was available, she was not long in arriving. Her face wore an uncharacteristic look of consternation as she settled herself somewhat rigidly into the chair beside Lars's desk. Her eyes glinted, perhaps like an eagle searching anxiously for an overdue meal. In all, she looked like someone ready to do battle rather than a person oppressed by difficulty.

Lars decided understatement was his wisest course of action. "You don't look happy," he said.

"You could say that," Connie responded with a slight nod. Lars thought it best to wait. "I'm so damn mad I can hardly stand it," Connie announced through clenched teeth.

"Something I can help with?"

"If we've off the record," Connie said, fixing her eyes to his, "maybe you will suggest what you think I should do."

Lars smiled, "I can't remember when you and I have ever been on the record. No need to start now."

Connie drew a deep breath, paused and then exhaled slowly. "You remember the Gonzales grievance," she began, her tone conveying her understanding that Lars needed no reminder. "I now find the facts somewhat different than I was told when we were making the case for Gonzales."

Lars could not resist sarcasm. "Misrepresentation in a grievance case? How unusual." Connie looked like she did not appreciate his attempt at humor. "I'm sorry," Lars retreated. "What are the facts as you now know them?"

"If you remember the sequence," Connie began, "the unaccounted for thirteen thousand dollars was first explained as additional salary to the professional set designer. Then we were told that the designer paid it to a student who actually did the design of the musical production. That was made kosher for use in Gonzales's defense by the student's admitting to the income and sacrificing the graduation credit that she otherwise would have earned for working in summer theatre."

"And now you find that these representations are not the truth?"

"Oh, it turns out that the student got the thirteen thousand all right," Connie reported with disgruntlement. "But not for theatre work. The set designer got her pregnant. Gonzales provided three thousand for her abortion and ten thousand to keep her quiet."

"And how did these interesting facts come to light now that the grievance has been settled in Gonzales's favor?" asked Lars.

"The young lady objects to paying taxes on this portion of her annual income. When both the designer and Gonzales refused to provide the additional money to pay the taxes, she came to me. She assumed that I knew the real story since I was the one who helped her write the statement used in the grievance argument."

This time, Lars was not able to refrain from sarcasm. "That is a very unattractive tale. It doesn't leave one with a favorable impression of any of the three of them, does it?"

Shaking her head in agreement, Connie asked, "The question is, what do I do about it?"

"Why would you do anything?" Lars wondered.

"Gonzales shouldn't have won his grievance, should he?"

"Connie," Lars answered, feeling the placidity of one familiar with the impure nature of justice through adversarial process, "can you prove that the young lady didn't design the set for the musical? Gonzales and the designer aren't going to admit to the real story. Regardless of the student's irritation at having to pay the taxes, she wouldn't be better off by going public."

"I know the true story. I could go on the record with what the girl told me."

"Was there anyone else there when she told you?"

"No," Connie admitted.

"So it would be just your word against her denial, which Gonzales and the designer would back up," Lars pointed out. He looked into Connie's eyes earnestly. "Let it go."

"That is hard to do," Connie said with disappointment blurring her voice. "This screws up the whole idea of what due process is supposed to result in."

"So one case went your way on dubious grounds," Lars argued. "If you stay in grievance work, you'll find some going the administration's way on equally dubious grounds."

"You make it sound like justice often gets lost in due process," Connie pointed out.

"Often," Lars repeated, "But not most of the time. You have to remind yourself of that to avoid getting cynical."

"Maybe I don't belong in this business," Connie sighed.

"If you eventually conclude that, I wouldn't be unhappy," Lars said. "I think that you've got better things to do with your time."

"I'll have to think about that," Connie said. She got up to go, her face showing that her mood had not lightened as a result of their conversation.

As she opened the door, Lars wanted not to end their visit on that note. "Hey," he said. "We've been talking about playing a round of golf for three years. Don't you think we should actually do it sometime? What do you say? As soon as the weather breaks?"

"I'll give you a call," Connie said. Lars was glad to see that she managed the slight beginning of a grin before she closed the door behind her.

Lars spent the next hour distractedly trying to prepare a lecture as he thought about Connie's disillusionment. He hoped that she would not be idealistic and officially reveal what she knew. No one, either within the administration that had conceded in the Gonzales grievance or the union which had prevailed, would thank her. She would be an irritation to all parties and an embarrassment to some. Lars hoped Connie would see that she would be the only loser if she did not let the matter rest. He had just given up on trying to concentrate on his notes and decided to go home when there was a knock on his door. Having resolved to escape, he considered waiting until the person concluded he was not in. However, his conscience prodded him. He did not want to avoid a student who needed his assistance.

He opened the door and was surprised to find Jim Haskell, who said that he hoped Lars might spare him some time to discuss an important matter. Lars responded that he certainly had time. He added that he was glad that Haskell had stopped by, since he had not yet had the opportunity to congratulate him privately on his selection as acting chancellor.

When Haskell was comfortably seated, he said that it was, in fact, a matter connected with the chancellorship that had brought him to see Lars.

"Heavens," Lars groaned and feigned an expression of horror, "don't tell me that the problems have started already when you are still several weeks from officially beginning the job."

"Actually, you could resolve this one very easily for me," Haskell stated amiably.

Lars was amused at the extent to which his afternoon had been devoted to requests to benefit from his sagacity. He would have to be careful not to think too well of himself, he mused frivolously. "I'll help if I can," he told Haskell.

"You know, of course, that this campus will need an acting president during the period of time that I am acting chancellor."

"Of course," Lars said.

"I would like you to serve as acting president," Haskell said with a broad smile.

Lars was too surprised to speak.

Haskell raised his hands palm out in an assuring gesture. "You wouldn't have to apply. I'll see that you are nominated. The committee would be certain to include you within the list presented to me, and I will, of course, choose you." Haskell clasped his hands together as though sealing a deal in accompaniment to his words. He looked well satisfied with himself as he continued to smile at Lars.

"This is quite a surprise," Lars said. He wanted to ask Haskell why he was making the offer, but decided to forego the question. All the likely explanations were improper reasons for appointing Lars to the North Shore State presidency. Maybe Haskell felt obliged because of the information Lars had provided him before Haskell's interview for the chancellorship. Maybe he assumed that Lars had provided one of the bare majority votes that had secured his election. Maybe Haskell felt some guilt over ending Lars's career in administration at NSSU. None of these reasons were ones that Lars would be comfortable with for making him the campus president, even if he were inclined to want the assignment.

Haskell must have assumed from the long silence that Lars was struggling with doubts of some sort. "You know that you are well qualified, Lars," Haskell encouraged.

"So is your academic vice president—and a couple of your deans, for that matter," Lars pointed out.

"None of them has your experience, or, more importantly, your ability," Haskell said with what appeared like conviction.

Lars was not pleased to hear his administrative ability praised by the man who had decided that expediency outweighed the value of that ability to the university and himself. It was tempting to conclude that Haskell's present offer was another expediency. Maybe his intention was to remove potential opposition from the board, since Lars's accepting the assignment would require him to resign as faculty trustee. The assignment would make Lars once again Haskell's subordinate rather than a member of the group to whom he was, as chancellor, responsible.

"This so unexpected, Jim, that I don't know what to say.," Lars responded. The indecisive statement had never been truer for Lars. It had been more than two years since he'd given a thought to returning to administration. Until his recent split form Marian, the time since leaving administration had been the happiest time he had spent in decades.

"Have you considered that a year in an acting presidency would make a wonderful stepping stone? After it, you'd be an experienced candidate for a presidency. Also, that you won't be a sitting president at the end of one year won't carry the onus of having been fired or been passed over in a selection process. You'd be a prime candidate for dozens of openings that will come up in the next year or two."

There was a great deal of cogency to what Haskell had just said. Realistic senior university administrators knew that every presidential selection committee preferred candidates with presidential experience who also did not bear the stigma of having been removed from a presidency. The interim replacement for a temporarily absent incumbent was therefore the kind of experienced, perceivably undamaged goods that committees were attracted to.

For the briefest moment, Lars was tempted. His estrangement from Marian had taken much of the livability out of being in St. Claude. New surroundings might remove more of the pain of the break up, even though he would gradually become reconciled to the break up if he stayed here. But, it occurred to him, there was a major omission in the case Haskell had made for Lars's taking the acting presidency. He was fully at peace with himself as he pointed it out to Haskell.

"I appreciate your thinking of me, Jim. Really, I do. But the reality is that I just don't want to do administrative work any more."

"Don't be too hasty, Lars," Haskell advised. He leaned toward Lars intent on continuing his argument. "You've every reason to feel negative about the last of your administrative experiences. But you shouldn't let that drive you away from doing work that you were extraordinarily good at."

Lars felt that he had ample reason to be angry at Haskell's last statement, since Haskell had not felt that Lars's was a valuable enough subordinate that he would endure the difficulty created by a single vindictive politician to retain him. But to point this out to Haskell required a bitterness that Lars had long since lost amid the satisfactions of teaching and the recreations that came with his freer life since leaving administrative work.

"Jim, I just don't want to meet the demands of administrative work any more. In fact, I don't know why you continue to do it. Trying to satisfy people's endless selfish demands, wrestling to make the money stretch, fighting the thankless battles to make sensible changes against selfish or ignorant resistance." Lars shook his head as he catalogued the distasteful aspects of university leadership. "Near the end of my days in administration, I used to describe administering as a football game in which I was playing four quarters of goal line stands. Again, thanks, but no thanks."

Haskell sighed resignedly and got to his feet. "Lars, the deadline for making nominations is two days off. I wish you'd change your mind. If you do, please let me know and I will see that you are nominated."

Lars smiled. "You're being very kind, Jim."

"Very kind, nothing," Haskell responded. "Some people might say that I owe you this."

Lars shook his head and smiled at the new acting chancellor, "You don't owe me anything," he said emphatically and sincerely. Haskell accepted that and left Lars to reflect with satisfaction that he had done and said the right thing.

CHAPTER 26

Northlander Pleased at Break in the Weather

The April trustees' meeting was so limited in substance that the usual cadre of media observers left an hour into the second morning's session.

The day before, the installation of Jim Haskell as acting chancellor and his remarks in accepting the appointment had provided them with a reportable story. Haskell had focused his statement on promising to be more than a mere caretaker during his interim appointment. To make that commitment concrete, he announced that the clean up of the polluted Little Moose Lake would begin at the beginning of the fiscal year on July 1, whether the state government provided additional funds for the task or not. He minimized the controversial aspect of the commitment by emphasizing that funding would be requested of the state. If it were not obtained, Haskell promised, the clean up would be funded by across-the-board re-allocation rather than the closure of any units or programs. Lars noted wryly that Haskell had not lost his skill of identifying the course of action that would please the largest number of influential people, or at least neutralize them.

Not only was the rest of first day soporific from the journalists' stand-point, the initial topic in the next morning's session soon convinced them that they should be elsewhere. Chair Appleby began the session by reporting that he had received a number of letters of protest about the new arrangements for the coming commencement ceremony in the college of arts and sciences at the Pauliapolis campus. The graduation event for this largest of the colleges at

Pauliapolis State had always been held in the intercollegiate basketball arena. That facility, which seated slightly over ten thousand, had always been considered large enough to accommodate all of the graduates' relatives and friends who wished to attend. Hence, graduates had never had to be issued a certain number of tickets to assure that a similar number of guests of other graduates would be admitted too. However, in recent years there had been complaints about over crowding and poor visibility. In response, the administration of the Pauliapolis campus had announced that for the first time tickets limiting attendance would be issued for the upcoming arts and sciences commencement. The seating plan, which would give each graduate the same number of tickets, had caused a furor among the students who wanted enough tickets for large groups of friends and family who wanted to come. Because both displeased graduates and their relatives had written to the board protesting the plan, Chair Appleby felt that the board should give the administration some guidance on the matter.

Lars's writhed inwardly as Appleby introduced the topic. The situation was a classic example of the kind of concern that a university public oversight group ought not to touch. The board should respond to the complainants that such matters were properly delegated to the administration of the campus and should not be intruded upon by the board. Lars was certain that the people responsible for the plan had considered all of the factors relevant to the decision, many of which would remain unknown to the trustees, even if the senior decision maker were summoned to report on the matter. Thus, a board discussion of the matter could be nothing more than a re-hash of alternative possibilities that had been thoroughly explored and found wanting for one reason or another. The discussion itself would inevitably show the board at its worst. Some would feelingly sympathize with friends and relatives who would be denied the opportunity to participate in the joyous occasion. Others would be certain that they had hit on an all-pleasing solution to the dilemma that had not been thought of. No one would bluntly recognize the situation as one of the unavoidable instances where even the most judicious solution—or several equally rational solutions—could not please every one. Finally, the matter would be sent back for re-examination to those who had already suffered the displeasure of the complainants. Most likely, even the most earnest reconsideration of all the possible courses of action would not result in a change. The only effect of all the talking and thinking would be a heightened mistrust of everyone involved in the process on the part of the complainants, many of whom were people who judged every displeasing outcome from the belief that, if their complaint had not succeeded, no one had really listened. It was a discussion, in sum, in which no rational person would take part. That was what Lars did until the lengthy dialogue reached its preordained conclusion.

After the endless and unproductive discussion, Appleby declared a twenty-minute recess. Lars decided to avoid being trapped in further dialogue on the non-issue. If he moved quickly, he could use the break to both relieve his boredom and possibly advance his new research project. The Pauliapolis campus bookstore, having a much larger inventory than the bookstore at NSSU, might have in stock a book that he had been told at home would have to be ordered. He decided that a rapid and refreshing walk across campus might save him several weeks' wait for the book by buying it today.

The walk in the breezy and mild spring air and a quick and successful search for the book had heightened Lars's mood as he hurried toward the bookstore check out. He rounded a set of shelves in full stride and tripped over a woman who was bent down examining the titles on a bottom shelf. He began his apology as the woman straightened and turned to face him and found himself face-to-face with Marian.

"You're in a hurry," she said with surprising amiability, considering that she had suffered an unexpected and hard jolt.

"My meeting's about to re-convene in five minutes, and I wanted to get this book," Lars said, hoping she would excuse his recklessness.

He realized that his explanation was no apology. "I thought I had enough time to get this book I can't buy at home. I hope you're not hurt."

"I'm fine," Marian answered reassuringly. She shook her head and smiled at him good-naturedly. "It's so like you to try to squeeze a time consuming chore into a tight time frame."

"Are you sure you're O.K.?"

Marian continued to grin at his embarrassment and concern. "Yes. Yes. Hurry off to your meeting." As Lars turned to go, she interjected, "Oh, I got your note. I'm glad Amy's made peace with you."

Marian was referring to Lars having written her to thank her for calming their daughter Amy about her parents' separation. Lars had received a conciliatory letter from Amy. He realized that Marian must have succeeded in convincing Amy that she should not be angry with her father over her parents' break up. Lars had quickly written his thanks for her effort.

"I do appreciate your reconciling her," Lars emphasized sincerely. Though conscious that he was out of time, he wanted to talk to Marian further. "Were you leaving just now?"

"Soon," Marian said, her mood remaining friendly. "But I think we're going in opposite directions. I'm headed back to the library."

"Oh," Lars said with genuine disappointment. "I guess I'd better run then."

He was already a few steps away when Marian said, "See you."

Lars turned back and waved energetically enough to convey his pleasure at their meeting.

The re-convened meeting proved no more stimulating than it had been earlier, and Lars was relieved when the last item on the agenda was introduced. In introducing it, Acting Chancellor Haskell added information to the printed presentation that brought the session out of the doldrums for Lars. The matter at hand was the board's endorsement of faculty leaves of absence for the coming year. The printed information was a list of names with brief explanations attached stating the reason for the requested leave. Haskell asked the board to add an additional name to the list of faculty to be granted a leave without pay. He explained that Dr. Costanzia Mercutio, a highly regarded associate professor of psychology at North Shore State had just been invited to be a visiting professor at Stanford University for the coming year. While a person of her considerable talents would be missed at NSSU, Haskell pointed out, Dr. Mercutio would be involved in an important extension of her research. The visiting professorship in itself was prestigious recognition for both the awardee and her home institution; however, the research involvement gave the award a special dimension of importance.

Lars was amused at how glowingly Haskell spoke of Connie. He recollected how difficult it had been during his last year as academic vice president four years ago to convince Haskell to award Connie tenure rather than terminating her. Lars was pleased at Connie's latest success. He wondered if her application for the visiting professorship had been made before or after her disillusion with union activity. Regardless, she would be separated from that thankless, time-consuming endeavor very shortly. Lars doubted that she would return to union involvement. In fact, a new concern might be that she would never return to NSSU after the level of professional involvement she was likely to have in the next year. Lars was genuinely happy for Connie whether or not her success would eventually be a loss to North Shore State. He resolved to call her on his return to St. Claude and congratulate her.

CHAPTER 27

Spring Lures Northlanders to New Activities

Possibly because of the early arrival of mild weather, Lars found Connie difficult to reach by phone during the weekend. He did succeed Sunday evening. After he offered hearty congratulations and his personal regard for the accomplishments that had brought her the recognition, Connie responded with playful mock humility, "I take it, then, that you didn't vote against my leave application, Trustee Paulsen?"

"I doubt that a trustee has voted against a leave request in decades, even ones that were requested for less stellar reasons than the one on which yours is based."

"I don't know how to respond to this flattery."

"No reason you shouldn't hear some praise. The athletic coaches shouldn't have all the glory," Lars said, touching one of the few subjects on which academics were universally agreed.

"Or all the money," Connie offered, continuing the theme which academics used as a subject for bonding.

"Oh, well, wait now," Lars responded with false-sounding opposition. "You're carrying the desire to have scholarship rewarded too far if you insist on its rewards matching those of the fundamental activity of a university."

Connie feigned regret. "Oh, sorry. I shouldn't have gotten carried away."

"These excesses sometimes occur," Lars said with a tone of absolution. "I'll tell you what I'll do, in the spirit of elevating regard for scholarship nearer the importance of athletic accomplishment. If you have the courage to accept, I'll pay for us to play that round of golf that we have been threatening to play for years."

"There," Connie sighed exaggeratedly, "is a reward far beyond anything I could have hoped for."

"Then you accept?"

"Of course," Connie said with a chuckle.

"O.K., then. I'll get us a tee time at Oak Ridge next Saturday morning and let you know."

"I'll get busy thinking about how many strokes, I'll get."

"No, no," Lars responded, "the verb is 'give', professor, not 'get'. A first rate scholar like you should be more careful with your use of language."

"I can see this is not going to be a friendly outing," Connie said, with a breathiness which played at dismay.

"Maybe you'll be surprised," Lars countered. "I'll get back to you on the time." He hung up feeling pleased at the prospect of the golf game, though his lack of golf skills would undoubtedly bring him some embarrassing moments.

The early spring had numerous northland golfers eager to enjoy their first round of the season. Thus, Lars had to report to Connie that their start time would be at eleven Saturday morning. Connie said that the late time suited her better, since she could get some chores out of the way before meeting him at the golf course. Lars bowed to the good sense of his also getting chores done before golfing, though his usual reluctance to use the weekend for unappealing household activity made him an unenthusiastic worker.

The rush of early morning golfers had slowed to a well-spaced number when Connie and Lars met at the clubhouse on the Oak Ridge course to begin their round. The pale blue of the spring sky was crowded with billowy white clouds that were moved along by a stiff wind. The pair shared an exhilarated feeling as they loosened up to await their turn on the first tee. Lars, judging by the fluidity of Connie's warm up swings and the easy grace of her movements, thought it wise to say something to prepare his colleague for the drastic limitations of his own skills. Connie responded with the usual banter responding to such a confession from a golfer one had not played with before. She charged Lars with trying to deceive her about his real capabilities, and assured him that she would not be lured into playing for money as the round progressed.

The playing of the first three holes proved decisively that Lars had not exaggerated the limits of his golfing ability. Though Lars had always enjoyed the game and had played it frequently and enthusiastically when he was younger, he had always been classically inconsistent. Each occasionally accurately hit shot was followed by several hits that were either sprayed off target, or bounced along a frustratingly short distance or sent beyond recovery into some thicket or pond. His partner, in contrast, was enviable to observe. Her lithe body coiled unhurriedly into a graceful back swing and unwound into an accurate and effortless contact with the ball, invariably sending it a considerable distance down the fairway toward the green. Each drive was followed by an accurate shot to the green. Her putting was true and consistent, leaving Lars to admire openly and record a score that was two or three strokes lower than his on each of the first nine holes. Lars could only take comfort in never having had any ego bound up in his golfing ability. Hence he could enjoy a game irrespective of his score, just so he did not have to spend too much time looking for his ball. What made his enjoyment greatest was having an amiable companion, and Connie was that, for she took neither his errors nor her accomplishments too seriously.

As they teed up for the tenth hole, Lars commented that the wind was getting much stronger. Unobserved, the white clouds had been replaced by dark gray ominous ones, and Lars observed that the sky looked as though it might rain. Connie chided that he shouldn't start hoping for a reprieve and should begin concentrating on his game. Lars responded with obviously false bravado that he was just about to hit his stride and was not in the least seeking escape. After his first respectable tee shot of the day, he turned serious long enough to ask Connie whether she was comfortable with the risk of getting drenched. He reminded her that the northland weather at this time of year was dramatically changeable.

Connie assured him of her desire to continue and teed up her ball. Lars warned her that he would soon start to exhibit his mid-season form. Before Connie hit her ball, she asked if she would be able to tell the difference from what she'd already seen.

In fact, she wouldn't have seen much difference between the mid season Paulsen and what she had already experienced, but whether she could was not put to the test. When they were half way up the tenth fairway, a heavy rain pelted down on them with a suddenness and force appropriate to reminding northlanders that an early interlude of good weather should not delude them into thinking that mild weather had come to stay. Lars and Connie, seeing no shelter nearby, headed for the clubhouse. Unfortunately, they were at one of the farthest reaches on the course from it. They were thoroughly soaked by the time they reached shelter. Observing to Connie that she had a much longer drive home than did he, Lars suggested that Connie come to his cabin to put her clothes in his clothes drier while they made themselves some lunch. As Connie studied him with raised eyebrows and a mysterious grin, Lars assured her that he was certain that he had a pair of jeans and a sweat shirt that she could wear while her clothes were drying. Connie agreed to the plan, provided that lunch be kept a simple affair. Lars assured her that based on his cooking skills, it could be no other.

Lars had just finished tossing a salad and was about to begin scrambling eggs when Connie entered the combined kitchen and living room area of the cabin clad in an oversized NSSU sweat shirt and a pair of his jeans, the legs of which had needed to be rolled up a narrow turn to fit. Connie surveyed the neat rustic interior—light oak paneling, a large stone fireplace, exposed beams, three oak captains' chairs, a leather recliner and the small but well equipped kitchen—and told Lars that she liked his accommodations. Lars responded that he had found the place comfortable and that he was sorry to have to give it up shortly since its owners would be occupying it for the summer. Noting Lars's preparations to scramble eggs, Connie volunteered to do that job if Lars would start a fire. Lars, who often ate from a tray on his lap as he sat before the fire, readily agreed.

Soon, they sat in the captains' chairs toasting their feet before the blaze and eating as the fire crackled noisily. The rain continued to fall steadily, adding its tapping to the lulling sound and sight of the flames. Lars and Connie lingered over lunch until the large pot of coffee had been consumed. Their conversation about their interrupted golf game was soon succeeded by a brief review of university gossip. Then interspersed questions and comments by each focused on learning about each other. They traded personal histories and views about the teaching and scholarly life in general. They became rather particular about which circumstances were appealing or annoying about the profession they had chosen and were delighted that their lists were identical.

Connie confessed that since she had initially known Lars as an administrator, she was still not accustomed to thinking of him as a political scientist. She asked if he had anything here that he had written. She thought it would give her a better sense of him if she read some of his work. Lars resisted showing her any of his writing, even though he had some old journals about that contained pieces he had written. He hadn't done any first-rate scholarship in fifteen years, he appealed. Furthermore, she would surely find it boring—didn't professors generally find their colleagues' specializations difficult to endure, he asked.

Connie persisted in wanting to read something of his work. Finally, Lars said that, if she really were serious, he would prefer to have her read an unpublished manuscript of his. Though he had never succeeded in getting it accepted for publication, it was nevertheless his favorite work. Connie said the manuscript was exactly the thing to read to get to know him better. Soon she was curled up in the leather chair, her feet tucked under her, reading what was a rather lengthy sheaf of typed pages. Lars picked up the novel he had been reading in short snatches for the last two weeks to occupy himself until Connie tired of what he expected her to find as too dry to stay with for very long.

In fact, it was Lars who tired of reading first. He sat studying his visitor as she continued seemingly absorbed in her reading. He wondered why he had never really looked at her before. Not that he hadn't noticed from the first time he saw her that she was very pretty. He had always been taken with her eyes. Were they not so sharp and challenging in impact, their sable brown would be devastating. The too large sweatshirt lent cuteness to her well-proportioned and attractive body. He was certain that Connie would be appalled to be described as "cute," but her relaxed and casually attired body curled up in the large leather chair brought the word unavoidably to mind. Of course, Connie's conviction of her competence usually molded her bearing and facial expression and suppressed any kittenish version of femininity. It was the dominant and appealing image that Lars had of her. Connie was altogether a most desirable woman, Lars concluded, as though he had uncovered a fact which was not obvious.

With a deliberateness much at odds with his warm feelings, Lars went to the chair where Connie was bent over his manuscript. He put a finger under her chin and gently tilted her face upward. He put his lips to hers gently and savored at length the sweet softness of her mouth. He ended the kiss and looked into those deep brown eyes and could not gauge her reaction. "Was that a mistake?" Lars asked.

"Only if you think you could have done better," Connie said. She studied his face with those probing eyes a long moment. Then she reached up and pulled Lars's head down. They kissed much more earnestly this time. The rainy spring afternoon became evening while Lars and Connie spent the entire time continuing to do the very best that they could not to disappoint one another with actions the sweetness of which was made even greater by their spontaneity.

CHAPTER 28

Seasoned Academics Lose Objectivity

Work and all pleasantries but one became mere distractions for Lars Paulsen as he was absorbed in his passion for Connie Mercutio during the two weeks after their first lovemaking on that rainy afternoon. He gloried in every moment that she would grant him her company. Interspersed between substantive conversations, he felt irrepressible and prolonged sexual desire the likes of which he had not felt for at least a decade. Connie enjoyed him, but laughed at him too. And Lars enjoyed and accepted that laughter, for she indulged him. She seemed to like best the conversations they had in the afterglow of making love. Connie told him that she had never known anyone else who could move in the space of an hour from intense sexual passion to equal enthusiasm about the intricacies of American politics in the Civil War reconstruction period.

The second week after the beginning of their affair, Lars convinced Connie that she should spend the weekend at his cabin. The early May weather was mild and sunny and Lars argued that it was a chance to enjoy the cabin by the lake before he had to move out and the mosquitoes moved in. Under a cloudless, pale blue sky, they breakfasted Saturday morning on the deck facing the lake. The birches and aspen were beginning to add a touch of light green that gave variety and brightness to the dark green of the pines that were in the mixture of trees along the shore. The surface of the water was rippled slightly by a warm breeze, which transformed the sunlight striking the water into a glittering silver. The whole visible world begged to be enjoyed. Whose idea it was to walk the entire trail that circled the lake, they would afterwards debate, but they both began the venture with enthusiasm.

They returned from the five-mile trek fatigued and thirsty but exhilarated. Each greedily drank several glasses of cold water as they argued over who had held up best and had to slow the pace not to leave the other behind. They returned to the chairs from which they had begun and lapsed into a contented silence.

"It's a shame I can't spend the summer here," Lars said as he continued responding to the bright colors and feel of the day.

"So you can fully enjoy the mosquitoes, the humidity and the occasional all-day rain?" Connie challenged.

"Don't go bringing reality into it," chided Lars. "Those are subjects true northlanders never discuss."

"Have you found a place yet?" Connie asked.

"Not one I would want," Lars nodded. "I'm trying to find something furnished. All of those seem to be rented by students and will be available shortly. But if you've ever seen what two or three collegians can do to an apartment in a few months, you know why I don't want to follow them as a renter."

"Surely there must be some places that have been rented to young ladies," Connie offered.

"You've a misperception of the domestic behavior of the contemporary coed," Lars pointed out.

"Wonderful," Connie grinned, "equality of the sexes at last."

"Unfortunately," Lars sighed, "the few places that aren't a shambles appear to be furnished with pieces that Goodwill rejected. I don't consider myself finicky, but there are limits to the ugliness I can endure."

"There's an easy solution to your problem."

"Which has apparently escaped me," Lars admitted. He looked at Connie with genuine curiosity.

"You could move in with me," she suggested. Her face had not turned from looking at the lake. Her profile told Lars nothing. He could not tell whether or not she was serious.

Connie did turn to face him then. When he continued his study of her, she said, "I'll only be there a month to six weeks before I leave to visit my folks and drive on to the west coast for my visiting professorship."

"How would it look?" Lars asked, to himself as much as to Connie.

"Looks like fun to me," Connie answered. "How does it look to you?"

"You know that isn't what I meant."

"Oh, God, Lars, St. Claude isn't a metropolis," Connie said. "There isn't anyone in town who doesn't know that you and Marian are separated."

"And, there isn't a one of them who wouldn't infer that you were the cause of it if I move in with you."

"And the relevance—let alone the accuracy—of that would be what?" Connie commented, her tone making clear that the matter under discussion was of little importance to her.

"I hope you realize that I've no concern about what people would say about me," Lars emphasized. "But you shouldn't be cavalier about what's said about you."

"It's a matter of no concern to me. Why should it be to you—unless you're just shopping for an excuse not to move in with me."

"Oh, yea," Lars said with the right touch of sarcasm, "I'm really turned off by an offer from a beautiful young woman to move in with her."

"So what's the problem," Connie encouraged. "I'm considerably neater than most coeds. I don't snore, and I'll only make mildly excessive demands on your body."

"Somehow," Lars began, donning a guise of deep reflectiveness, "that last condition doesn't frighten me, but I don't think that you've thought about the implications of this."

"We're a couple of grownups who are fond of each other."

"Very fond," Lars corrected. He thought for a moment. "Tell you what. I thought of a way you can sample what our taking our relationship public would be like."

"Oh, gee," Connie interjected with widened eyes as she came over and sat on his lap. "A scientific experiment." She kissed him quite distractingly. "And will there be appropriate controls?"

Lars kissed her and searched her body with eager hands. "I'll put you in charge of controls, or lack of them, as the case may be."

"In that case, I'll participate in this experiment," Connie said. "What is it?"

"Come with me to dinner next Thursday night."

"This is a test?" Connie smiled derisively.

"It's the annual dinner of the university trustees celebrating the end of the academic year," Lars said, watching for some sign of unpleasantness in Connie's expression. "At the chancellor's residence in Pauliapolis," Lars continued, still on the look out for a look of distaste. "Hosted by Acting Chancellor Haskell and Mrs. Haskell, of course."

Connie remained inscrutable. "And this experience will permit me to gauge what?"

"If we're going to live together, we're going to have a social life."

"I would hope so," Connie said.

"This little soiree will give you a sample of how people who know our circumstances are going to react to us as a couple," Lars pointed out.

"How is it you expect them to behave?"

"I'm not sure," Lars admitted. "What's important is how you will feel, however they act, particularly the Haskells."

Connie looked into his eyes earnestly. "I'm not going to care whether they are accepting or asinine."

"Better wait and see before you're sure of that."

"I'll tell you what I'm not sure of," Connie said. Her air of deep thought was clearly playful. "Do you think that the people in those cabins over there would see us if we did it out here on the grass?"

Lars's eagerness for her almost prompted him to ignore whether they might be seen, but he soon carried her into the cabin for a private expression of their rites of spring.

CHAPTER 29

Cordiality Counters Queries at U Dinner

Since Connie had no reason to be in Pauliapolis other than to accompany Lars to the trustees dinner, she drove there separately to meet Lars in the lobby of his hotel so that they could go on to the event together. Lars had not long settled into a chair the lobby from which he could see the hotel entry, when Connie appeared and looked about. When she turned toward him, the full effect of her appearance stunned him. On campus, Connie was always stylishly but understatedly dressed and attractively groomed. To see her groomed and dressed for a special occasion, Lars found her exceptionally pretty in a sophisticated way and alluring to an extent that her casual daily appearance did not emphasize. As she approached Lars now, her smile reflecting her awareness of the effect she was having on a man whose appreciation of her charms was intensified that such a much younger woman had blessed him with her attentions. Her dress was a royal blue silk sheath that reached mid calf but was slit on one side to mid thigh. The vee neckline dropped just low enough to stimulate male interest but not invite unwanted attention. The dress was sleeveless, and she had a stole of some gauzy material draped across her shoulders and around her arms. Lars could not believe that the wrap was any comfort against the chill of the spring evening, but he liked the effect it gave of Connie's being caressed by her own cherishing mist.

"Aren't you going to say anything," Connie said as she stopped before him.

He had been so engrossed drinking her in that he was still sitting and staring. He scrambled to his feet and confessed, "It would only be inadequate."

"Ah, you political scientists," Connie sighed, "evasive, but nevertheless ingratiating."

"I may sound a typical political scientist, my dear professor," Lars responded, "but you look like no other psychologist that I've ever seen."

"That could mean anything," Connie pointed out, "including a number of things that are not flattering."

"We have three choices," Lars said. "We could stand here until I hit on a satisfactory compliment; I could carry you upstairs and ravish you right now; or we could go to the dinner."

"The second choice is definitely my preference, but I suppose going to the dinner is the sensible thing to do."

Lars agreed, both with Connie's preference and what was sensible. He asked her to wait until he brought his car around. She said she would walk along with him to the car. In the elevator of the parking garage, they did not behave like the sensible people who had chosen the dinner over lovemaking.

They were among the last to arrive for the dinner. As they approached the Haskells, who were stationed in the entryway of the chancellor's residence to greet their guests, Lars could see the surprise and alarm on the face of their host when he recognized Lars' companion. Jim Haskell whispered to his wife as Lars and Connie approached.

"Good evening, Jim," Lars said as he took Haskell's hand. "I believe that you know Dr. Mercutio."

"Indeed I do," Haskell responded affably. "My dear," he said turning to his wife, "here is the outstanding North Shore psychology professor I've been telling you about." Mrs. Haskell looked blank. Haskell added, "You recall, the one who'll be a visiting professor at Stanford next year."

With a purr of pleasure, Mrs. Haskell broke into a broad smile. "Of course," she said, taking Connie's hand in both of hers. "And how thoughtful of Lars to bring you so that we could show off our exceptional young scholar to the other trustees. So helpful to our campus, you know, to remind the trustees that we have faculty of your caliber at North Shore."

It was obvious to Lars and Connie both that the Haskells had grasped an impersonal reason for Lars's bringing Connie to the dinner. The Haskells knew that Lars and Marian had separated. However, they apparently did not want the gathering to surmise that Lars and Connie were involved with each other. With the instantaneous defensiveness developed during long years in university administration, they had rationalized an explanation for Connie's being with Lars that would deflect inferences of a personal involvement. No doubt they would use the rationale with every person to whom they introduced Connie throughout the evening, along with using it as an explanation to anyone who inquired about her to them.

Lars and Connie were but a few steps beyond greeting their hosts when a server approached with a tray of filled champagne glasses. They each took one and moved to an open spot among the clusters of guests engaged in the kind of lively conversations likely between long time acquaintances who only periodically saw one another. They had enjoyed their first sip of wine when they were approached by Trustee Harlan Cartwright and his wife. "Well, Dr. Paulsen, we haven't seen your charming wife since your very first meeting last fall."

Connie looked at Lars with a devilish expression, apparently amused in anticipation of what he would say. "In fact," Lars began, showing as much external tranquility as he could muster, "my wife isn't with me this evening. Let me present Dr. Constanzia Mercutio, who is also a professor at North Shore State."

Cartwright's face brightened, "You're the one who's going to Stanford next year." He explained briefly to his wife Connie's activities for the coming year and how prestigious the invitation was.

Mrs. Cartwright studied Connie coolly and asked, "And will your husband be going to California with you?"

"Oh, I'm not married," Connie replied.

"I'm sorry," said Mrs. Cartwright, perhaps apologizing for her presumptuousness.

"So am I," Connie responded. "I guess we academics just get too absorbed in our work."

"My dear child," smiled Mrs. Cartwright, who looked old enough to address Connie maternally, "your colleagues' absorption in their work must be very intense not to have noticed you. Perhaps you should work in the corporate world. Beauty doesn't go unnoticed there, does it, Harlan?"

Cartwright looked as though he would rather not answer. Maybe he had been too observant of beauty in the corporate world, Lars thought.

"What is your specialization, Dr. Mercutio?" Cartwright asked.

"I'm a cognitive psychologist."

"That explains it," Cartwright stated. "I'm afraid you understand men too well. It frightens them away."

"With due respect for the professor expertise, Harlan, I doubt it requires knowledge of psychology to understand the male animal," said Mrs. Cartwright. "Forbearance rather than knowledge is the essential virtue."

Cartwright looked something less than the successful corporate dragon that he was. Mrs. Cartwright began to maneuver her husband away. "I hope, my dear," she said to Connie, "that your entire stay in California is not devoted to academic matters."

Lars lifted his glass to Connie. "Chalk one up to female bonding. You've added a couple admirers."

Connie tapped her foot against his. "Oh, please," she murmured, "you ain't seen nothing yet." In fact, Connie soon demonstrated the point amply as she charmed several other wives of male trustees during the social interlude before the group was invited to dinner.

Lars and Connie were seated at separate tables. Lars conversed fitfully and ate distractedly as he looked repeatedly across the room at Connie's table, wondering how her evening was going. He doubted that all of her considerable tact and unshakable aplomb would be sufficient to avoid boredom. Worse, if her tablemates inferred her to be displacing a loyal wife of longstanding, she might be spending a very chilly evening. He was not a relaxed diner, a situation not ameliorated by one of his dinner partners being Trustee Pete Henderson, who devoted his evening to one of his favorite topics, the excessive pay and the light workload of university faculty.

The dinner broke up after Jim Haskell's brief remarks thanking the trustees for their dedication to the university throughout a year of considerable difficulty. Lars stood at his table as the room cleared. The only others remaining besides him were Connie and three women who were talking spiritedly and laughing heartily at Connie's contributions to their conversation. Lars moved to the edge of the group, which was still seated. Trustees Marsha Brandwyn and Martha Collins sat on one side of Connie and the wife of James Middlebrook, the other academic on the board, on the other.

"It sounds like your going to have a wonderful year, Connie," Mrs. MIddlebrook said as she stood.

"And your research sounds so important," Marsha Brandwyn added.

"I just hope that I can make some progress," Connie said modestly.

"Of course, you will," Brandwyn said affectionately. She patted Connie's hand as she stood to leave.

Connie and Martha Collins joined the others on their feet, as Collins contributed, "Just don't you forget where home is when you're out there, Connie. We need you and want you back here."

"I promise not to let them seduce me," Connie said, then looked impish, and added, "Well, I mean about staying there, that is."

The others responded with a burst of laughter before they started slowly to make their exit. Connie came to Lars and gave him a playful poke on the arm. "Hello, you."

"Well," Lars asked, "did they make plans to nominate you for governor?"

"We did get along," Connie grinned.

"Very well, I'd say."

Connie gave Lars a satisfied look. "These ladies, Trustee Paulsen, unlike Mrs. Cartwright, don't think I am looking for a husband. Solid scholarship and commitment to the cause of equality for women is what scores with them."

"I can't imagine why I was afraid that they might be cool to you," Lars said with relief. "Apparently it doesn't ostracize a lady to have a married man pursuing her."

"Maybe they don't think that you are any threat to my virtue," Connie smiled wickedly.

"Let's get out of here," Lars said with determination. "I'll show them."

CHAPTER 30

Early Spring No Guarantee of Hot Summer

June 1 neared and Lars's thorough study and follow up of the for-rent ads in the St. Claude paper turned up nothing suitable. He placed an ad describing the kind of apartment he hoped for. For several days he impatiently awaited the first phone call offering some possibility. On the last day that the ad ran, he hoped that a response had finally come when his office phone rang as he was about to leave for lunch. He was momentarily disconcerted when the caller was not someone with an apartment to rent but Marian, who invited him to dinner that evening.

When he was slow to respond, Marian offered, "If you're busy tonight, maybe we can do it tomorrow."

"No, no," Lars interjected, "tonight would be fine." Then he paused again, unsure that he was being wise.

"Shall we say seven, then?" Marian suggested.

"Fine," Lars answered, "where shall I meet you?"

"Lars," Marian chuckled at his seeming obtuseness, "I'm going to cook. You do remember that I know how."

"I remember," Lars said with some embarrassment. "You cook very well. Always have."

"Well, we'll see if I still can."

"Can I bring anything?" Lars offered.

"Just yourself," Marian answered amiably. "See you then."

Lars devoted so much time to wondering what had prompted Marian's invitation that the time for his next class arrived before he could get lunch.

Armed with a bottle of Marian's favorite wine, Lars approached the door of his former residence that evening feeling rather strange. The place where he had lived of over a decade until seven months ago seemed strangely like unfamiliar territory. In the dim evening light the yard and shrubbery that he had always tended lovingly looked well cared for. The flower beds looked ready to be planted now that the danger of killing frost was past. Surprisingly, he did not feel regretful that the care of the grounds—or the house—was no longer his responsibility, though he's done it passionately for years. Perhaps it was because of having to ring the bell like any other visitor.

Marian was quick to open the door and invite him in. She smilingly welcomed him and asked him to settle himself, for the preparation of dinner required her immediate attention at the moment. Lars offered to open the wine he had brought, apologizing that it was not chilled. Marian said that there was a bottle of the same variety in the refrigerator and suggested that he open it. In a few minutes, they were moving around the kitchen and chatting in relaxed fashion as had been their custom before their estrangement. The exchange of information about campus minutia soon exhausted itself, and they moved on to discussing the latest doings of their children.

Expressing their parental pride was a topic that lasted Lars and Marian throughout dinner, supplemented only by Lars's complements about the meal and Marian's comments about culinary matters. As they lingered over coffee, Lars concluded that there must have been no reason for Marian's invitation other than the desire to maintain contact. Then she set her coffee cup aside with a deliberateness that seemed preparation to change the mood of the evening.

Marian looked at him earnestly. "Lars, I've something to tell you." Her expression indicated a mixture of gravity and delight. "I've been offered a job—a very good job."

"That's good news," Lars said because he was sure that was what Marian wanted to hear.

"A very senior position, at half again my present salary, at the University of Michigan." The information tumbled out of Marian, reflecting her pleasure and excitement.

"It sounds great."

"Their college of education wants to develop some research strength in just the areas that I've been publishing in. They approached me. I hadn't applied or anything."

Lars smiled and nodded approvingly in recognition of the implication of what Marian said. "That's really a tribute to your accomplishments. Their approaching you is what happens when a prestige university wants to excel in a particular area. They identify the people who're top notch. Then they go after the person they want." Lars was not saying anything that Marian did not know. He wanted her to know that he understood.

"If I were to accept it," Marian said after pausing and scrutinizing Lars's face intently, "would you come along with me?"

The question was so unexpected that Lars could only return Marian's stare. "I'm thinking of a complete reconciliation, of course," Marian emphasized. "I want to—I want us to renew our vows, Lars."

Lars was incapable of direct response to the heart of Marian's question. There were some things he felt that would be easy to say. He could say that he was glad she had this opportunity. He could truthfully say she had really earned it. He could sincerely say that the sensible decision was not to turn it down. He said none of these things as he smiled at his estranged wife.

"It would be perfect if you were there too," Marian offered.

Lars avoided addressing the intimate aspect of Marian's proposal. "What would I do in Ann Arbor? Or in the commuting area?"

"You'd find a teaching position, just as I have every time we've moved before," Marian reasoned.

"Marian, you know that at my age and in my circumstances I'm not marketable for a senior position at anywhere near the salary I'm getting now. I haven't done any research—respectable or otherwise—for over fifteen years, since I went into administration."

"But you don't need a senior position, just an enjoyable one. Our combined incomes would be about the same as they are now," Marian pointed out. Her voice was neither calculating nor pleading. "You've always been a fine teacher, Lars. You'll get something that you like. We'll be together again. It will be just as it was before—before we split up."

Lars could see that Marian was earnest; it was harder to judge her sincerity. He was unprepared to assess what Marian was offering, since he had, during their separation, given no thought to reconciliation.

"If you're waiting for me to admit I was wrong, Lars, I know that I was. I got involved with someone—"

Lars interrupted. "You don't have to tell me anything."

"I want to," Marian said. She lowered her gaze to the tablecloth. "I led you to believe I wanted to be free for casual sex. The truth is, I'd met someone. Someone from the Pauliapolis faculty, and we were involved for several months. It's over now, Lars. I want to be the loyal wife I was for thirty years."

Lars was filled with respect for Marian. His anger over the circumstances of their parting had dissolved over the last few months. He had warm memories of the affection and happiness they had shared over the years. The separation had also given him a keener awareness that Marian had sacrificed more to the maintenance of their marital relationship than he had. He had always reasoned that the financial benefits to their family justified putting his career first and that the liability to Marian's hopes was unfortunate but necessary. He now had to admit that that line of reasoning was more convenient than compelling on his part. During those long, black winter evening in his lakeside cabin, he had come to admit to himself that he had exploited Marian.

Lars looked at Marian squarely. "You were more than a loyal wife for thirty years. You were a treasure. The truth is, you were much more than I deserved." Lars saw Marian looking at him with wide and hopeful eyes. He returned her gaze and said in all sincerity. "I never really appreciated you. I apologize for having had my way at your expense so much."

Marian reached across the table for his hand. "Can't we start over then? Let's?"

"We shouldn't," said Lars, surprising himself.

"You don't want to," Marian stated, rather than asked.

"No," Lars said, pausing to try to understand himself. "I said we shouldn't." He squeezed Marian's hand as she tried to pull it away. It was important to continue touch her. "If I thought about reconciling very long, I'd probably want to. God knows, you gave me a lot of happiness for thirty years."

"You're not thinking about us," Marian said with a touch of bitterness. "It's about that young psych professor, isn't it?"

"It isn't, really," Lars said with conviction. He was not surprised that Marian knew of his relationship with Connie. Once he and Connie had become intimate, they had made no attempt at secrecy.

"I'm going to break that off," Lars said, surprising himself a second time. He had not given a moment's thought to anything of the kind before he had said it. "If we kept on, I'd be exploiting here even more than I did you."

Lars needed to explain his unexpected assertion to himself as much as to Marian. "Our marriage of thirty years was based on a myth. It's probably a tribute to us—more so to you than me—that we did keep it alive for thirty years. We always said ours was a marriage of equal partners. I now think that there can't be any such thing, or at least I don't know how to do it."

Lars found no difficulty in continuing to look at Marian squarely. "In the inescapable compromises required to maintain a marriage, someone's always going to have to give at least fifty-one percent while the other gives no more than forty-nine. You gave a hell of a lot more than fifty-one percent. I see that now."

"Lars," Marian began, now no longer trying to withdraw her hand from his, "I'll admit there were many times over the years that I felt exploited. I've no doubt that my resentment often showed. But we stayed together. However we did it can still work if you're willing to say it's your turn to give fifty-one percent. Is it unfair to ask that of you, after I've done it for thirty years?"

"It's not unfair," Lars admitted. "But I have to admit that the major giver role would do the same thing to me that it did to you."

"Have I been so bad?"

"Certainly not," Lars said emphatically. "Probably a lot better than I'd have been under similar circumstances."

Lars steeled himself to make a confession. He did not want to make Marian angry, but he had to risk it to make himself understood. "You know, I've never really felt that you trusted me."

"Of course I have."

"I think you tried—tried very hard," Lars assured her. "But even though both our names are on everything we own; and even though we have joint bank accounts and have avoided ever talking about "your money" or "my money," you occasionally worried—never directly, I admit—that I'd cheat you, if not literally, then psychologically."

"You imagined that, surely," Marian said. "You can be over-sensitive."

"I can't deny that," Lars admitted. He added, "I'm thinking of how you always wanted to know what you salary had been used for."

"Wasn't it always used for us jointly, or for the kids?"

"Yes."

"I never made an investment that wasn't in both our names."

"That's true."

"I don't see where the mistrust was, then," Marian said with apparent bewilderment.

Lars realized his point had not been made, but his conviction developed over many years remained. "You always seemed on guard that one day I might perpetrate on you the unfairness that men have dumped on women since time began. Maybe what I'm trying to say is that I always felt that you saw me as one of them—the male users of women, rather than just me. Me, the one who could be trusted."

Marian squeezed his hand now. "I don't want to get angry and I don't want to make you angry, but isn't this all a rationalization to justify that you're giving me up for a much younger woman?"

Lars nodded, recognizing the legitimacy of her question. "It would be, if I didn't mean it about ending it with her, but I do, believe me."

"You'd rather be alone than have either of us?" Marian asked disbelievingly.

"I don't want to be alone. I just don't want to take advantage of anyone any more—or seem to be, in that person's mind." Lars took Marian's hand in both of his and rose from the table. "I want you to be happy. I'm honored that you think that you could share your happiness with me, but my going with you would be a mistake." Lars smiled at Marian. "Go, and be happy. Really."

As he turned to leave, Marian asked, "Lars, do you want a divorce."

"No," he answered, "unless you do."

"If I go," Marian reasoned, "there'll be all sorts of details."

"I don't want to get legal," Lars said, the idea striking him as completely unattractive, "unless you think it's necessary."

"Friends can work these things out," Marian said.

"Right," Lars agreed with a broad smile.

Lars got his coat from the closet. Marian followed him toward the door. "Lars, the house," she began, "you could move in—after I go, of course—" Lars smiled again, at her wanting to make clear she was not proposing they share a house, even for a short while.

"That would be a help," Lars said before he bid Marian good night and good luck.

CHAPTER 31

Prof Arranges for Productive Year

During the entire two weeks of her stay with her parents, Connie had anxiously waited for the letter that now lay unopened on the night-stand beside her. Though her parents had been effusive in expressing their pride over her visiting professorship for the coming academic year, they also had questioned her about her obvious distraction and surprising moodiness for one soon to begin the peak year of her professional career.

Depending on what the letter said, she might or might not have to surprise her parents with the news that she was changing her plans. Otherwise, she would proceed with the plans already arranged for her year in California and present them with a surprise upon her return to the Midwest. Of course, there was a third course of action, one that would avoid surprising anyone, but she had firmly decided against it. She was proud that it had been a reasoned decision, as that decision especially ought to be, she believed.

She was amused at herself for delaying so long over opening the letter. Actually, what was already settled in her mind was much more meaningful than what the letter would say. That had been decided without the agonizing delay she was now experiencing. And once decided, never doubted. Connie chided herself over the absurdity of fretting so long over opening a letter responding to the question she had written to ask. She had mailed her inquiry the day after her arrival to spend some time with her parents and had anxiously awaited the response ever since. Muttering an uncharacteristic expletive, she grabbed the letter and quickly tore it open. Under the Stanford University psychology department letterhead, the brief contents did not take long to absorb.

Dear Connie:

I appreciate the candor of the information in your recent inquiry. It is wise for either party in these visiting professorship situations to avoid surprising the other. I have explored your circumstances with all the relevant parties: the departmental research committee, the dean of the college, and the academic vice president of the university. All have agreed that your pregnancy should pose no problem in your serving your visiting professorship as originally planned. It is fortunate that you were not expected to teach at all, since research activities are somewhat more flexible than fulfilling the more rigid schedule of instruction.

We look forward to your arrival sometime around September 1. Please get in touch with me in the near future about the details of your housing and other matters.

Sincerely,

Arthur Brandeis
Chair, Dept. Of Psychology

Connie felt a rush of relief. The letter was exactly what she hoped for. She would serve her visiting professorship while having her baby in February. When she returned to her parents' home next summer with their six month old grandchild, the existence of the child would forestall their debating the wisdom of what she had chosen to do. The same logic held for her return to North Shore State in the fall fourteen months hence. She had not lightly decided to accept the difficulties of being a single parent. And a single parent she intended to be—though she suspected that Lars might make some proposal out of a sense of duty if her plan to understate the baby's age by three months did not succeed in convincing him that he was not the father. Now that her plans were both clear and desirable in her own mind, she suddenly had the thought that some misguided pro-lifers might use her choosing to have a child as an example for opposition to abortion. She hoped not, for it would force her to take time from her commitment to research to correct their erroneous thinking, and she was firm on wanting to leave all of that sort of thing behind her.

0-595-28305-5